C8 000 000

KU-511-648

PUNISH THE DEED

A Lucinda Pierce Investigation

When children's charity worker Sharon Flemming is brutally murdered and a note found by her mutilated body bears the words 'I was left behind', Lucinda Pierce must track down this violent killer before he strikes again. And when a series of notes are also left on her car windshield, she knows this has got personal. Comfort comes from a most unlikely source but can only lead to further complications...

Diane Fanning titles available from
Severn House Large Print

The Trophy Exchange

PUNISH THE DEED

A Lucinda Pierce Mystery

Diane Fanning

Severn House Large Print
London & New York

This first large print edition published 2011
in Great Britain and the USA by
SEVERN HOUSE PUBLISHERS LTD of
9-15 High Street, Sutton, Surrey, SM1 1DF.
First world regular print edition published 2008 by
Severn House Publishers Ltd., London and New York.

Copyright © 2008 by Diane Fanning.

All rights reserved.
The moral right of the author has been asserted.

British Library Cataloguing in Publication Data

Fanning, Diane.
  Punish the deed.
  1. Women detectives--Fiction. 2. Volunteer workers in
  child welfare--Crimes against--Fiction. 3. Detective and
  mystery stories. 4. Large type books.
  I. Title
  813.6-dc22

  ISBN-13: 978-0-7278-7930-1

Except where actual historical events and characters are being
described for the storyline of this novel, all situations in this
publication are fictitious and any resemblance to living persons is
purely coincidental.

Severn House Publishers support The Forest Stewardship Council
[FSC], the leading international forest certification organisation. All
our titles that are printed on Greenpeace-approved FSC-certified paper
carry the FSC logo.

MIX
Paper from
responsible sources
FSC® C018575
www.fsc.org

Printed and bound in Great Britain by the
MPG Books Group, Bodmin, Cornwall.

NORTHFIELD LIBRARY
Tel: 4641007

To Liz and Alex –
may their love wildness never die

One

The shrill of the alarm clock pierced Conrad Fleming's sleep. He slapped the snooze button and rolled over. He reached for his wife, longing for the touch of her skin, the warmth of an embrace. But there was no one there.

He sat upright, confused. He listened but heard not a sound. Worse, he didn't smell coffee brewing. If Shari were here, the aroma would fill the house. *Where was she?*

She often worked late – very late. But she always came home. Maybe Monica was right. Maybe Shari was having an affair with the school district superintendent. He'd laughed at Monica yesterday when she told him that rumor. He wasn't laughing now.

He called the direct line into Shari's office. It rang four times and clicked to voice mail. He hung up without leaving a message. He clicked the speed-dial button for her cell. It, too, went unanswered.

He paced the bedroom then slipped into the master bathroom seeking signs that she'd been there and had left already – arriving and leaving while he slept. The shower was dry, as were the sink and all the towels. *Where was she?*

He walked into the kitchen, poured water into

the coffee maker and flipped the switch. He watched his feet move back and forth on the kitchen tiles as he waited. He pulled out the carafe, interrupting the flow of the brew. He started to pour but stopped mid-tilt. Dingy hot water. Nothing more. He hadn't put in any ground coffee.

He turned off the pot and went down the hall to the home office, grabbing the school district directory as he walked through the door. He punched in the numbers for the home phone of Superintendent Robert Irving.

A woman answered. 'Mrs Irving?' he asked.

'Yes,' she rasped.

'Is your husband there?'

'Do you know what time it is?'

'Is your husband there?' he repeated.

'It's not even five thirty yet.'

'I know. It's important. Is your husband there?'

'Yes. Who is this?'

'Are you sure he's there?'

'Yes, I'm sure,' she snapped. 'He's right here next to me. Who is this?'

Conrad blinked, speechless. He was so sure Irving wouldn't be at home either.

A male voice came on the line. 'Who is this and what do you want?'

Conrad hung up, burning with shame. *More than twenty-five years of marriage and now my first thought is to distrust Shari?* He scratched infidelity off his list of reasons for his wife's absence.

His thoughts turned dark and fear churned the

acid in his empty stomach, creating a burn in his throat. He called both hospitals to check on overnight admissions. No Shari. No Jane Does. Again he hit speed dial for her cell phone. Still no answer. The sound of her voice on the recorded greeting plunged into his heart like a dagger of ice, evoking images of Shari in a dark alley, bloodied with a knife protruding from her chest. He shook his head hard to chase the vision away.

He went back into the kitchen and properly prepared the coffee. He dressed while the coffee brewed. When it was ready, he bolted down a cup so fast he scalded his mouth.

Maybe she had an overnight business trip and he'd forgotten. *Or maybe*, he rebuked himself, *I just wasn't listening when she told me. If she was away on work-related travel, the superintendent might know.* He picked up the phone and called his number again. Robert Irving answered, 'What?'

'I was wondering...' Conrad began.

'Who is this?' Irving interrupted.

Conrad hung up, grabbed his keys and headed out to his car to drive downtown to the police station.

Two

Sammy Nguyen entered through the basement door in the back of the school district building. He punched his time card at 5:56 a.m. A small and wiry man, his wrinkled, weathered face barely peered over the top of the big trash receptacle as he wheeled it down the hall and into the elevator on his way to the second floor.

There were few offices on the upper level. Meeting rooms of various sizes consumed most of the space. Since the school board had not met the night before, his job there was quick and easy. He emptied waste baskets, gathered up three used coffee cups in one hand and went down to tend to the dozens of offices on the first floor.

He parked the trashcan in the hallway outside the kitchen. In the doorway, he spotted a woman's brown shoe lying on its side. Puzzled, he bent down to pick it up. As he stuck it under the arm holding the dirty mugs, he saw spots on the floor. He squatted down and swiped at one of them. Dry. He licked his index finger and wiped at the stains again. Bright red blazed on his fingertip. *Blood?*

He stood up and stepped through the kitchen doorway. When he saw the bare foot, the cups

10

fell from his hands to the floor. Two of them shattered on impact, sending cold droplets of creamy brown and black coffee up in the air, across the floor, on to his shoes and up his legs. The third mug bounced twice, spewing liquid on the path of its trajectory before landing and rolling to rest in the arch of the naked foot.

His eyes started their journey there, tracking up the woman's leg to her skirt, hiked up to mid-thigh. Then on to hands crossed on her chest, where stained fingers stuck up at unnatural angles. His gaze lingered on those bloodied digits and then moved on, up to the pool of blood radiating from her head like a demonic halo, to the mangled mess of smashed nose, swollen eyes, blood-crusted lips and matted hair. He did not recognize the woman but he knew the face of death.

He stumbled backward until he could no longer see the length of battered body – just the arch of one delicate foot curled around a coffee-stained mug. He gawked at it as if the power of his stare could animate both to life. Then fear eclipsed his shock. He turned and ran for the side door. He fumbled with the keys clipped to his belt loop, unlocked the door, ran down sixteen broad steps to the sidewalk and pulled out his cell phone.

He kept an eye on the wood and textured glass door, prepared to flee if the door moved at all. He scrolled down to the superintendent's home phone number in his electronic directory and pushed the call button.

Irving's voice exploded in Sammy's ear. 'You

11

son of a bitch. I'm calling the police. Leave us alone.'

'Mr Irving? Mr Irving?' He said no more. No one was on the other end of the line.

Calling the police? Good. He folded his cell and slid it into his pocket. He stood sentry, his eyes never straying from the door, his head cocked as he listened for the sound of approaching sirens. After a moment, he questioned what he heard. *How does Mr Irving know where I am? How does he know who I am? Why did he call me a son of a bitch?*

Sammy pulled out his cell and pressed 9-1-1.

Three

Homicide Detective Lucinda Pierce pulled up to the curb in front of the old high school that now served as the administration building for the school district. She flipped down the visor to check the mirror and make sure she hadn't forgotten anything essential in her rush from home that morning.

Hair was combed – not as perfectly in place as the hairdresser managed, but good enough. Two naturally arched eyebrows soared over two gray-shadowed lids. No clumps of mascara hung in blotches on her long lashes and the eyeliner was straight and thin.

She checked the positioning of her prosthetic eye to make sure it was properly centered. She tilted the mirror down. On one side, a prominent cheek bone, smooth, silky skin and plump full lips. On the other, the destruction of a shotgun blast, cratered, molten skin led down to a cruel thin slash like a lump of hardened wax lying where bountiful lips once smiled.

She traced a finger across the remnants of her mouth. She had a second round of surgery scheduled in a couple of days to attempt to make it look normal again. She was skeptical that the doctor could accomplish the miracle a return to 'normal' required. She hated the down time from work and loathed the idleness demanded for healing.

With a deep sigh, she snapped up the visor, clicked open the door and threw out one long leg and then another. She clipped her gold badge to the waistband of her khaki skirt, brushed the heavy cotton smooth with a downward swipe of her hands. She reached in the back seat, picked up the jacket of her suit and slid it on to cover her shoulder holster from nervous civilian eyes.

She strode the length of the sidewalk and up the broad granite steps to the front entrance of the building. The two uniforms flanking the door said, 'Good morning, Lieutenant,' in unison as they pulled open the double doors.

She nodded at them in response and stepped inside. Her heels clicked on the granite floor as she walked up the entryway toward the reception desk where the hall stretched out in both directions, traversing the length of the building.

She heard a familiar voice calling, 'Good morning, Lucinda.'

She turned toward Sergeant Ted Branson and smiled. 'Are you responsible for my rush out of the house this morning?' In her heels, she could look the 6'3" officer in the eye.

'Could have been,' he said with a grin. 'But they told me you were next up before I had a chance to ask.'

'If I hadn't been?'

He shrugged his shoulders.

'Yeah, right,' she said. 'What've we got?'

'Blunt-force trauma. Female vic. Kitchen/ lounge area, down that way,' he said, gesturing to the west side of the building.

'Know the vic's identity?'

'Think so.'

'And?' Lucinda asked.

'There are two cars in the parking lot. One's registered to the custodian who discovered the body, the other to Conrad and Sharon Fleming. A patrol car is on the way to the Flemings' address now.'

'Who is Sharon Fleming?'

Branson flipped open his notepad. 'Fifty-six. Married. Executive Director of the Communities in Schools program for the district...' A shrill ring interrupted his recitation. He clicked his cell open and said, 'Branson.'

He listened for a minute and then asked, 'Do you know where Conrad Fleming works?' He said 'OK' a few times then clicked the phone shut. He turned to Lucinda. 'No one's responding to the doorbell or knocks at the Fleming house. One of the guys shone a flashlight in the garage window and there aren't any cars there either.'

'That's mighty interesting,' Lucinda said as she mentally entertained the possibility of spousal homicide.

As if reading her mind, Ted said, 'Doesn't look like it, Lucinda. The front gate said Fleming didn't leave the community once from the time he arrived home from work at six last night until about five minutes before we got the 9-1-1 call, and he lives a good twenty minutes from here.'

'Are they sure?'

'Yeah, this is a high-security gated community. Multiple cameras at the gates and a couple at each intersection. They're downloading the tapes now for patrol to take back to the station.'

'So where is he? At work?'

'Don't know. The phone at Cenco Labs clicked over to a recorded message saying their offices don't open until eight thirty. There's a car heading that way now to check it out.'

'Good. What's going on here? Techs? Coroner?'

'The tech team checked in, at the station, inspected the crime-scene truck and is in transit as we speak. Because of the location, I figured this murder would be high profile so I asked for Doc Sam. He, too, is supposedly on the way here.'

'Good,' Lucinda said. They stepped around the green trash receptacle and Lucinda peered down inside it. She saw nothing but crumpled paper. 'Make sure the techs process this can.' Ted jotted this on his notepad.

They stepped up to the kitchen doorway. Her eye scanned across the scattered pottery shards to the body. 'A bit of a struggle here, it seems,' Lucinda said.

'Hard to tell,' Ted said.

Lucinda glanced at him sideways as if he'd taken leave of his senses. Shattered mugs, spattered coffee, splattered blood all intermingled in a mess that stretched across the room...

Ted saw the look and laughed. 'Well, unless the custodian did her, the coffee-related mess is

16

not part of the crime scene. He was carrying the mugs to the sink and dropped them when he saw the body.'

Lucinda winced. She spotted a shoe off to her left on the end opposite the body. 'What about that brown pump?'

'He found it in the hall, picked it up and dropped it in here.'

'Oh, jeez.'

'It gets worse. He saw spots on the floor beside the shoe and rubbed on them with a saliva-moistened finger.'

Lucinda shook her head. 'The spots were blood, right?'

'Oh, yeah.'

She rolled her eyes. 'I don't want to set foot any deeper in this room until Doc Sam gets here. We've got enough problems already. See if the custodian will voluntarily give up a DNA sample. Where is he?'

'In the parking lot. We're holding all the arriving employees there until you say otherwise.'

'I want to take a look,' she said, leading the way behind the reception desk to a large, curved multi-paned window that overlooked the parking lot a floor below on the same level as the basement. 'Where's the custodian?'

Ted pointed to a cluster of marked cars and the small man standing beside them, looking lost. 'There, the Vietnamese guy in the blue coveralls.'

A black Escalade pulled into the lot, sending gravel flying as it came to an abrupt stop in the middle of a lane. The door flew open and a large man stepped out waving his arms and moving his mouth. 'I wonder who that is,' Lucinda said.

Ted leaned forward, squinting his eyes. 'Looks like the superintendent to me.'

'Lord, help us all. I probably have to talk to him first. What's his name?'

'Irving. Robert Irving,' Ted said.

At the sound of opening doors at the front entrance, Lucinda and Ted turned around to see a team of five Tyvek-suited techs marching down the hall with matching blue booties over their shoes, surgical gloves over their hands and lugging enough equipment to put the Ghost-busters to shame. The front door opened again and Doc Sam shambled inside. 'Lieutenant,' he barked.

'Hey, Doc Sam, follow me.' Turning to Ted, she said, 'Brief the team and make sure they collect a sample from the spit and blood spot in the hallway before anyone tramples it.'

Lucinda and Doc Sam slid on booties and pulled on gloves before walking into the kitchen. He knelt down to examine the body while Lucinda stood by his side. After he grunted a few times, Lucinda asked, 'What's it look like?'

'She sure wasn't beat to death with those coffee mugs,' he grumbled.

'She was beaten to death, though?'

He turned his head and looked at her with disgust. 'Come on, Lieutenant, you know I won't tell you the cause of death until I do the autopsy. What d'ya think I have? A crystal ball?' He turned back to the body, knowing fingers palpated the skull beneath the blood-saturated hair.

Lucinda swallowed a grin. *Good old Doc Sam. Some things never change.* 'What *can* you tell me, Doc?'

'She was beaten, all right. But you don't need me to tell you that. Feels like the blunt object that struck her had curved edges. Like a pole. But it would have to have been something solid; these fractures are bad. Your people find anything like that lying around?'

'No. But they've just started.'

'Well, I'll get out of your way then,' he said as he stood upright with a deep groan. 'Whenever you're done here, I'll be waiting down at the morgue. I'd like to get this done before lunch.'

'We'll finish up as soon as we can, Doc.'

'Yeah, yeah, yeah. You'll do it in your own sweet time like you always do,' he said as he headed down the hall ripping off his gloves. He handed them to an officer at the door and went down the steps with the blue booties still wrapped around his shoes.

Four

He huddled under cardboard, peering out at the community of the left behind. He wanted to punish them for the ways they were just like him. He wanted to stomp them into the ground for the ways they weren't like him – for the courage they lacked to strike back.

Instead he observed their movements, wrapped in a tattered blanket of pity for the pathetic nature of their lives. Each man who shuffled past his makeshift home bore the stench of a misbegotten life. All had the repulsive smell of the never washed but each foul odor bore its own distinctive accents of personal musk. He could close his eyes and still recognize each man by the fragrance that traveled in his wake.

The women were different. Each left a rancid feminine perfume on their trail – an alien aroma that overpowered any individual nuance that left him feeling lost in a jungle of desire and loathing. The last one he abolished was a woman. It was hard to sniff her sins beneath the mask of femaleness that emanated from her coppery blood. It took too much of a toll. The next one would have to be a man. The scent of woman dead robbed him of his sleep.

His eyes darted back and forth from the

pathetic souls who moved about or sat still under moldy cardboard shelters or huddled beneath crinkly garbage bags. He watched them with as much interest in their welfare as he expended on the scurrying beetle that struggled through the dirt and mud. He was of them. Yet he was above them.

He hated them all. He loved them all. He did what he did for each and every one of them. *I am the snake that slithers in on angel wings seeking vengeance for the world of the forgotten.*

His lips curled as the rain stirred up the scent from the above-ground latrine – nothing more, really, than a spot behind the bush. That solitary bush of modesty made the dirty two-legged creatures superior to the rats, stray dogs and feral cats that darted in and out of the night. But not by much. Not enough to count. Not enough to matter to the world outside, which continued to turn and thrive by ignoring those lost in the shadows.

When the rain stopped, he'd move on, seeking another village of the damned in the center of a city of conspicuous consumption – a place where both goods and souls were consumed with little distinction between the two.

He'd acclimatize to the new place. Then take his time to sniff out another Pharisee and lead yet another lamb to slaughter.

Five

Lucinda gave the go-ahead to the team of techs to process the crime scene. She watched as the first suited-up body videotaped their approach and another followed in his wake shooting still shots with a digital camera. Once they'd passed into the kitchen, another tech got busy with the contents of the trashcan, and yet another gathered samples of the blood and saliva stain on the floor beside the door.

Lucinda followed the first two techs into the room but stood back while they worked. When they had completed their documentation of the scene with the body *in situ*, the team leader, Marguerite Spellman asked, 'Lieutenant, we're ready to call in the coroner's guys to remove the body. Do you need some time first?'

'Yes, Marguerite; just a few minutes. Thank you.'

Lucinda absorbed the image of the victim from every angle. Because of the location of the body in the small room, she couldn't do a 360-degree circuit of the body as she preferred. Her eye was drawn to the fingers, splayed at unnatural angles with her hands folded on her chest. *Had to have been placed there after she died. What else did he do to her after he killed her?*

She observed the victim's skirt riding halfway up her thigh. *Did that happen in her fall to the floor or in a struggle? Or did the perpetrator do some exploration after her death? Was she sexually assaulted?* The answer to that would have to wait until after the coroner completed the autopsy.

She crouched down to examine the coffee mug nestled in the arch of the victim's foot. *Is it what it seems? Did it simply come to a stop right there? Or is its position trying to tell me something?*

She stood and bent forward to look at the dead woman's face. It was hard to call it a face any longer. Brutal force had turned her features into raw meat – nose broken, teeth chipped, cheek bones crushed flat, eyes covered in rivers of blood and her skull caved in at several locations. *There's a lot of anger here. Is it personal toward the victim? Or is it unfocused, internalized rage and the victim was just at the wrong place at the wrong time?*

She straightened up, sighed and gave Marguerite the go-ahead to have the body removed. Lucinda moved over to the far end of the kitchen counter. There she spotted a legal pad with the first few pages curved over and back. On the top of the flat section, there were four words printed in caps in the middle of the page: 'I WAS LEFT BEHIND.'

Do those words have anything to do with this crime? Using the tip of a pen, she eased out and flipped over the bent pages. Across the top binding, she spotted more printing in all caps:

'FLEMING.' *Must belong to Sharon Fleming. Were both printed by her hand?* She flipped through the remaining folded-over pages and saw someone's notes – presumably the victim's – sprawled in sloppy cursive racing across the page, ignoring the lines as they went. *Dramatically different from the printing but that does not automatically lead to a different author.*

She flipped the pad over and back, looking for any signs of evidence from the crime. She did see clusters of small, dark spots on one edge but they looked more like old splashed coffee than dried blood splatter. *When did it get here? How did it get here? Did the victim carry it into the room? Or was it already here and she came into the room to retrieve it when she was attacked? Was that her printing on that page? Or the perpetrator's. Did he use what was at hand? Or did he bring it in here after the crime? Am I sure it was a male who committed the crime? Most likely, but not definitely.*

The two men in white overalls took pains not to disrupt the crime scene any more than necessary as they lifted the body up off the floor and placed it in an open body bag on the stretcher. Lucinda took a last look at the devastation on the victim's face then stepped back to allow the men to zip up the bag and roll it away. She closed her eye and still saw the ravaged features. As the image faded, the spark of anger in her chest flamed as hot as extreme heartburn. She pushed a fist into her chest, opened her eye and swallowed deep. She watched as a tech shot photos of the bloody floor where the body used

24

to lay.

Marguerite turned to Lucinda again. 'Lieutenant, I've got a blood-spatter expert at the state lab on stand-by. You want me to bring him in for analysis and possible stringing?'

'I'm not sure if that's necessary,' Lucinda said. 'But then, I'm not sure that it's not. Better do it to be on the safe side. When the state guy gets here, let the methods he uses be at his discretion. Make sure you bag up the cups on the floor. I'm not sure that they'll matter either but I'd rather err on the safe side. And that legal pad on the counter? Make sure it gets taken to the lab for fingerprint and body fluid analysis – and try not to damage any of the writing. Matter of fact, you might want to copy it all before you do any testing.'

Marguerite nodded and got to work bagging the evidence. Lucinda hung back observing the team at work and taking in the details of the scene, hoping that all the pieces would come together into a clear picture that would lead to an arrest.

Satisfied with the thoroughness of the team's evidence gathering, Lucinda went to the door at the end of the hall and checked it for any signs of forced entry. Finding none, she moved into the office beside the entrance to inspect the windows. Her cell phone interrupted her. 'Pierce,' she said.

'Lieutenant, Officer Colter. The school district superintendent is insisting that we allow him into the building.'

'The answer is no, Colter. Spell it for him if
25

you have to.'

'Yes, sir...'

'Is that all, Officer?'

'Ma'am, he's written down my badge number and said he's calling the mayor and the police chief.'

Lucinda sighed. 'Tell him I'll be right there, Officer.'

'Yes, ma'am.'

Lucinda headed back to the door she'd checked a few moments before. On the sidewalk at the foot of the steps, she saw the back of patrol officer Robin Colter, her elbows jutting out from her sides, her legs spread wide, her feet firmly planted. In front of her, inches from her face, a hefty man in a blue suit and bright yellow tie towered over her, ranting.

'Superintendent!' Lucinda shouted from the top of the stairs.

Robert Irving turned his gaze upward. 'I demand to be allowed into my office.'

'Where is your office?'

'What are you? An idiot?' he said, waving his arm in Lucinda's direction. 'In there.' He tried to side-step Officer Colter. She stepped in front of him, blocking his way.

He laid a hand on Colter's shoulder but before he could push, Lucinda said, 'I wouldn't do that, Superintendent.'

'Tell her to get out of my way and let me into my office.'

'No, Superintendent. Take your hand off that officer or I'll have you arrested.'

He glared at Lucinda before moving his arm

down to his side. 'I'm superintendent of this school district and I demand that you vacate this building or show me the search warrant that entitles you to be on the premises.'

'No, Superintendent. We are not leaving until we finish our investigation. And under the circumstances, we don't need a warrant,' Lucinda said as she walked down the steps in his direction.

As she got closer, Irving's eyes widened. 'I recognize you. What are you doing here? I thought you were in homicide.'

'I am. That's why I'm here. I'm investigating a murder in this building.'

The blood drained from Irving's face, taking all signs of belligerence with it. 'Murder? Here?'

'Yes, sir.'

'Who? How?'

'We have not confirmed the victim's identity.'

'Why not? Who do you think it is?' Irving asked.

The screech of tires pulled Lucinda's attention away from the superintendent. A boxy hybrid made a u-turn and sped off. In seconds, patrol cars gave chase with lights flashing and sirens wailing. Lucinda walked down the sidewalk to the curb.

'Lieutenant! Lieutenant!' Irving shouted after her.

Lucinda waved him off without looking back in his direction. The high-pitched sound of metal scraping metal ripped through the air followed by a thud and the tinkling noise of broken glass. Irving walked down the sidewalk and tapped

27

Lucinda on the shoulder. 'Lieutenant?'

'Not now, Mr Irving. We've got a situation here. Go stand by Officer Colter. I'll be with you as soon as I can.'

He blustered a protest but Lucinda turned away from him, stepped into the street and walked down to the corner without comment. Her cell phone rang. 'Pierce.'

'Lieutenant, the vehicle side-swiped a television satellite truck as it turned into Third Street. It careened off of there and smashed into a telephone pole.'

'Any injuries?'

'Just the driver of the fleeing vehicle but he's just got a few small cuts and scratches and a chaffed face from the airbag deployment. And right now, he's being badgered by reporters.'

'Get him into a patrol car and bring him up here. Block the road to keep the media away. And get someone to search that vehicle. The murder weapon is heavy with a rounded edge.'

'Yes, ma'am. We're on it.'

Moments later, the patrol car pulled up in front of Lucinda. She pulled open the back door, placed a hand on the roof, leaned forward and peered inside at the cuffed man in the back seat. He looked in his early thirties even though his hairline was obviously receding. Pulled back straight from his crown were strands of mousy brown hair cinched in a ponytail at the nape of his neck.

'Who are you?' Lucinda demanded.

'Sean Lowery, technology director for the schools. I work here.'

'I see. And why did you rabbit out of here so fast?'

'Listen, are these cuffs really necessary? I'm aching from getting knocked around in the accident.'

'Mr Lowery, why did you flee the crime scene?'

'Crime scene?'

'Mr Lowery, please answer the question: why the hell did you peel out of here?'

'I was flustered,' he said.

'Flustered?'

Sean nodded his head and gave her a weak smile.

'Why would you be flustered?'

'I saw all the police cars and panicked.'

'Why, Mr Lowery? Why did the police presence make you nervous?'

'Well, you know. It was just a normal reaction.'

'Mr Lowery, look toward the parking lot. Do you see the other school district employees out there?'

'Uh, yeah.'

'So why did they all pull into the lot without hesitation while you ran away? What's the reason? Do you have something to hide?'

'Oh no. Nothing to hide. No reason,' he stammered. 'It was just a reaction. A stupid reaction. You see cops, you see trouble. There's always a problem. Something wrong.'

'So instead of coming back to help us solve this problem at your workplace, you decided to become part of the problem. Is that what you're telling me, Mr Lowery?'

'Uh, no. I didn't mean to cause a problem. I just didn't want to get involved.'

Lucinda sniffed and smelled the vague remnants of a familiar odor. She crouched down beside him and looked straight into his eyes. His focus was off. Redness permeated the whites of his eyes. He turned away from her. 'I didn't mean any harm, I just wanted to...'

'Mr Lowery, are you under the influence?'

'I haven't been drinking, I swear.'

'I'm not talking about alcohol. Are you stoned?'

His eyes darted up to her face then bounced away and he looked down at the floor by his feet. 'Uh, no, of course not.'

'You are in serious trouble, Mr Lowery.'

'Trouble? Just because I ... I ... I...'

'The combination of your flight and your obvious lie have just made you a prime suspect in a murder.'

He looked at her with a blank expression. 'What?'

She rose, slammed the door and pushed the button on her cell phone to redial the last call she'd received. 'Have you found anything in the car search?'

'No weapon, Lieutenant. But found a small roach in the ashtray and three neatly rolled joints in the console.'

'Thanks,' she said as she disconnected and walked back toward the building. 'Mr Irving, I've got someone out here claiming to be your employee. You want to confirm that for me?'

When Lucinda opened the car door, Robert Irving's eyes widened. 'Sean?' he said.

'Mr Irving, I don't know what is going on. I didn't kill anybody. Tell her, sir; tell her I wouldn't kill anybody.'

'Lieutenant, what is going on here?' the superintendent asked.

'Do you recognize this man?'

'Yes. It's Sean Lowery, our technology director. What has he done?'

'Nothing,' Sean interjected. 'Nothing, sir. I swear.'

Lucinda slammed the door. 'Thank you, Mr Irving.'

As she walked back to the building, the superintendent followed behind her. 'Why has Sean been arrested? You don't really think he killed anyone, do you? What is going on? How long are you going to keep my people in the parking lot?'

'As long as I need to, Superintendent. I...' She stopped when the unmistakable sound of an approaching helicopter pulled her eyes upward. 'Shit,' she hissed under her breath as she spotted the television call letters on the chopper. 'Mr Irving, is there a place on the top floor or in the basement where we can bring everyone inside in one place?'

'There's the school board meeting room upstairs.'

'Gather your staff together on the sidewalk in front of Officer Colter. Do not discuss anything I've told you.'

Robert Irving sighed. 'Lieutenant, you haven't

told me anything.'

'You know there's been a murder. You know Sean Lowery has been arrested. That's all you need to know right now. But the rest of these folks don't need to know that. Can you keep your mouth shut?'

Irving bristled, opening his mouth to snap back at her before thinking better of it. 'Yes,' he said through pursed lips.

Lucinda went inside and briefed Ted Branson on the situation outside. 'I'd like you to go back to the station and get a warrant to search Lowery's office for drugs. And make sure you get the language broad enough to include a possible murder weapon, just in case.'

Uniformed police officers escorted the school district employees through the side door and up the stairway just left of the entry. Lucinda followed at the tail end of the group but stopped on the landing when her cell phone rang.

'Lieutenant, Conrad Fleming is not at his workplace.'

'Are you sure?'

'Yes, ma'am. His car's not in the parking lot. Security said he didn't use his entry card to get in this morning and to be doubly sure, I checked his office and lab. No sign of Fleming.'

'This is not good. Get out an alert on his car. Call me right away if anyone spots it. Approach the vehicle with care. If he did this, he'll be a desperate man.'

Six

Lucinda scouted the second floor and found a room to use for questioning. She positioned a long table with a chair on one side where she could sit with her back to the window and another on the other side where the early-morning sun would shoot bright rays into the eyes of the person she interrogated.

She went down the hall to the school board meeting room where she ignored the superintendent's attempts to get her attention. She put officers to work getting names, job positions and contact information for all the people in the room and asked Officer Kirby to stand guard down the hall. Then she called Sammy Nguyen.

He rose and walked to the front of the room with hunched shoulders and downcast eyes. He followed Lucinda down the hall with steps as short and quick as a geisha. His dark green work pants were lighter at the knees – faded to a near-white shade. The legs of his pants were rolled into cuffs. Frayed edges rested on the top of scuffed work boots. His matching work shirt displayed signs of wear at the cuffs and across the top of the collar. Lucinda offered him a seat at the table and sat down opposite him.

'Mr Nguyen, I know you've been through this

already, but if you could please tell me everything you did, everything you saw, from the
moment you pulled into the parking lot until the
time the police arrived.'

Sammy related his story again, his voice
getting higher and faster as his story progressed.
The stress of the morning's discovery was apparent in the whiteness around his nostrils and
the tightness constricting his lips.

'Mr Nguyen, are you certain that the basement
door was locked before you entered the building?'

'Yes, yes,' he said with a nod.

'Did you unlock the side door before you left
the building?'

'Yes,' he answered.

'And you unlocked the front doors?'

'When the officers asked me to, yes.'

'If the doors are locked, do you need a key to
get out of the building?'

'Yes,' he said. 'When the bolt is thrown you
cannot open the door at all.'

*Then whoever killed Fleming had to have had
a key.* 'How many people have keys to the
building, Mr Nguyen?'

'I don't know. Lots of people. Most everybody.'

'Mr Nguyen, what time did you leave work
yesterday?'

'Me?' he asked, pointing a finger to his chest.

'Yes, Mr Nguyen.'

'I left usual time – about three o'clock.'

'What did you do then?'

'I went home. I watch news on television. I

34

have dinner with wife. We watched television shows and go to bed.'

'Which television shows did you watch last night?'

'Ahh, ahh, don't remember – was something wife liked. I not pay much attention. I do cross-word puzzles.'

'Your wife will corroborate that, Mr Nguyen?'

'Yes, yes. She always tell truth. She's good woman.'

'Thank you, Mr Nguyen. Could you please return to the meeting room?'

'Yes,' he said. As he rose, he jerked his head forward in a half bow.

Lucinda jotted down a few notes about the interview then went back down the hall. She stood quietly in the doorway, unnoticed as she observed the behavior of the unwilling congregation. Sammy Nguyen stood with his back to a corner, shaking his head back and forth. Superintendent Robert Irving stood in front of him, badgering him with questions.

'Mr Irving,' Lucinda said.

He turned toward her with a fast flush rising from his neck to his cheeks. 'Yes?'

'This way, please,' she said and turned on her heels without waiting for his response.

As he stepped into the makeshift interrogation room, Irving said, 'Lieutenant, you've put me in an awkward position. I should not know less than my own employees. What is going on in my building?'

'Have a seat, Mr Irving.'

He slid into the chair but Lucinda remained

35

standing, her arms folded across her chest. 'The moment these premises became a crime scene, you ceded control and authority to the police department. I am in charge now, because, sir, you are a suspect – one of many, but a suspect nonetheless.'

'That's preposterous.'

'Do you have a key to this building?'

'Of course I do.'

'Since we've not found any indications of a forced entry so far, your possession of that key makes you a suspect.'

'Do you know how many people have keys?' Irving objected.

'No. But I'm hoping you'll provide us with a list.'

'Of course, but who was killed?'

'We are still trying to locate the next of kin for the likeliest individual.'

'Lieutenant, I have narrowed it down to a handful of people who are not in the meeting room up the hall. I may be able to help you.'

Lucinda turned her back on him and walked in front of the windows and looked down into the parking lot as a car pulled into a slot and was surrounded by a sea of blue. She spun around and snapped, 'Why did you call Mr Nguyen a "son of a bitch" this morning when he called you about the murder, Mr Irving?'

'I did no such thing. He never called me. I would never call Mr Nguyen...'

Lucinda raised an eyebrow. 'Really? Then Mr Nguyen is lying to me?'

He shaded his eyes from the sun. 'Could you

36

lower the blinds?' he asked.

Lucinda did not respond. She didn't move. She continued to stare as she congratulated herself on the way she had positioned the chairs.

Irving broke the silence. 'I admit I was pressuring him to tell me what he knew, back there in the meeting room. But I have never, ever called him names.'

'Once again, you are telling me that Mr Nguyen is lying?'

'If he said I called him a "son of a bitch", yes, he is.'

'We've checked his cellphone log, Mr Irving. We know he called you this morning. And, from your response to him, it sounded as if you already knew why he was calling. In fact, at first, he thought you'd already called the police.'

'Why would I call the police?'

'You tell me, Mr Irving. Did you know what Mr Nguyen discovered before he called?'

'He didn't call me,' he said, rising to his feet.

'Sit, Mr Irving,' Lucinda ordered and waited for him to comply.

He glared at her before sinking back down into the chair and shading his eyes with his hand.

'Mr Irving, we have documentation of Mr Nguyen calling your home this morning. You're wasting my time and yours by denying that phone call. Someone answered your home phone. And according to Mr Nguyen, it was you and you said, "You son of a bitch, I'm calling the police. Leave us alone." And then you hung up the phone. Now if that is not an accurate representation of what you said to Mr Nguyen, you

37

tell me what you did say. But don't tell me it didn't happen.'

Irving stood to his feet again and leaned forward with his fists resting on the table in front of him. 'Lieutenant, if you are not going to believe anything I am telling you, perhaps I need a lawyer. But I will insist again, I did not talk to...' The blood drained from Irving's face, and he slumped down into the chair. 'Ohmigod.'

Lucinda leaned into his face. 'Yes, Mr Irving?'

'I didn't think it was Nguyen. I thought it was the other person calling again.'

'What other person, Superintendent?'

'I don't know,' he looked up at her, a pleading look in his eyes. 'Honest, I don't know.'

'Tell me about it,' Lucinda urged.

'The first call came before five thirty. My wife answered. The caller wanted to know if I was there. I took the phone but he wouldn't tell me who he was. He just hung up. Then he called again and hung up again. I thought the third call was from the same person. And, yes, that is just what I said. But I had no idea it was Nguyen. The first two calls certainly weren't him. I'd recognize his voice. He has a slight accent.'

'I suppose your wife will verify your story?'

'Of course, Lieutenant,' Irving bristled. 'But do you really need to drag her into this? It's school business not personal business.'

Lucinda sighed. 'Did you really need to ask that question, Superintendent?'

Irving flushed again. 'Sorry. Stupid of me. I really do want to help, Lieutenant. I just don't know how I possibly can without a better idea of what is going on – of who died here last night.'

Lucinda stared down at him, contemplating the wisdom of providing him with more information. Her reverie was interrupted by a knock on the door frame. She looked up at Ted Branson.

'I've got the warrant and brought along a couple of detectives to execute the search. Should I assist them or is there something else you need me to do?'

'Thanks, Ted,' Lucinda said. 'I could use your help with these interviews. Could you pick a room, set up and get started?'

'Consider it done,' he said as he turned and walked away.

'I thought you didn't need a search warrant, Lieutenant,' Irving said.

'We probably don't but we have a side issue in addition to the homicide and I didn't want to take any chances.'

'A side issue? You mean Sean Lowery, the tech guy?'

'Yes,' Lucinda said.

'Please, Lieutenant. Tell me what's going on. Let me help you,' Irving pleaded.

She studied him for a moment and said, 'OK, Superintendent, but it has to stay in this room.'

'No problem, Lieutenant.'

'Illegal drugs were found in Lowery's car. We need to search his office for any additional drugs or drug paraphernalia and any information we might find to help identify his supplier. And, just in case, we're also searching for a murder weapon.'

Irving gasped. 'Drugs? Are you serious?'

'So far, just a small amount of marijuana.'

'There's nothing small about that. He will be fired immediately.'

'That'll have to wait. We're holding him on resisting arrest, reckless driving, interfering with a homicide investigation, obstructing justice, driving under the influence and anything else we can think of to pile on top of the possession charge. He'll be busy for a while.'

'I can't wait to take action, Lieutenant. I would be underestimating the reaction of some of the parents if I did. If they even suspected that any-one on our payroll ever inhaled second-hand pot smoke at a college party, they'd be demanding termination. But this? If the school district is slow to take action, they'll be lined up on our doorstep with pitchforks.'

'I thought most of your parents would have experimented with drugs when they were younger.'

'A lot of them did, but at times I get the im-pression that some of those who didn't are bitter that they missed out on the fun,' he said with a laugh.

'Fun, Superintendent?'

Irving sighed. 'Just a joke, Lieutenant. Now, are you going to tell me who died in my building?'

'We think it's Sharon Fleming,' Lucinda said.

'Shari? Are you sure?' Irving asked.

'Pretty much. Her car was the only one in the lot besides Mr Nguyen's when the first officers arrived on the scene.'

40

'You haven't told her husband?'

'Can't find him, Superintendent. Have you got any ideas about that?'

'Have you checked the lab where he works?'

'Sure have. He's not there. He's not at home. We have no idea where he might be.'

'So you think ... No, no, Lieutenant. Not Conrad. He adored his wife. And he put up with a lot.'

'What do you mean by that, Superintendent?'

'She works all the time. She stood up Conrad at company events and on social occasions. Shoot, if the poor man won a Nobel prize, she'd probably miss the flight to Sweden.'

'Do you encourage your employees to work that hard, Superintendent?'

'She's not my employee. Sure, she works in my building and provides a program in my schools but she's not on the district payroll. She works for Communities in Schools, a non-profit organization with its own local board of directors.'

'Are you on that board, Mr Irving?'

'Well, yes,' he admitted. 'But I'm just one of nine members.'

'Why are you trying to distance yourself from the victim?'

'I'm not.'

Lucinda's shot up an eyebrow in disbelief. 'Oh, really?'

'Look, Lieutenant, I have to distance the school district from this crime.'

Lucinda laughed. 'Mr Irving, the *crime* happened in your building. The list of possible

41

suspects includes every one of your employees.'

'I know. I know. But I have a board to answer to, too.'

'OK, Superintendent. Let's get down to basics. Can you think of anyone who'd want Shari Fleming dead?'

'No. She was idolized. The social workers she hired to work at each school acted like they were working for Mother Teresa. The teachers and administrative staff think she walks on water. The parents of our at-risk students treat her like she's omnipotent.'

'But you, Superintendent? You don't seem to share their unqualified adoration of Ms Fleming.'

'Listen, she was fabulous. She was dedicated. She really cared about our at-risk students. But like I said, she worked too hard. She was supposed to be an administrator and quite frankly, she was too hands-on. I tried to counsel her to focus on her job, which in some ways is just like mine; but she always wanted to get involved with the work in each of the schools, with parents in the schools. She instituted a number of remarkably successful programs, but she could have turned over some of the responsibility to staff once she got them up and running.'

'Like what, Superintendent?'

'Well, she set up an annual field trip with the kindergarten classes. She'd take these little at-risk guys and as many parents as she could cajole into attending to an area college or university and give them a tour. It was the first time a lot of these parents – many of them high school drop-outs – ever considered the possibility of college for their children. Over the years, many students, who might never have graduated from high school, went on to four-year schools. She credits the parents' involvement from an early age. She says that's the key to every child's success.'

'You doubt that?'

'I think it's one of the keys.'

'OK. Did you ever have any other problems with her?'

'When she was in the office, she had a constant stream of parents before, during and after office hours.'

'Aren't you all here to serve the community, Superintendent?'

'Yes, but it's usually handled on the school level. People who work here go to the schools to meet with the parents. With the exception of the ones coming to see Shari, they rarely come here except for when the school board meets each month.'

'She'd let parents in here after hours when no one else was in the building? She had her own key?'

'Yes, to both questions.'

'Are there any parents who might hold a grudge against her? Who might be dissatisfied?'

'I know where you're going with that, Lieutenant. But I can't say that I've heard of anyone. I could ask her staff. They might know of someone.'

'You do that, Superintendent. That's all for now.'

'Can I go down to my office and get to work?' Irving asked.

'Oh no, sir. You just go back to the meeting room. We may need to talk to you again.'

Irving opened his mouth to object, shook his head and walked away. Before Lucinda could return to the room to fetch another interview subject, her cell phone rang.

'Lieutenant, we found Conrad Fleming's car.'

Seven

Ted stepped into the doorway of the conference and asked, 'Is the Human Resources Director present?'

A woman in a red suit exhaled a long 'yes' as she uncrossed her legs and rose to her feet. Placing one hand on her hip and tilting back her head, she added, 'I'm all yours, Officer.'

'That's Sergeant Branson, ma'am. And your name?'

'Monica,' she said, arching an eyebrow.

Ted scrawled on a pad of paper as he asked, 'Last name?'

'Theismann,' she answered with a strong emphasis on the first syllable.

'Come with me, please,' Ted said, stepping back into the hall. Although totally aware of her slow walk and swaying hips, Ted gave no outward indication that he was paying any attention to her at all. He led her down to another room and stood by the door. 'After you,' he said.

Monica walked past him, making sure she brushed against his body as she did. She smiled up at him but he ignored that, too.

'Please have a seat over at that table,' he said, gesturing to the middle of the room.

Monica took her time settling into the chair.

Ted remained patient and seemingly oblivious until she was still.

First, he established Monica's claim that she knew nothing about what had happened in the building the night before or even what was going on right now. Then Ted took her a step forward. 'If I were to tell you that someone was murdered in this building last night, what would come to your mind?'

'Mmmm?' Monica hummed and looked upward, swinging a foot back and forward in the air.

Ted was surprised by her lack of emotional reaction to the news of a homicide in the place where she worked. He folded his arms across his chest as he studied her for any other suspicious reactions.

Suddenly, she looked straight at him and winked. 'I think I know what happened,' she said with a coquettish grin.

Good grief, is she flirting with me? Ted struggled to maintain the passive expression on his face to hide his shock from her. 'Ms Theismann, what do you know?'

'Well,' she simpered, 'I don't *know* know.' She uncrossed her legs and placed an elbow on one knee and tapped a bright red fingernail against her lips. 'But based on who was not in the meeting room and the logical process of elimination, I'd say someone killed Shari Fleming.' She beamed at him as if awaiting a pat on the head.

At first Ted was too stunned to respond. *How did she know? Did she kill her? This silly, vain woman? But maybe her behavior is all an act –*

46

an act designed to divert suspicion away from her. If it is, it's not working.

Monica continued to smile at Ted. She tilted her head to one side, raised an eyebrow and asked, 'Well, Officer, am I right?'

'What makes you think Ms Fleming is the victim, Ms Theismann?'

'So you're not going to answer my question. I could assume that your silence means I'm right.'

Ted looked at her with a blank expression and waited for her to continue.

'Well,' she said, brushing her skirt smooth with two manicured hands. 'Of all the people not in the room down the hall, Shari Fleming is the only one I know who is engaging in risky behavior.'

'What do you mean by "risky behavior", Ms Theismann?'

'Monica, Sergeant. Please call me Monica.'

'Please answer the question, Ms Theismann.'

She rolled her eyes and tutted. 'Very well, Ms Fleming was engaged in an extramarital affair.'

'An affair?' Ted echoed. 'Are you sure about that?'

'Oh, definitely. I suspect she was killed by her husband, or her lover or her lover's wife.'

'Just who do you allege is her lover?' Ted asked.

'This is not gossip, Sergeant. This is straight from my personal observation.'

'Please, Ms Theismann, who do you believe is the other party in this affair?'

'Robert Irving,' she said with a sneer.

'The superintendent?' Ted asked, already

dreading the political ramifications of this tidbit.

'Oh, yes, Sergeant. Aww, but come on, you already knew that, didn't you?'

'What leads you to believe they were having an affair?'

'All those one-on-one meetings behind closed doors. The secret, private smiles they exchanged in meetings all the time. And the fact that neither one of them ever made any decision without consulting with the other person.'

'Did you witness any overt displays of affection?'

'They are not stupid people, Sergeant Branson. But then, neither am I. I'm in Human Resources. I'm trained and experienced at reading people. Their shared smiles and exchanged glances spoke volumes.'

'I see. So it's just speculation on your part?'

'Puh-lease, Sergeant. I am a trained professional. Which of the three do you think did it?'

'Ms Theismann, what time did you leave the office last night?'

She threw back her head and laughed long and hard. 'Really, Sergeant, you can't cow me with that red herring. You've got three likely suspects here and I am not one of them.'

'Ms Theismann, I am serious. Please answer the question: what time did you leave work last night?'

Monica rolled her eyes. 'Very well, I'll play your little game, Sergeant. It couldn't have been more than a minute or two after five o'clock when I walked out the door.'

'What did you do then, Ms Theismann?'

She sighed. 'I headed home. On the way, I stopped at the liquor store for a bottle of wine and some Amaretto.' She leaned forward and whispered, 'It's *the* liqueur for lovers. Have you ever had any? And would you like to try it?'

Ted straightened up, pressing his back to the chair. 'What did you do then?'

She sighed, even deeper this time. 'I went home, read a magazine while I sipped on a glass of wine. Fixed a salad for dinner. Took a shower, read some more, drank more wine and went to bed.' She pouted her lips and added, 'All by my lonesome.' She paused for a reaction from Ted, got none and continued. 'I slept all night, got up, got dressed, pulled into the parking lot about eight thirty and have been under the watchful eye of the cops ever since.'

'You didn't leave your home all evening?'

'No, Sergeant! I'm getting very tired of this game. Can I go now?'

Ted gave her a tired smile. 'Not just yet. You wait right here for a moment. He walked out of the room to find Lucinda and brief her about the interview. To his surprise, he encountered her in the hall heading in his direction.

'You're not going to believe this...' they said in unison and erupted in mutual laughter.

Eight

'You first,' Ted said.

'They found Conrad Fleming's car,' Lucinda said.

'Where?'

'After looking all over town, a returning patrolman spotted it in our parking lot.'

'At the police station?'

'Yeah,' Lucinda said with a shake of her head. 'If the media gets hold of this, we're gonna be laughed out of town.'

'What was it doing there?'

'Fleming was inside filing a missing-person's report on his wife.'

'You're kidding,' Ted said.

'I wish. He arrived there at about the same time the first officer arrived here. I've gotta head down to the station to talk to him. I need you to keep the situation here under control.'

'No problem.'

'So what did you get?'

Ted related Monica's story about Robert Irving and Shari Fleming.

'Do you believe her?' Lucinda asked.

'I'm not sure. Maybe she's guessing. Maybe she's making it all up. And maybe she's right but it has nothing to do with Shari Fleming's death.'

'Aw, c'mon, Ted. What are the odds that they're having an affair and it has nothing to do with this homicide?'

'Slim. I know. But, it's also possible that, true or not, the story is a smoke screen thrown up by Theismann to conceal her own involvement.'

'And what would be her motive for killing Shari Fleming?'

'At this moment, I have no idea,' Ted said, shaking his head.

'Follow up on that, Ted. Ask some other people about Theismann's story and about Theismann. See what you find.'

'So what do I do with her now?' Ted asked.

'Do you trust her not to talk to anyone about your conversation if you send her back to the meeting room?'

'I hardly trust her to keep her mouth shut sitting in a room all alone.'

'Oh, one of those,' she said with a laugh. 'Stick her in the room I was using. Kirby's still there. He can keep an eye on her.'

Lucinda walked out to her car. Before she was halfway down the sidewalk, she spotted something stuck under her wiper on the driver's side. It seemed irreverent to be soliciting so close to where someone had died a violent death. *No one knows that, though.* She thought. *Not yet.* She sighed. *But they will soon.*

She turned and looked down the street to the barricade where uniforms stood vigilant to prevent reporters from nudging the white sawhorses forward. She spotted a camera with a very long lens moving to point in her direction. She turned

51

away and snatched the glossy sheet of paper off her windshield. She was starting to crumple it into a ball when she realized that none of the other vehicles around hers had anything under their wipers.

She smoothed the paper out – it was just a flyer for a battery sale at Sears. She flipped it over and saw words printed in black ink in the white margin of the ad. 'STOP IT. STOP IT NOW OR ELSE.'

Stop what? She knew whoever had left that on her car was sure to be long gone by now, but she scanned the area anyway, turning quickly away when she spotted a media camera again. *Was this note intended for me specifically? Looks like it. Does it have anything to do with this investigation? Who knows? It could be a coincidence – and nothing more.* Coincidences always made Lucinda nervous. She decided to hold on to the note just in case.

As she pulled away from the curb and headed to the station, she didn't notice that beyond the barricade, another car started up, circled the block and fell in behind hers.

Nine

Lucinda stood on the viewing side of the glass and observed Conrad Fleming. He rose from the table, circled the room and sat back down. He rested his elbows on the surface and his face in his hands. He ran his fingers through his hair and stood again. He repeated this pattern seven times in the five minutes Lucinda watched him.

The stress was apparent in more than his actions. His hair stuck out in all directions. His eyes reminded Lucinda of a panicked rabbit as they darted around the room. He wore a rumpled Duke University T-shirt and a slouchy pair of sweatpants – his clothes looked as if he'd slept in them.

Is he distraught? Or is he feeling guilty? Or is he just putting on a good show? Lucinda wondered.

Fleming was on his feet with his back to the door when Lucinda opened it. He spun around at the sound. He stared at her, his eyes wide, his lips parted.

'Conrad Fleming?'

'Y-y-y-yes,' he stammered.

'I'm Lieutenant Pierce,' she said as she strode across the room with an outstretched hand.

He slipped his hand into hers but his handshake was weak and his palms cold and clammy.

'Have a seat, Mr Fleming.'

His movements were clumsy, as if someone tugged a rope and jerked him into the chair. 'Did you find Shari?'

'We think we have...' Lucinda began.

He threw his head and exhaled loudly as he placed a hand flat on his forehead. 'Oh, thank God. Thank God. Thank God.'

'Mr Fleming, if we are right, it is not good news.'

He dropped his head forward. 'What do you mean? What are you saying? Is Shari hurt?'

'If we are right, yes, she is. She—'

'How badly?' Conrad interrupted. 'Is she in the hospital?'

Lucinda pursed her lips and took a deep breath through her nose. 'Mr Fleming, we fear that your wife has been murdered.'

'Murdered? No. You're wrong.' He thrust out his arms and pushed away from the table. Turning his back on Lucinda, he hung his head and swung it from side to side. 'No. No. No. No. No. No.'

'Mr Fleming, please. Please sit back down. We are not sure if it is your wife. We need to find out. Please sit down and help me.'

He returned to his seat. 'It's not Shari. It can't be.'

'How was your marriage, Mr Fleming?'

'It's good. Really good. The only disagreement we ever had was over her long hours at work. We really don't get to spend as much time together as I would like. But Shari's job is demanding and she really cares about the students. And that's part of who she is – of the woman I love.'

'Have you had any arguments recently?'

'Arguments? No, we hardly ever argue. What? Are you thinking I did something to Shari?'

'We have to check out all the possibilities, Mr Fleming. If you argued, she could just be missing right now. She may just have gone out of town to think.'

'Oh, I hadn't thought about that. No. No arguments. I was hoping she'd get home before too late last night 'cause there was something I needed to ask her. I guess that could have been an argument if we had a chance to talk, but we didn't.'

'What did you want to ask her, Mr Fleming?'

'Oh, it doesn't matter now. It bothered me last night but not now.'

'Why, Mr Fleming? What happened to change your mind?'

'Oh, I found out it wasn't true,' he said.

'Found out what wasn't true?'

'The stupid stuff Monica said.'

'Monica Theismann?' Lucinda asked.

'Yeah. She called last night. She's not a very nice person.'

'What did she tell you, Mr Fleming?'

'She had some ridiculous story about my wife and Robert Irving having an affair.'

'If it bothered you last night, why doesn't it bother you now?' she asked him but her thoughts were more direct. *Is it because you know she's dead – because you killed her?*

55

'Because I know they didn't spend the night together.'

'And just how do you know that?'

'I called his home this morning. He was there.'

'Did you talk to him?'

'Actually, when he came to the phone, I hung up.'

'You just called once?'

'Well, actually, no. I called again to ask him if he knew where Shari was but when he answered the phone he was so angry, I just hung up again. I'm usually not that rude, honest.'

Well, that answers that. Or does it? 'When was the last time you spoke to your wife, Mr Fleming?'

'Uh, let's see. Right after I got home from work. I couldn't have been home more than fifteen or twenty minutes. It was sometime before six last night.'

'Where was she when she called?'

'At work. She said she'd be there for a while. She told me to go ahead and eat dinner. I was worried about her. About whether she'd get something to eat or not. She told me not to worry. She said she'd grab something when she got home.'

'Did she say when she expected to get home?'

'Uh, she said she wasn't sure. She said she had some paperwork to do and a parent conference and she'd be home as soon as she could.'

'Did she mention the parent's name?'

'Uh, uh,' Conrad bit his bottom lip and shook his head. 'No. No she didn't. And, damn it, I didn't ask.'

'That's OK, Mr Fleming. Stay calm for me, OK?'

'Yeah, yeah,' he said, shaking his head, but his ragged breathing belied his words.

'Do you remember what she was wearing when she left for work in the morning?'

'Uh, I was still in bed. I-I-I, uh, she kissed me goodbye. I, uh, I told her I loved her. I didn't pay any attention. I don't know.' He threw his head on folded arms and sobbed. 'It is true, isn't it? She is dead.'

Lucinda reached across the table and patted his forearm. 'I'm still not certain, Mr Fleming. But, yes, I think so.'

'Oh, God,' he wailed as he raised his head. 'Why didn't I notice? I never paid enough attention to what she wore. She always looked so good and I hardly ever told her. Can I see her now?'

'Mr Fleming, you don't want to see her.'

'Yes, I do,' he said in an angry voice. 'In fact, I demand to see her. She is my wife.'

Lucinda shook her head, 'No, Mr Fleming, you don't. You really don't. Please trust me on this.'

'What? Oh my God. What do you mean?' Conrad shouted. His mouth hung open. His eyes filled with tears. 'What happened to Shari?'

'We have the body of a woman. We have reason to believe it is your wife. But we can't be certain just by looking at her.'

He stood and paced back and forth in front of her, wringing his hands. 'Ohmigod! What did they do to her? No, I don't want to know. How

57

will I ever know it's her? Or maybe it's not her? How will we ever know? Maybe this is a big mistake. A case of mistaken identity? That's possible, isn't it?'

'Anything's possible right now, Mr Fleming. Let me check and see if her personal effects are available. You would recognize her watch and jewelry, wouldn't you?'

'Uh, some of it. Some of it, not. I bought some of it for her. I would remember that. She usually wore the watch I bought her two Christmases ago but not always. What – what did she have on?'

'I don't recall offhand, sir. Let's see what I can find out from the coroner's office.'

'The coroner's office? Oh my God!' He slumped back into the chair and rested his head on the table, sobbing quietly.

When the phone answered, Lucinda said, 'Pierce here. Are Shari Fleming's personal effects ready?'

'Yes, ma'am, all wrapped up and ready to go,' the tech said. 'If you're in the building, I can bring them up.'

'Thanks. I'm in interrogation room B.'

'Be there in a flash.'

Lucinda disconnected and turned to Conrad Fleming. 'Is there anyone you need to call while we wait? Any family members that need to know?'

He raised his hands and waved outward-facing palms in the air. 'No. No. Not now. Not until we know for sure. Oh, God, I don't know if I want to know,' he said, bowing his head.

'We need to know, Mr Fleming. If it's not your wife, we need to be looking for her.'

'Really?' his head lifted, his eyes brightened. 'That officer who took my report said it had to be at least twenty-four before they'd do that.'

'Things have changed, Mr Fleming. She was last known to be in a building where someone was murdered. If she's not the victim, she could be a witness, or, quite frankly, she could be responsible. But either way, we'll need to find her immediately.'

A rap on the door brought Lucinda to her feet. She signed for the small box wrapped in brown paper. She sat at the table and broke the seal. She slipped the contents out for Conrad to see.

He grabbed the thin watch, held it up and stared at its face. Then he clutched it to his chest and wailed. Lucinda had her answer. Shari Fleming was dead. Now she had to figure out why.

Ten

Before leaving the station, Lucinda stopped by the forensic technology center. The review of the tapes from the Flemings' community confirmed Conrad's alibi. And Shari's cell phone confirmed the call to her husband at five fifty-six the evening before.

After interviewing Conrad, Lucinda thought he was blameless in his wife's death – these details reinforced her opinion. The only doubt she had about his story involved the reported affair between Shari and the school superintendent. *Was Conrad in denial? Or was he right?* Time to pay a visit to Robert Irving's wife.

Again, as Lucinda pulled from the curb, she did not notice the silver Honda that started up and followed in her wake. She lost her tail, though, when she pulled up to the guard booth of the gated community that the Irvings called home.

She stood on the front porch of a mock-Victorian house and rang the bell. The door was opened by a chubby elf of a woman with high-lighted blonde hair and a pixie smile. 'Yes, may I help you?'

'Mrs Irving?' Lucinda asked.

'Yes, I'm Trudy Irving – and you are?'

'Lieutenant Pierce, homicide,' she said as she flashed her gold shield.

'Oh, your scars! You're the detective who was shot in the face by that abusive husband, aren't you?'

Lucinda swallowed hard. Her hand made an involuntary move toward the damaged side of her face. She nodded in response.

'I'm so sorry,' Trudy said. 'That was very rude of me. Please, come in,' she said with a smile. 'This way, please.'

Lucinda followed Trudy through a spacious foyer with a grand staircase and into a book-lined room with large windows curving outward on the far wall. Trudy gestured to an overstuffed chair. 'Please have a seat, Lieutenant, and tell me how I can help you today. Did something happen to one of my neighbors?'

'No, ma'am,' Lucinda said, but before she could continue, Trudy blanched and clutched her throat, 'Robert?' she gasped.

'No, ma'am. Your husband is fine. Nothing has happened to him.'

Trudy exhaled loudly, 'Oh, thank heavens. Oh my, you gave me a scare for a moment.'

'Sorry, ma'am, but your husband is involved in my investigation.'

'Robert? Involved in a homicide investigation? How could that be?'

'It happened in the school district building. The body was found this morning.'

'Oh, my! I shouldn't have skipped watching the news this morning. I wonder why Robert didn't call me and let me know?'

'We haven't been allowing any calls, ma'am.'

'Oh, I see. Who, who...?'

'Shari Fleming was murdered sometime last night.'

'Shari? Murdered? Are you certain it was Shari? How could anyone possibly want to hurt Shari?'

'We're trying to find that out. And part of that process is to check up on everyone's whereabouts at the time of the crime. What time did your husband return from work last night?'

'I don't think I recall exactly. I was on the phone with my sister. I know it was after six o'clock, but definitely before seven.'

'Did he go out anywhere that evening?'

'No. We had a quiet evening at home. Went to bed after the eleven o'clock news.'

'When did you get up?'

'When some rude crank caller woke us up this morning.' At Lucinda's prompting, she described the conversation she had with the anonymous man on the phone and reiterated her husband's story about the two additional calls.

'How would you describe your marriage, Mrs Irving?'

'My marriage?' she said with a laugh. 'I do love my husband, Lieutenant. And I believe he loves me. But after thirty years together, it's pretty predictable – almost boring.'

'Boring enough to make it easy to succumb to temptation?'

'Oh, heavens, no. It would be the death of Robert's career. He's so close to retirement now. That's not something either one of us would want to put at risk.'

'Are you sure you can speak for your husband, Mrs Irving?'

'I trust my husband. He's not a lusty kid anymore. He is honorable, thoughtful and considerate. No, Lieutenant, I have no reason to believe he's cheating on me.'

'What do you know about his relationship with Shari Fleming?'

'With Shari?' she said with a grin. 'Oh, good grief, you've been talking to Monica, haven't you?'

'Why do you say that, Mrs Irving?'

'Who else? Make sure you get Monica to tell you about the three or four other affairs my husband has had. Good heavens, to listen to her you'd think old Robert was a stud muffin.'

'So this isn't the first time Ms Theismann has suspected your husband of an affair?'

'Oh, no. And she never tells me directly, but she always makes sure someone will.'

'Why are you so certain she's wrong?'

'Because it's Monica. She cornered my husband one day in his office and pressed her body up to his. He rebuffed her advances. And since then he's declined her invitations to meet her off school district property nor will he even meet with her at the office unless someone else is in the room. So, to salve her damaged pride, Monica spreads rumors about any woman she ever notices behind closed doors with Robert. She is rather vindictive. Not a nice person, at all.'

'Why does your husband keep her on his staff?'

'You tell me. I've asked the same question over and over, Lieutenant. He says that she does a good job and although he is willing to dismiss someone for performance problems, he would never fire anyone for personal reasons.'

'Is there anything else you can tell me about the environment in your husband's workplace? Is there anyone who had a problem or disagreement with Shari Fleming?'

'You mean besides Monica? No, no one. She was universally admired. And Monica, well, let's just say that I think she's a coward and too passive-aggressive to actually *do* anything. Unless it was poison. Now that would be Monica's style. Was Shari poisoned?'

'No, Mrs Irving.'

'Then, you can scratch Monica off your suspect list, in my opinion. But what about me? If you suspect Robert of having an affair with Shari, wouldn't I be a suspect, too? And what about Shari's husband? I'd think we'd both be at the top of the list.'

'Both of you, and your husband, Robert, are persons of interest at this point in the investigation.'

'How exciting!'

'Exciting?'

'I told you my life was a bit boring, Lieutenant. I'll grab at any diversion from the daily routine.'

Lucinda left the Irving home shaking her head. She was certain that Trudy Irving had nothing to do with Shari Fleming's death. She felt the same way about Robert and Conrad. Her leads were

64

drying up fast. She needed to get back to the school district offices and see if Ted had uncovered anything new.

Eleven

Back at the site of the murder, Lucinda stuck her head into the room where Ted sat, interviewing a woman on the staff. He ducked out to the hall where they compared notes. The information the two had gathered about Monica Theismann was remarkably similar. At Lucinda's request, Ted reiterated the details from his interview with Monica.

Lucinda went a few steps down the hall to where that woman paced under the watchful eye of Officer Kirby. She'd barely passed through the doorway before Monica erupted. 'Why am I being held prisoner here?'

'You are not under arrest, Ms Theismann. You are here to help us with a murder investigation.'

'Why am I being isolated? Why am I separated from everyone else?'

'You made some statements earlier that requir-ed follow-ups with others. We did not want you repeating those statements until we had the opportunity to talk to the people you identified as possible suspects. Now, will you please take a seat?'

Monica folded her arms across her chest and said, 'I don't think so.'

'You really don't want to make this difficult,

Ms Theismann.'

'Arrest me or let me go.'

Lucinda sank into the chair on her side of the table. 'It's not that cut and dried. If you won't sit down and talk to me, I'll have you taken to the station and talk to you later after I finish up here.'

'You have no right.'

'Yes, I do, Ms Theismann. You see, at this moment, you are the only person we know with a possible motive for killing Sharon Fleming whose alibi cannot be verified by another source.'

Monica's mouth flew open and her hands dropped to her sides. She couldn't bring herself to say a word.

'Please have a seat,' Lucinda asked again.

Monica slouched into the chair, her posture limp, her face ashen. 'You must be kidding, right?'

'Not at all, Ms Theismann. Right now, you could look pretty good for the murder of Shari Fleming.' Lucinda concealed her serious doubts that her involvement was possible.

'What motive could I possibly have?'

'Your belief that Robert Irving and Shari Fleming were having an affair, for one.'

'Well, that makes him, his wife and her husband much more likely suspects than me.'

'Not necessarily. You see, Ms Theismann, we are aware of your unrequited lust for Superintendent Irving.'

'How dare you?' she said, jerking to her feet.

'Please sit, Ms Theismann.'

'I will not. Not until you apologize.'

Lucinda stared at her. Monica looked away but didn't soften her rigid posture or the stubborn thrust of her chin. Lucinda pushed back from the table and walked towards the door. 'Kirby, could you run her down to the station?'

'You can't do that!' Monica shouted.

Lucinda turned and faced her. 'Yes, we can, Ms Theismann.' She turned her back to Monica and spoke to Kirby. 'Cuff her if you have to.'

'Don't you dare do this to me,' Monica shouted at Lucinda's back. Then she turned a smiling face toward the patrolman and simpered, 'Officer, you know she's only doing this because she's jealous of me.'

Kirby reached for her elbow and she shrugged him off. He pulled the cuffs out of his belt and dangled them in the air. 'Your choice, ma'am.'

'But officer, don't you understand? She's just getting back at me because she has such a hideous face. And, well, me on the other hand...' she said, tilting her head and giving him her most seductive smile.

Kirby didn't bat an eye. He just jingled the cuffs again and repeated, 'Your choice.'

Monica snorted and stuck out her elbow, allowing him to escort her, uncuffed, to his patrol car.

Twelve

Lucinda and Ted finished up the staff interviews without uncovering any new, relevant information. The only other people left in the building were the techs on the second floor and the superintendent and the custodian still in the meeting room with a patrolman.

'I don't like the way this is shaping up, Ted. We don't know much more than we did when we got here this morning.'

'We do have one suspect.'

'Pfft. Monica Theismann?' Lucinda asked.

'Yeah.'

'Oh, please. Did you see how perfect her manicure was? No way she just beat someone to death last night. No, we're left with the slim, almost negligible possibility that the tech guy we busted early this morning did her in 'cause she uncovered his drug habit.'

'Well, the tech guy is possible, I guess,' Ted admitted. 'Although they didn't find a stash of drugs in his office anywhere, they did find a half-straw and a white-dusted mirror.'

'Cocaine?'

'The vice guys took it to the lab. Could be traces of meth. Could be something he confiscated from a student.'

'Yeah, but to kill her with that much brutality would have to mean he had a great deal of hostility towards her and nobody indicated that at all. In fact, I don't think they really knew each other beyond a "hello" in the hall.'

'So, where do we go now?' Ted asked.

'We'll have to talk to all of Shari Fleming's staff and see if they know anyone – a teacher, a parent, a student – anyone she might have met with last night or who was angry with her about anything. Then, we'll follow those leads. Hopefully, one of them will lead somewhere.'

'What about Irving and Nguyen?'

'Send them home. We know where to find them. I'm heading back to the station. Hopefully, by now, Theismann's learned her lesson and I can send her home, too.'

Outside, something fluttered on Lucinda's windshield. This time it was a torn piece of newsprint. In the margin she read another note: 'I AM SERIOUS. STOP IT NOW.'

Block printing? Any connection to the legal pad in the kitchen? No. Too obvious. She looked down the street both ways for anything that appeared at all suspicious. Her eye passed right over the silver Honda. The driver ducked down before the vehicle came into Lucinda's view. She sighed and stepped into the car.

She pulled out her cell and keyed in Ted's number. When he answered, she asked, 'Have you found any note stuck to your windshield recently?'

'They call them parking tickets, Lucinda,' Ted said with a laugh. 'No, I haven't. Need me to fix

70

one for you?'

'No, Ted,' she snapped. 'I am talking about notes – vague notes.'

'Is someone threatening you?'

'Yes. No. I don't think so.'

'Is it connected with this investigation?'

'No. It's probably nothing. Forget about it.'

'Forget about what?'

'Sorry I bothered you, Ted. Bye,' she said, flipping her cell phone shut and starting her car. She drove back to the station with her silver shadow running close behind.

Thirteen

In the elevator of the Justice Complex, Lucinda pressed the Down button. She had decided to stop by the morgue before she'd let Theismann off the hook. She pushed open the swinging stainless-steel doors and called out for Doctor Sam.

'Back here, Lieutenant. How am I supposed to do my job if you keep interrupting me?'

'I haven't bugged you for hours, you old curmudgeon. Have you finished the autopsy of Shari Fleming?'

'How slow do you think I am? I finished with her hours ago.'

'So what's the verdict?' she asked.

'Verdicts are for court,' he snarled back at her.

'Doc, cut me some slack. Cause of death, manner of death, whatcha got?'

'Someday I won't be around here anymore and then you're gonna wish you treated me nicer.'

'C'mon, Doc. You know you're my favorite ghoul. What did ya learn? What do I need to know?'

'I have half a mind to ignore you for that "ghoul" remark, but in the name of justice, I'll let that slide. She died from blunt-force trauma to the head. The weapon was probably a baseball bat – not definitely now; it could have been any club-shaped object. But there were no splinters in her hair and so, whatever it was, it had a smooth, finished, rounded surface like a bat. And her hands, you remember her hands?'

Lucinda thought for a moment and said, 'Yes. Across her chest. The fingers bent strangely.'

'Well, it looks like your guy broke her fingers after she was dead and then put her hands together like that.'

'A guy? Not a woman?'

'Possibly a woman but not likely. Whoever did this used a lot of brute force. Looks like you've brought me the handiwork of yet another sicko, Lieutenant. Thanks a lot,' he said as turned away to return to the autopsy table.

'Why, Doc, do you always blame me for the bad guys?'

He turned around and looked at her over the frame of his half-glasses. 'Can't blame the victim now, can I?'

Lucinda rolled her eyes and headed back to the elevator and up to the fourth floor. She observed Monica through the glass. Her shoulders slumped, her gaze cast down on the table and her hands folded on uncrossed legs that stood primly side by side. Lucinda walked into the room and Monica didn't even raise her head. 'Ms Theismann, can we talk now?'

Monica nodded her head.

'About you and Superintendent Irving...?'

'Yes. You are right. I threw myself at him and he rejected me,' she said with bowed head. She turned her face upward and continued. 'I swear

73

to you, though, I had nothing to do with Shari Fleming's death. You have to believe me.' Her eyes filled with tears.

Lucinda could see the tracks of those previously shed trace a line through the make-up on her face. She felt a moment of sympathy for the frightened woman before her and then remembered what a spiteful gossip monger she was. 'You are still a person of interest and even if you are cleared of murder, you may be charged with obstructing justice for that rumor you started about Irving and Fleming.'

'Oh, please, please. I'm sorry,' Monica pleaded.

'It's not up to me. It's up to the District Attorney. But I have no further need to hold you here for now. You can leave,' Lucinda said and walked away from the table to the door.

'You're not going to give me a ride back to work to get my car?'

'Not me. Not hardly.' Lucinda said, knowing any patrolman would gladly do just that but wanting Monica to have to figure that out for herself. Lucinda just walked out the door and didn't look back.

Fourteen

Lucinda went to her desk, searched through her in-box and pulled out the contact list for all of Shari Fleming's staff and headed out to visit their homes. She whispered a 'thank you' into the air to whomever it was that had dug out the list she'd requested earlier that day. She drove off to start visiting their homes.

By nine fifteen that night, she had completed six visits to social workers and received four names – three parents and one teacher – to check out as possible suspects. None of them sounded very likely but at least she had some leads. She decided she could squeeze in one more staff member before it would be too late to be disturbing people at home.

She rang the bell beside the door to the apartment of social worker Melanie Thomas. She heard the cover sliding off the peephole and a muffled voice asking, 'Who is it?'

'Lieutenant Pierce. Homicide,' she said, holding her badge and identification in clear view.

The deadbolt clunked open, the chain slid out and the door opened. Melanie's hair was jet black, straight and down to her waist. It contrasted sharply with a face as pale as a new Easter lily bloom. Her dark blue eyes were mesmeriz-

75

ing in the midst of that all that drama. 'Are you here about Shari?'

'Yes, I am,' Lucinda said.

'Come in. What can I get you? Coffee? Tea? A soft drink? A glass of wine? Whatever you want, it's yours.'

'Just a little time and some information,' Lucinda said, following her into the living room.

Melanie plopped down on the sofa, stretched her legs out across the cushions and pointed to an adjacent upholstered chair. Lucinda took a seat and could tell the other woman was studying Lucinda's face. The question marks in Melanie's eyes were as obvious as dog drool. *I am so tired of answering questions about my face.*

Before Melanie could verbalize what was on her mind, Lucinda asked her about her job responsibilities and daily routine at Olde Towne Primary School, then asked her about her whereabouts the night before.

'I was right here. My sister and her boyfriend were here, too. They came down for a long weekend – almost a week, actually – and didn't leave until this morning. Her boyfriend went to bed around ten last night but we were up till two in the morning talking about everything.' Melanie grabbed a notepad and pen off the coffee table. 'Here's my sister's phone number and I think I've got his number on my cell.' She pulled it out of her pocket and scrolled down. 'There it is.' She jotted it down on the pad, tore off the sheet and handed it to Lucinda.

'I usually have to ask first,' Lucinda said with

a chuckle.

'Hey, why waste time? I guess my eagerness could be misinterpreted as a cover-up for a grand conspiracy. But shoot, if that were true, I'd be a goner all ready; my sister is such a blabber-mouth. What else can I tell you?'

It was refreshing and maybe even a little dis-arming to find such a cooperative witness, but Lucinda worked on being grateful instead of skeptical. 'Are there any parents at your school with a reason to be angry at Ms Fleming?'

'Oh, wow, you've got to be kidding. These are all young parents with little kids in the program at my school. Some of them were kids when they had kids – some of them still are kids. Shari and the program are their salvation. They love it when she comes by the school for one of our parent meetings. They call her "Tia Shari" and gather round her like kittens to a bowl of milk.'

'Most of the families are Hispanic?'

'Heck no, not at this school, just a handful are. Most of our families are African-American. But one Latina started calling her "Tia" and now everyone does.'

'What about the teaching staff and the school's administrative staff, any problems there?'

'Jeez, no. We solve so many problems for them from head lice to absenteeism to behavior issues. The only problem we have from the faculty is excessive demonstrations of grati-tude.'

'No behavior problems you couldn't solve – one that caused a teacher to blame you or Ms Fleming?'

'We don't really have the serious issues that are common at the middle schools and high schools. These are little guys, Pre-K, Kindergarten and first grade. A little acting out from a need for attention. If you take action right away, and get the parents involved, it usually clears up in no time. And unless Mr and Mrs Satan move into the neighborhood and enroll their little minionettes, I don't expect any life-threatening problems.'

'OK then, what about the staff of Communities in Schools? Anyone discontent, annoyed, angry?'

Melanie looked down and contemplated the lines in the palm of her hand. Lucinda waited in silence.

'Have you talked to any other staff members?' she asked without looking up.

'Yes, I have. A few of them.'

'Did any of them mention any problems with co-workers?'

'No, they didn't.'

Melanie grimaced and looked up. 'I'm really not comfortable answering that question.'

Lucinda sat still, holding her gaze but not saying a word.

Melanie sighed. 'I really don't think it's relevant.'

Still Lucinda did not utter a word.

'But if it popped up at another time, it might throw you off the track. So, here goes. Timmy Seifert.'

'What about Timmy Seifert?'

'Timmy is a social worker like me. But he's at

Timberlane High School. He's always complaining about not being the Executive Director.'

'He wants Ms Fleming's job?' Lucinda asked. *Possible motive?* she wondered.

'Well, he certainly did. Timmy's been around as long as Shari, since the very beginning. In fact, he applied for her job then. He was one of the three finalists but Shari got the job and he's been ticked at the board of directors ever since.'

'Has he been angry at Shari, too?'

'He's never expressed that. He always talks and acts like he owes Shari a debt of gratitude. According to Timmy, he appreciated Shari for hiring him despite the fact that he competed for her job and in defiance of a board of directors that believes he's gay.'

'Is he gay?'

'No. He's just a mess. He's a real homophobe, actually, with insecurity about his own gender identity. Then, God only knows why, he got into a profession where most practitioners are female. It makes him real defensive and he's always suspecting discrimination because someone, somewhere, thinks he's gay. He believes that's why he didn't get Shari's job in the first place. I tell him he's silly. The board flat out doesn't care one way or another just what his sexual preference is, just so long as it doesn't involve kids. He's paranoid about it. Always saying this person or that person thinks he's gay 'cause he's a social worker.'

'How can you be sure that the board didn't discriminate against him?'

'Because there is at least one woman who is

79

lesbian and a guy who's gay on the board. And there are rumors that another guy dresses up like a woman when he's out of town on vacation.'

'Nonetheless, do you think there is a possibility that he might take his resentment toward the board out on Ms Fleming?'

'I don't think so. In fact, I'd bet on it. Then again, I'm just a social worker, although I have a really good intuitive feel for people. Still, I'm not a mind reader.'

'Anything else you think I should know?'

Melanie shook her head. 'I wish I did, Lieutenant. I wish I had all the answers for you. As a social worker and a Christian, I am all about redemption. But not for this guy. Not for whoever killed Shari. Catch him and put a bullet in his head if you get half a chance. I kinda felt guilty thinking that, but now I've said it and I guess that makes it even worse. I should be ashamed but I'm not.'

'You're just human, Ms Thomas; no need to be ashamed of that,' Lucinda said as she stood and handed Melanie a business card. 'You think of anything, give me a call.'

Melanie nodded, stood and placed a hand on Lucinda's forearm. 'Listen, Lieutenant. I do referrals all the time. If you need any help hooking up with a surgeon or a counselor, just let me know. I'd be glad to help.'

Lucinda wanted to scream, but instead, she forced a smile, said 'Thank you' and let herself out of the apartment as quickly as she could.

Back at the station, Lucinda ran a criminal background check on all the names she'd gathered that evening. Besides a few minor juvenile infractions, only one of the parents on the list popped up with an adult offense: Clarence Dumas. He was arrested and convicted of DUI six years earlier. Probation served without incident. No repeat offense. Not exactly a precursor for violent homicide. Still, she'd have to give him special attention. She had just signed out of the database when Ted walked in the door.

'Hey Lucinda,' he greeted her. 'The techs have finished up at the scene and the whole building has been searched for a possible murder weapon. They brought in a couple of baseball bats they found in offices throughout the building and a couple of pieces of pipe from the basement. None of them appeared to have blood on them but they'll do a thorough check in the lab.'

'Did you release the building?'

'Oh, no. I figured you'd want to do a walk through in the morning. I left the tape up and patrol folks on duty. You can release it when you're satisfied. I know better than to second-guess you,' he teased.

'Oh yeah, Ted. I'm so difficult to work with.'

'Nah, not really. But you are demanding. As you should be.'

Lucinda gave him a smile and brought him up to date on her end of the investigation. They agreed that Ted would visit as many of the Communities in Schools staff as he could the next day and Lucinda would follow up on the new leads she'd got from her interviews.

'I'm heading home, Ted. My cat awaits and is

81

probably in a foul mood since I've been away and he's been without tuna for...' She stretched out her arm and looked at her watch. 'Close to eighteen hours. And if there were anything else I could do tonight, I still wouldn't be going home – so, he should consider himself lucky, but he won't.'

'Want to grab a drink first?'

'No. I just want to go home, Ted.'

'Not me. Home is a messy apartment I share with a guy who snores louder than I thought humanly possible.'

'You still haven't patched things up in your marriage?'

'My marriage is dead, Lucinda.'

'Have you been to counseling with Ellen?'

'No. It would just be a waste of time. End of discussion, Lucinda.'

'Damn it, Ted. You owe her. Ellen is still grieving over the loss of the baby. If you don't help her get past this, you will regret it.'

'I guess that means you're not going to invite me to your place for a drink, either.'

'Shut up, Ted,' Lucinda said and stomped out of the office.

Fifteen

Lucinda opened the front door of her apartment and heard the pounding of cat paws galloping through the kitchen in her direction. Chester mewed and rubbed against her shins. She crouched down to greet her gray tabby, scratching the spot that he loved so well on the back of his neck. When it felt too good to keep standing, Chester plopped on the floor and rolled on his back, displaying the white belly that now needed attention. Lucinda stroked on it while he stretched and purred out his appreciation.

Lucinda stood and Chester dashed over to his food dish and gazed up at her with avid expectation. Lucinda reached into a cabinet and pulled out a tin of tuna feast. Chester performed figure eights as he waited for her to open the can. His manic movements brought on an unsettling surge of vertigo. She'd learned the hard way to hold perfectly still and not look down when Chester performed these gyrations. If she moved, the vertigo took hold. When she first lost her eye, the dizziness was so intense it drove her down to her knees. Now it was merely unsettling, but still she tried to avoid the sickening sensation whenever she could.

She breathed in deeply and it passed. It stirred

up her feelings of gratitude for the monocular vision therapy she'd received. Without it, her recovery from a moment of physical disorientation would not be as automatic or as complete. She bent down and plopped two spoonfuls in her cat's dish.

'Good grief, Chester, you act like you're starving. You still have half a bowl of dried food. If you were really that hungry, you would have eaten that all up.'

She laughed at the half-growl, half-purr noise that rose from his throat while he chewed. She walked down the hall to her bedroom shaking her head. After slipping on a pair of sweats and a T-shirt, she came out to the living room where the answering machine blinked at her.

She played back her messages. There was a reminder of her pre-op visit for the scheduled plastic surgery for her lip reconstruction, a whiny message from her sister chastising her for not calling, and a lot of other stuff she really didn't care about. But there was one that mattered – it was from Charley, the nine-year-old girl whose life she'd barely managed to save the year before during an investigation into the death of the child's mother. The bond that grew between them took Lucinda by surprise. She didn't think she'd ever develop deep feelings for someone else's daughter but she sincerely loved that little girl.

'Hi, Lucy. This is Charley. I just wanted to say hi! I miss you. Call me soon, please. Just to talk. I love you.'

It was too late now to return the call but

Lucinda made a note to remind herself to do so. She poured a glass of one of her new favorites, an Australian red blended wine from Peace Vineyards. She stretched out in her recliner and sipped on it while she reviewed the case in her head. She had eliminated more suspects than she still had on her list to interview. That worried her but she reminded herself that scratching people off the list of possibilities was progress. She'd talk to the five remaining tomorrow and maybe Ted would get more names from the Communities in Schools staff he visited. And maybe she'd get a hit back from the national crime database. Maybe.

Lucinda had a bad feeling about this case. The usual suspects were all eliminated. The second tier of less likely prospects was under review but none held clear promise.

The crime scene felt like a repeat offender. The post-mortem broken fingers seemed like a signature. Had she already spoken to this socio-pathic killer and not seen behind his mask? Was it someone who hadn't and wouldn't cross her radar? Was she going to let someone get away with murder? With a brutal, savage murder? 'No,' she said out loud. 'Absolutely not.'

She was tired and sleep came easy. But it didn't stay with her long. At four o'clock, she was up again, getting dressed to return to the front line.

When she got into the office, she found two hits from the crime database – a pair of unsolved cases in the region where the weapon in the beating deaths appeared to be a baseball bat or something similar. But that was where the similarity ended. Both victims were men. One was homeless. The other lived out in the boonies in a sagging farmhouse with no running water or central-heating system.

She checked for criminal records on her list of five potential suspects and nearly shouted out her excitement when she found that Mickey Justin had an extensive record with multiple counts of domestic violence and assault. Her excitement was short-lived, though. A further search led her to more pertinent information. Cops had arrested Justin on yet another assault charge two days before Fleming's death. He was still in county lock-up, unable to make bail. *Damn!*

She checked on where the remaining four lived and worked and mapped out a plan for talking to each one of them. She saved Timmy Seifert until last. She didn't want to talk to him at work where, with his professional standing, he might feel in control. She'd save him until after school and approach him at his home. As she pulled out of the Justice Complex parking lot, a silver Honda slipped into the road behind her.

It was close to lunchtime when she finished up her fourth visit. She had learned nothing new – she was hoping that one of the parents would lead her to others that needed to be investigated. But no luck there. She moved all four of the people she interviewed to her mental 'very unlikely' list.

She remembered that she needed to talk to Charley but that would have to wait until later – Charley would be at school now. She called the office of her surgeon, Dr Rambo Burns, and cancelled the visit scheduled for that afternoon as well as the surgical procedure planned for Friday. She used the intensity and unknown duration of her current homicide investigation to put off their attempts to get her to reschedule.

She called Ted next and arranged a quick meet for a lunch-on-the-run where she could get the contact information for the two parents and a teacher that had come up in Ted's interviews that morning. Lucinda was gratified to find out that another staff member had corroborated Melanie's tale of Timmy Seifert's aspirations and paranoia. After gobbling down a burger and fries, she was off again to talk to potential suspects. By the end of the school day, the only viable name remaining was Timmy Seifert.

On the drive over, she didn't notice that halfway to her destination the silver Honda peeled off and was no longer following her. She parked on the street in front of a well-maintained Craftsman bungalow. The paint was fresh, the grass manicured, the shrubbery neatly trimmed, the flowerbeds mulched and free of weeds. She stepped on to a broad front porch complete with intricate wooden railings and four rocking chairs, sitting side by side, facing out to the front yard.

The woman who opened the solid wood door appeared to be close to sixty. Her light brown hair was streaked with gray and she had pronounced laugh lines beside her eyes and around her mouth. *Too old to be Seifert's wife.*

'May I help you?' the woman asked.

'I'm Lucinda Pierce, homicide,' she said as she flipped open her badge. 'I'm looking for Timmy Seifert.'

'Why do you want Timmy?'

'Then I do have the right place?' Lucinda asked.

'Yes, he does live here in my house. I'm his mother,' she answered. 'But what do you want with my Timmy?'

He still lives with his mother. That could explain his insecurity. 'There was a woman killed at the school district office building and we're talking to a lot of school district employees.'

'He's not in any trouble, then?'

'No, ma'am, I just want to ask him a few questions.'

An older face surrounded by a halo of bright white hair peered around the corner of the door. 'Dora, make sure this is not a trick to get a false confession. You know, like on those shows we've seen on the television.' She turned her face to look straight at Lucinda. 'I'm not just talking about those TV dramas, mind you. We've seen those shows about real cases, too. I know what you all are capable of. So don't even think about pulling any fast ones, here.'

'Oh, Mother, look at her,' Dora said.

Oh, good grief. He lives with his mother and *his grandmother?*

'With a face like that,' Timmy's mother said,

'she couldn't possibly tell a lie and get away with it.'

Lucinda rolled her eyes. She'd heard at lot of comments about her face over the years since the accident, but this was a first.

'You're right, Dora. Where are our manners? Open the door and invite the poor woman inside.'

Dora lifted the latch that held the screen door shut and opened it. 'So sorry, Lieutenant. Yes, please do come in. I'm Dora Seifert and this is my mother, Ruth Perchase. Come right this way.'

Lucinda started to follow Dora but was stopped when Ruth grabbed her arm. 'Does it still hurt?' she asked as she peered at the scars.

'No, ma'am, not at all.'

'Those lips? They don't hurt? They look awful painful.'

'No, ma'am, not at all,' Lucinda repeated calmly but inside she was screaming – *nothing is worse than pity.*

'Mother, please,' Ruth said. 'Let the poor woman come in here and sit down.' She directed Lucinda to a wooden chair with an upholstered seat and back. 'You wait right here; I'll go get Timmy. He's in the kitchen doing prep for dinner. He always does that when he first gets home. He says it calms him after a day at school surrounded by teenagers.'

For a moment, Lucinda and Ruth waited quietly. Then Ruth asked, 'You're not married, are you?'

'No, ma'am, I'm not.'

'I can sure see why.'

Lucinda bit her tongue and forced her facial features not to react.

'Now, our Timmy, he's not married either. The woman who marries him will get to live right here,' she said to Lucinda with a wink.

'Grandma, cut that out,' said a male voice from the doorway.

Lucinda looked over in the direction of the sound and saw a lanky man with blond flyaway hair wearing a red and white checked apron with a white ruffled edge tied around his waist. He walked into the room then stopped and his jaw dropped as he focused his gaze on Lucinda's face.

Lucinda barely noticed. She was too busy ogling Timmy's apron and wondering why he was surprised that anyone would question his sexual preference.

Dora came through the doorway and flicked a tea towel at her son's arm. 'Don't stare, Timmy. It's not polite.'

Timmy stammered, 'Sorry,' then followed Lucinda's gaze to the apron and his face reddened. He untied it as quickly as he could and tossed it on to an empty chair. 'There,' he said, brushing his palms across one another. 'Now, what can I do for you? Mother said you had some questions.'

Lucinda listened patiently as he ranted and raved about his discrimination at the hands of the Board of Directors. When she asked him about Shari Fleming, he prattled on and on about her sainthood here on earth and the lofty position she must now hold in heaven. Lucinda was so bored with his droning that she wished he would go back to staring rudely at her face. *Or maybe Grandma will jump in with an inappropriate question.* When Lucinda asked about anyone who might want to harm Shari Fleming, she heard instead a litany of all the people who loved her and why.

Finally, they got to the question about his whereabouts on the night of the murder. Timmy hardly said a word. His mother and grandmother raved on and on about the dinner he'd made that night. Then about the snacks he prepared for their bridge party and how he always kept the trays full of food and their glasses full of drink. Then they'd all watched the news and a half-hour of some talk show that they just had to tell her about in excruciating detail.

With relief, Lucinda finally rose to her feet and handed Timmy a business card.

'Oh, you're not going to stay for dinner?' Dora asked.

'No. I can't. But thank you very much.'

'Officer, you have to eat,' Ruth said. 'Tell her, Timmy. Tell her to stay,' she said to her grandson, then turned back to Lucinda. 'Timmy really wants you to stay. He'll make something special.'

'I'm sorry, I can't. I have an appointment,' she said as she backed out of the room. Out on the porch she took a deep breath and regretted leaving a business card – it might lead to more invitations she didn't want to receive.

Sixteen

He danced a frenzied jig around the park bench. *At last. At last.* For days, he'd searched discarded papers. He'd stopped by hotel lobbies and bus stops. He'd found a coffee shop next to a newsstand and hung out there until they ran him off. Then he came back when a different shift worked and did it again.

He picked up discarded newspapers, most from up and down the east coast but he also ran across a partial copy of the *Houston Chronicle* and another of the *L.A. Times.* He finally found the story he sought and it sent shivers of anticipation up and down his spine. It was in the *Washington Post.* He ripped the whole page from the newspaper and carefully folded it to fit in his shirt pocket. *Time to head north. But how?*

He sat on the bench and breathed deeply in and out, focusing on the breathing and nothing more. He needed to relax, to be calm, to think. *Aw, the hell with that. I just want to fly. To be there. To be there now. I just want to jump up and run and run and run until I reach my destination and spit again in the eyes of fate.* The compulsive energy agitated his adrenalin into action. It coursed through his bloodstream making his left knee jiggle up and down, one hand wring against the other, his breathing turn ragged. Passers-by gave him a wide berth.

He noticed their odd stares. *No! No! No! I must be calm. Must be patient. Must think. Breathe in. Breathe out.* He closed his eyes and deepened his inhale and his exhale until his heart stopped pounding and his knee and hands came to a rest. He regretted continuing his deep breathing when a woman walked by and her essence penetrated into his lungs. It made him nauseous and renewed his impatience.

All good things come to those who wait, he muttered for reassurance. He stood and went back across the street to the coffee shop. He slipped a newspaper off one of the wrought-iron tables on the sidewalk in front of the little cafe. He walked past the store front and leaned against the brick wall, pretending to read while observing every small detail in the vicinity of his gaze.

It took longer than he hoped but he maintained his vigil and was rewarded. A young woman pulled the front end of her tan Saturn into a parking space. She locked her car and stepped into the outdoor dining area, dropping a newspaper and her keys on the table and her purse on a chair. Her face brightened as another young woman approached from the other side. They embraced. The driver of the Saturn grabbed her bag and they went inside.

The loitering man walked up the sidewalk, between the shop and the table. He scooped up the newspaper with the keys in one smooth move. He continued in the same direction until he reached the corner of the block. Then he crossed the street and headed the opposite way. When he was aligned with the tan Saturn, he jaywalked over to it. He glanced up the sidewalk – the women had not yet returned.

He opened the driver's door, slid behind the wheel, backed up and turned right at the first intersection. Before he completed the corner, he looked back and saw that the table was still vacant.

He estimated that he had at least fifteen minutes before the radio call to look for the stolen car went out to officers in the field. That was not quite enough time to get to the north side of town. But if he was lucky, the woman wouldn't notice the keys were gone until she got back up to go to her car – a delay that would buy him more valuable minutes.

Exhilarated about the upcoming hunt for and destruction of his new target, he didn't have the inclination to worry about the passing time. Fifteen minutes went by, then twenty, and still he drove on. At last he made it outside of the city limits and on to Interstate 95. He exited at a truck stop. They'd be looking for the car now. The risk was too great to drive it all the way to D.C.

He parked behind the building where motorists and patrol cars on the highway would not see it. He wanted to be far from here before the car was discovered. Then, he went looking for a truck driver to give him a ride.

The first two he approached looked at his tattered clothes and wouldn't even listen to him.

They just hopped into their rigs and slammed the door. The third guy was far more receptive.

'Hey, man, I'm in a fix,' he told the driver. 'My mama is dying up at this hospital in D.C. My car broke down. I don't have no money for a bus. Could you give me a lift up the highway?'

The driver looked him over and slowly nodded his head. 'I reckon so. But I've got a gun and I won't hesitate to use it if you try anything.'

The hitch-hiker held up both of his hands defensively. 'Hey, man, I just want to see my mama before she dies.'

'Alright then, we'll get along fine. I can't go into the city, though. But I can drop you at the exit closest to it.'

'That's great, man. Thanks a lot.' He turned and looked back at the two drivers who'd dissed him. He wanted to rush over and snuff them both on the spot. But the waiting target was the most important priority. He sighed and stepped up into the rig.

As they headed up the highway, he contemplated killing this driver. He ran the list of pros and cons through his head. He decided not to decide just now. He'd just wait till the truck stopped to let him off and go with the flow. Follow his feelings at the moment he felt them. He was pleased with that plan. He liked surprises – even from himself.

Seventeen

The next morning, Lucinda didn't notice a silver Honda shadowing her every turn as she drove from the station to the school district building. But when she pulled to a stop, she spotted that car slipping into a parking slot a block away. It looked familiar but she could neither recall where she'd seen it before nor decide if it really mattered.

She stepped out into the street and glanced back. The car's front end was blocked by the one parked in front of it, making it impossible for her to read the license plate. She could walk back and openly jot it down. But there was a person in that car. *Why hassle someone, maybe ruin their day, just cause I'm feeling squirrelly? It's probably nothing.* She shook off her paranoia and walked up the sidewalk into the building.

Outside of the break room door, she imagined the victim entering first and the assailant standing here in the doorway. *What did her attacker see? What was he thinking? Did he come here to see her? Or did he see her because he came here?*

She stepped inside the room and tried the opposite scenario. She looked for a hiding place – any spot where the perpetrator could have stood and not been noticed when the victim approached the threshold. *That was easy. There were two major areas blocked from view by the angle of the entryway. OK, where could he hide so that the victim would not see him until she was well inside the room?*

Ah, there's a dilemma here. As long as the lights were on – and I'd have to assume she'd flip the switch at the door – there is no place to hide except inside the cabinets under the sink. Lucinda strode over and pulled open the big doors. A clutter of cleaning supplies on the left. A trashcan on the right. All of that would have to be removed for anyone to fit in the space.

But then, afterwards, he would have to put it all back in place. Does that make any sense? Not really. Too complicated. She peered at the bottles and canister and saw ridges of dust on top of several of them. She scratched that possibility off of her list. So, he either attacked her as she entered or he sneaked up behind her after she was in the room.

She stood on either side of the doorway and searched the walls and floor around it. *If he struck her here with the bat, or whatever, there would be blood spatter all around here.* She saw none. She pretended she had a cylindrical object in her hand and swung on one side of the doorway, discovering there wasn't enough room without banging it into the wall behind her and there were no marks there. Then she swung on the other side and realized that unless the victim entered the room backwards, a strike from that side would not match the evidence on her body.

So, he sneaked up behind her. What does that tell me? She must have heard him and turned her head slightly. That's it. It was a slight turn. The kind of turn you make when someone you know is there approaches you. Not the kind of turn you make if an unexpected visitor startles you. Lucinda sighed. *Back where we started. It's either an employee or a person she allowed into the building. But who?*

She crouched down and studied the evidence and markings on the floor, pleading with them to speak to her, to give her answers, to point to a clear suspect. But not even a murmur arose. She sighed again.

A clearing throat interrupted her reverie. She turned and a patrol officer spoke. 'Ma'am, Superintendent Irving is out on the steps by the side door. He asked if he could see you.'

She nodded her head as she rose. 'Yeah, let him in. I'll meet him in the hall.'

Irving walked into the building talking loudly. 'Lieutenant, when am I going to get my building back?'

'Soon, Mr Irving. Probably a little later today.'

'When, Lieutenant?'

Lucinda folded her arms and stared at him.

'OK, OK. I give,' he said. 'What can I do for you? How can we speed this up?'

'I need a list of names with contact information for all the staff that were not here yesterday morning.'

Irving pulled a folded sheet of paper out of his pocket and opened it up. 'Here is the list I made of the people who were in the meeting room

98

yesterday. And on the other side, a list of the names of everyone I could think of who wasn't there. I know at least one of them is out in the parking lot right now. If I can go into my office, I can check the database on my computer and see if I forgot anyone and pull the phone numbers and addresses you need.'

Lucinda agreed and followed Irving into his office. As his computer powered up, he asked, 'So where do things stand? I'm guessing you don't have a suspect yet or you wouldn't be asking for more names.'

'Actually, I have a lot of possible suspects right now, Mr Irving. Including you.'

'But, but...' he blustered. 'I have an alibi.'

Lucinda pointed to his monitor and said, 'Looks like your computer is ready.'

Irving gave her a hard look and shifted his eyes over to the monitor where he pulled up his employee database.

After eliminating all the staff on his list of those present, he printed out the rest and handed it to Lucinda. She looked at the five names with social security numbers, addresses and phone numbers on the sheet of paper. She mentally scratched off Sean Lowery. She knew exactly where he was – in the county lock-up on drug charges. That left four.

'You said that one of these people was out in the parking lot?' Lucinda asked.

'At least one.'

'Who?'

Irving pointed to a name. 'He's here.'

Lucinda walked to the bank of windows across

the room from Irving's desk. 'Look down there. See if you spot anyone else.'

Irving looked down into the parking lot, pointing out two others on the list until only one remained: Steve Broderick.

'Who is he? What does he do for the district?' Lucinda asked.

'He's our Enrichment and Extra-curricular Director. He has oversight of all school activities outside of the classroom. From field trips to a park across the street to overnight trips out of state, he sets up processes for each school and makes sure district policies are followed. He is also responsible for the smooth operation of on-campus before- and after-school activities – athletic competitions, club meetings, music lessons, the free breakfast program and the day care at some of the elementary schools.'

'And he wasn't here yesterday and not here today?'

'Well, not here yet, anyway.'

'Have you heard from him?'

Irving sighed. 'We haven't been taking phone calls here since you took over the building yesterday, Lieutenant.'

'But he didn't call you at home to find out what's going on here or let you know what's keeping him away from work?'

'No. I haven't heard from him,' Irving admitted.

'What about those others out in the parking lot? Did you hear from any of them?'

'Actually, you're right. They all called just after dinner last night. Two of them saw something on the news and the other one was concerned because she hadn't been able to reach a real person at the office all day.'

'How well do you know Broderick?'

'I don't socialize with him one-on-one. He's divorced. I'm married. Doesn't usually work well at intimate dinner parties and stuff like that. But I do see him out at major events and around town. We met at a conference four or five years ago. I hired him to his position with the district actually.'

'But you don't know him well?' Lucinda said with raised eyebrows.

'Oh, I do, professionally. I know about his education, his experience in the field and his performance – more than competent by the way. I can put a project on his desk and stop worrying about it before I leave his office. But personally? No, not so much.'

Lucinda thought about his response then asked, 'Could you round up those three people in the parking lot and bring them in here so I can talk with them?'

'Sure. What about the offices?'

Lucinda pointed an index finger at his chest. 'You. And only you can come in and work in your office. But stay in your office and don't go wandering around the building. Clear?'

'Yes, Lieutenant,' he said with a sigh. 'When?'

'Soon. Unless something unexpected comes up in these interviews, I can probably release the building to you when I finish.'

Irving nodded and headed out the door. Lucinda looked out the window, watching him gather up the three employees she needed to question. *What about Broderick? Is his absence as suspicious as it feels to me?*

She met Irving and the staff members just inside the entrance. She directed the man and two women up to the meeting room on the floor above. As they started up the stairs, Lucinda turned to the superintendent. 'Could you try to reach Broderick? And if you do, ask him to come in?'

'Sure. Should I tell him you want to talk to him about Shari's murder?'

Lucinda thought for a moment. 'You know him better than I do, Mr Irving. Feel him out. If you think that will make him rush over here to help with the investigation, tell him. If you get a hinky feeling, a niggling worry that he might run, keep it to yourself.'

Upstairs, Lucinda learned nothing new, just more of the same – shock at the crime, positive feelings toward the victim, and an eye-rolling response at the mention of Monica Theismann. None of them knew anything about Broderick's whereabouts and not one seemed to find that suspicious.

Lucinda met back up with Irving, who'd had no luck hunting down his missing director. She unraveled the remaining yellow crime-scene tape and released the building. When she left, she headed straight to Steve Broderick's home.

His house was a small brick ranch with a carport in a neighborhood full of more of the same. A car sat in the driveway. She called in the plates – registered to Steven Broderick, no surprise there.

She rang the doorbell twice without getting a response before she knocked, politely and then again with both fists. She grabbed the knob and twisted but the door was locked. She felt uneasy about not getting an answer while the subject's car still sat in the driveway so she circled the house, peering inside.

She saw nothing untoward through the front windows or in the ones on the side. In the back, she walked on to a small flagstone patio and looked through the opened vertical slats that hung across a sliding glass door. She saw a dog's bowl full of water and a dish next to it licked clean. *But where was the dog? Why wasn't it barking?*

Nothing in any of the rooms gave any indication of foul play. *Broderick would never be nominated as housekeeper of the year. But then, there have been times when my place has looked even worse.*

Still she felt uneasy. *What if he's in there and he's hurt? Or gagged so he can't speak? Or someone's holding a gun to his head? Or maybe he's dead already. He could be dead. And the dog. The dog would have to be dead, too, wouldn't it? Otherwise, he'd bark. Maybe I should force my way in. Break a window. Remember the time you wouldn't let Ted do just that? Remember?*

'Stop it!' she said out loud. *You are not looking for a possible victim here. You are looking for a suspect. And he might not even be a serious suspect. A private citizen has every right to leave*

103

his home and leave his own car behind. He has the right to take a dog with him if he wants. There is no sign of any disturbance inside. No indication of any kind of confrontation. Reasonable cause for a forcible entry does not exist.

But to go AWOL the day after a woman is murdered at his place of work? The timing could simply be a coincidence, she argued to herself. *There is such a thing as coincidence.*

But no matter how many times she repeated that phrase, she never really believed it.

Eighteen

On the drive home, Lucinda stopped at the market. Chester greeted his heavily laden roommate at the front door as if he knew she had something for him in one of the bags. His movements around her legs became frenzied when she pulled out the can of treats and shook them in her hand. Then he lay down with the side of his face on her foot, rubbing and purring. When she pulled off the lid, he jumped to his feet and stared up at her.

'Is that smell appealing?' she asked with a laugh. He answered with a loud meow as he twined around her legs again. Careful to avoid the onset of vertigo, she knelt down and gave Chester a handful of crunchy, anti-tartar treats, put away her groceries and checked her voice mail.

The third message was from her surgeon's office. 'Ms Pierce, this is Michelle at Doctor Rambo Burns' office. I am calling about the cancellation of your procedure. We would like to reschedule your surgery and, of course, your pre-op visit, but if you are not ready to do that yet, we could give you a referral to a counselor who understands the issues you are facing, who has experience helping people with the anxiety and fear generated by facial reconstruction. Just give us a call at your earliest convenience and let us know how we can help you.'

Lucinda slammed down the receiver. 'Damn you,' she shouted at the telephone. Chester ran for cover. 'Damn you. Damn you. Damn you. I am not afraid. I am not anxious. I am busy. Busy. Busy. Busy. Counselor? What do you have? Shit for brains? I told you I was busy. I told you I had an active homicide investigation. Damn you!'

No matter how she raved, she knew she raged because Michelle had happened upon the truth – the truth of the fear she denied to everyone, the nervous apprehension she tried to deny to herself. But it was real, no matter how hard she tried to repress it.

She knew plastic surgery was part science, part art. She trusted the technical side that required knowledge and skill sets. She knew Rambo possessed both in abundance. The artistic part of the process, however, terrified her. In attempting to restore her looks, to make the damaged side look like the natural side, the smallest mistake or even a glitch in the healing process could make her face look even worse than it did now. A mirthless chuckle rocked Lucinda. *Yeah, right. As if that's possible.*

Mumbling, she walked away from the phone and into the kitchen. She pulled out cheese, bread, lunch meat and condiments to fix a sandwich for dinner. The sounds and smells of food preparation lured Chester out of hiding. He waited at Lucinda's feet for a tidbit.

She usually obliged but tonight her thoughts

were too dark to notice Chester's discreet begging. *Did I really cancel because I was busy? Or because I was afraid of the procedure? Or is it deeper than that? Am I still struggling with survivor's guilt all these years after my mother's death? I thought I'd dealt with that. But have I really?* She chastised herself for worrying about herself at a time like this – she had a homicide case on her hands and it required all of her attention.

She took two bites out of her sandwich and abandoned it on the kitchen counter. Pulling out her notes on the investigation, she sat sideways on the sofa with her legs up and knees bent, the Fleming file balanced against her thighs. She went through page after page, searching for something she might have missed. Anything she could have misinterpreted. But every time her thoughts stalled on the question of the perpetrator, her mind drifted over to the lip reconstruction surgery now on hold.

She slept fitfully that night, waking up several times with non-productive thoughts about the investigation or the procedure. But when her eyes popped open just after five a.m., she was thinking about the board of directors of Communities in Schools, Shari Fleming's employers, and she knew exactly what to do next. She dressed quickly and headed into her office.

At her desk, she dug through her in-box and found the Board of Directors list she had requested. To her delight, it was right there as promised. She whispered 'Thank you' into the empty room but knew she'd have to do more to express her gratitude to the research and documentation staff just as soon as she closed this case. She scanned over the list, noticing a few familiar names of people who were notably active in the community. It was too early to start stopping by homes – well, she could, but she was certain they'd be more cooperative if she didn't wake them up at an unsociable hour on a Saturday morning.

While she waited for a more reasonable time to come around, she checked each director for a criminal record. She found a few minor traffic violations but nothing more. No surprise there. Uncovering a violent felon on the board would be nice, but the odds were stacked against that.

She took out a city map, plotted the different addresses of the directors and planned the order of each visit. When she finished that up, she remembered that she hadn't returned Charley's call, grabbed the phone and dialed the Spencers' number. When Charley's father answered, Lucinda said, 'Hi Evan! I was thinking about taking Charley out this evening, would that work for you?'

'Sure would,' he said. 'In fact, you could do me a big favor.'

'What's that?' Lucinda asked.

'She really wants to see the new *Pirates of the Caribbean* movie and I really don't want to sit through another couple of hours watching Johnny Depp reprise his hero pirate role.'

'Johnny Depp is kinda cute and appealing in an offbeat way.'

'Doesn't do a thing for me, Lucinda. Now,

you, on the other hand...'

Lucinda cut him off. 'Later, Evan. I've got to run – duty calls. Tell Charley I'll pick her up around six or so tonight.'

Lucinda didn't know much about the politics of boards but instinctively knew the wisdom of putting the board president at the top of her list. Thomas Klein was upper management for the regional telephone company and he lived in a suitably large and ostentatious home in a gated community. She disliked him from the moment she saw his up-tilted, puggish nose. She found him annoying from his first words. He tilted up his chin, looked down at her chest and said, 'And what do you want?'

Lucinda tried to get him to look her in the eye throughout the interview but she could never get him to look at her face at all. It was even more irritating than the stares and rude questions she got from others. None of that would have mattered, though, if he had given any useful information at all, but he was exceedingly unhelpful.

Like a politician, he never answered any of her questions; he just used each one as a springboard to talk about what mattered to him. He complained of hearing about Shari's death on the news – somehow, he took that oversight as a personal insult – and he worried about the impact of the murder on donor dollars. He did not, however, express any concern about the grief of the new widower or the emotional impact of the crime on staff of the organization he represented, even when Lucinda gave him the oppor-

109

tunity. All he wanted to talk about was his inconvenience, his embarrassment and the difficulty of maintaining his image when his position forced him to become involved in what he called 'a sordid mess'.

Lucinda walked out of Klein's front door shaking her head. *Did he avoid my questions simply because he's an egocentric asshole? Or was he evasive because he has something to hide?* When she reached the car, she wrote Thomas Klein's name on her list of suspects. She laughed at herself. *Suspects? Not hardly. All I've got are one missing employee of the school district and two people I can't eliminate – whose worst crime is probably habitual obnoxiousness which, unfortunately, is not a felony.*

Nineteen

By geographical serendipity, the next four board directors were all men. Although each one of them could account for their whereabouts at the time of the murder, not one had any useful information to impart. Unlike Klein, however, they showed appropriate empathy for the victim's family and staff. The five she interviewed that morning along with Superintendent Irving were all of the men in the group and only the first one was at all suspicious. Next up: the three women on the board.

Lucinda pulled up to the home of Estelle Castro. White strands streaked through once pitch-black hair and a warm smile beamed from a kind face. When Lucinda introduced herself and displayed her badge, Estelle's *cafe-au-lait* complexion turned ashen gray.

Estelle would not answer any of Lucinda's questions before she asked some of her own. 'How is Conrad Fleming holding up?' 'Have you talked with her staff?' 'How are they?' 'What about the people at the school district? Are they traumatized?' 'Have counselors been provided?'

Lucinda realized that Estelle wouldn't be able to concentrate until her concerns were addressed

111

so she responded to the flurry as best she could. Then she managed to steer Estelle back to the reasons for her visit. Estelle readily admitted that she didn't have an alibi – her husband had been out of town on a business trip, leaving her home alone.

'Did anyone drop by that night?' Lucinda asked.

'Not a soul.'

'Any phone calls?'

'I had several,' Estelle said. 'But I couldn't even estimate when I talked to anyone without checking around with them. Except for the first call that night,' Estelle said with a nod. 'Oh yeah, that one was a bit different. I couldn't forget that. It came in right around six fifteen.'

'Why does that call stand out?'

'It was Monica Theismann. I thought her brother the attorney was a pain. But that woman! All she ever wants to do is stir up trouble and tear people down.'

'Why was she calling you, Ms Castro?'

'She thought, as a board member, I should be aware of the immoral conduct of my Executive Director.'

'Immoral conduct?'

'She said that Shari Fleming was having an affair with Robert Irving. Preposterous. I hung up on her.'

'Why were you so certain that it wasn't true?'

'I've known the Irvings forever – Trudy better than Robert. I knew the background of Monica's infatuation with Robert. Trudy and I had talked about it before – rather cattily, I must admit.

112

Trudy and I thought Monica was a joke.'

Very interesting, Lucinda thought. *The same night of the murder, Monica was attacking Shari Fleming's reputation. Maybe there is a possibility there.*

Estelle continued. 'I got a couple of calls from friends, one from another non-profit organization looking for donations, volunteers and potential new board members. Then the last call I got was from my daughter out in Texas. I'm not sure when she called but it was late enough that she apologized for calling at that time.'

Estelle promised to provide her with phone numbers for all her callers that night. She moved to the highly improbable list in Lucinda's mind.

'How well did you know Shari Fleming?' Lucinda asked.

'Not well at all, really.'

'Really?'

'You've got to understand a little about the organization. Sure, I knew Shari by reputation and how she conducted herself in meetings. But personally, no. Over the three years I've spent on the board, I have seen her only at board meetings and events. She was pleasant, competent, knowledgeable and obviously committed to the work. But we never chatted together at all. Have you talked to any other board members?'

Lucinda rattled off the list of the six men.

Estelle laughed. 'Oh, the Boys' Club. I'm sure they all gave you the impression that without their individual presence on the board, the organization would disintegrate – some probably were less subtle about their importance than others. But the bottom line is that all of us could disappear overnight and there wouldn't be a single ripple effect on the program.' A shadow passed over Estelle's face. 'Well, anyway, we could have as long as we had Shari.' She sat quietly for a moment with her eyes closed.

'The board members serve a maximum of two three-year terms. That means the most long-standing director has been involved for six years – less than half the time of Shari. She's the founding executive director and has total control of the program. All we do is come to monthly board meetings and fund-raising events.

'Sure, we take our fiduciary responsibilities seriously. We review the financial reports and audits, ask the appropriate questions and make minor suggestions. Make sure that Shari had everything she needed to keep working her magic. To keep the funding rolling in, we make annual major contributor calls, but considering most of those folks are former members of the board it isn't exactly a hard job. In fact, I've served on several boards throughout the years and this one is no work at all in comparison. We just sit back and bask in Shari's success.

'We have absolutely nothing to do with the day-to-day operations. We never visit the schools or talk to the other staff members unless Shari brings them to a board meeting to make a presentation or get an award. Except for the board president. He does visit the different locations but he doesn't really do anything. He just struts around making a nuisance of himself and acting important.'

'What do you mean "making a nuisance of himself"?'

Estelle grimaced. 'That would be violating a confidence.'

Lucinda stared at her.

Estelle squirmed. 'Well, it's third-hand information, anyway.'

Lucinda did not move or make a noise.

Estelle sighed. 'OK. But I was told this by Trudy. She heard it from her husband. Shari had gone to the superintendent for advice about her concerns.'

'What concerns, Ms Castro?'

'Tom Klein, the president of the board, was hitting on some of the younger social workers on Shari's staff. A couple of the women went to Shari about it because Klein made them worry that if they didn't give him what he wanted, they might lose their jobs.'

'What did the superintendent tell her to do?'

'Trudy said that he told Shari to confront Klein and give him a copy of the organization's policy on sexual harassment. He said she should make it clear to him that he would modify his behavior or she'd tell the entire board about it. And the superintendent told her that if necessary, he'd help her make that happen.'

'Do you know what Shari did?'

'She thought about it for a few days because she was worried about being fired – Klein was her boss, after all. But then she told the superintendent that she'd thought about it and was ready to face off with him.'

'Had she done it?'

'I don't know. Trudy doesn't know. She said the superintendent didn't know. He was just aware that she planned to confront him sometime this past week.'

Wonder why Irving didn't share that piece of information with me? And why didn't his wife? To Estelle, Lucinda said, 'Thank you very much, Ms Castro.' Handing her a card, she added, 'Please call me if you think of anything else.'

Lucinda learned nothing new from the interviews with the two remaining women on the board. They did corroborate major pieces of Estelle's story and shared her scornful opinion of Thomas Klein, but for entirely different reasons. They knew nothing about the suspicions of sexual harassment. *But three people did,* Lucinda thought. *I can understand why Klein never brought it up. But why didn't either of the Irvings? Was there a reason they concealed it from me?*

Twenty

Lucinda had time to do little more than dash by the apartment to feed Chester and then head downriver to the Spencers' loft. Evan opened the door when she rang the bell, then he yelled down the hall, 'Charley! Lucinda's here!'

'Hurry up, girlfriend,' Lucinda chimed in. 'We want to have time to grab a bite to eat before the movie starts.'

'Oh, no hurry,' Charley said with a giggle. 'I can fill up on popcorn and candy at the movies.'

'Yeah, right, kiddo,' Lucinda responded.

Evan put a hand on Lucinda's arm. 'Lucinda?' he said in a voice tone more tender than she wanted to hear. *Oh please, Evan, don't go there.* She was relieved when Charley chose that moment to gallop into the living room and save her from having to push Evan away.

A tricorne hat was perched on top of Charley's head. Her face wore a big grin and Lucinda's old eye patch. 'Aye, me hearties,' she said.

Lucinda and Evan burst out laughing at the little girl's pirate impersonation and the tension that filled the room just a moment earlier disappeared as they shared the pleasant moment together.

In the car, Charley bubbled over with excitement about seeing the movie then moved on to how happy she was to see Lucinda. 'I knew you were busy trying to catch bad guys but I still missed you a lot.'

'I missed you, too, sweetie.'

'But, Lucy, I thought you'd be in the hospital this weekend.'

'The hospital?'

'Yeah, on account of your surgery was supposed to be yesterday.'

'How did you remember that?'

'You told me, Lucy.'

'But that was weeks ago.'

'I wrote it on my calendar so I wouldn't forget. How come you're not in the hospital?'

'I had to change that, Charley.'

'Why, Lucy? Were you scared?'

'No, no.' Lucinda shook her head. 'I'm just really busy and couldn't get away.'

'Another bad guy?'

'Yes, another bad guy.'

'Can't somebody else take care of the bad guys for a while so you can take care of yourself?'

'It's not quite that simple, Charley.'

'Oh,' Charley said with a nod. 'You are scared, aren't you?'

'I wouldn't say I was scared...'

'Um hum. You're scared all right. Now, Lucy, you need to do this no matter how scary it is. You'll be very glad you did.'

Lucinda almost laughed out loud at that trite adult assurance coming out of a young girl's mouth but a glance at Charley's face saw the intense earnestness there. She knew she had to

118

respond seriously to Charley or hurt her feelings. 'You're right, Charley. I need to feel the fear and do it anyway, right?'

'Yes. And if you need me, I'll be there. My daddy's a doctor so I know he can sneak me into the hospital. I can hold your hand and take care of you and everything.'

A tear welled up in Lucinda's eye. 'I know you will, honey,' she said as she pulled into the theater parking lot, knowing the arrival here would shift Charley's attention away from her and on to the movie.

Charley entertained Lucinda, jabbering about the movie all the way home. When Lucinda pulled the car into the condo's parking lot, though, she could see the tiredness in the little girl's eyes. *That makes two of us,* Lucinda thought. *I'm lucky I stayed awake through the movie.*

The Spencers' front door opened before Charley could insert the pass card. 'Good evening, ladies. Did you have a good time?' Evan Spencer asked.

'Oh, Daddy,' she said, giving him a hug. 'It was a super movie. Can we get the DVD? I want to see it again.' She turned to Lucinda. 'Thank you, Lucy.'

Lucinda crouched down to her level. 'You're welcome, Charley. I had a great time.'

Charley leaned forward and placed a soft kiss on Lucinda's damaged cheek. 'I love you, Lucy.'

Charley always kissed that side of her face but every time she did, Lucinda was overcome by intense emotion. No one else does that. *Even my own sister is careful to bestow a peck on the smooth side of my face.* She smiled at the little girl. 'I love you, too, Charley. Now you head off to bed. You need to get some rest before that birthday party tomorrow.'

Charley smiled and scampered off, shouting 'Goodnight, Lucy' as she went.

Lucinda stood and felt Evan's hand touch her between her shoulder blades and slide down to the small of her back. She wanted to push him away and snap out something rude. But she knew if she did she risked losing Charley. She wouldn't look at him because she was certain her negative reaction was flashing across her face.

'You know, Lucinda, if you ever want any adult companionship, I am always here for you,' Evan said.

Lucinda looked at him then. She winced at the soft eagerness in his voice. 'Oh, you know me, Doctor Spencer, I don't have a life,' she said as she eased herself out of his reach and placed her hand on the doorknob. 'I barely have time for an occasional outing with Charley.'

'Doctor Spencer? I thought we were beyond that level of formality, Lucinda.'

'Sorry,' she said, donning a rueful smile for his benefit. 'I am just beat. I really need to get home.' She turned the knob and pulled open the door. 'Thanks again for sharing Charley.'

He reached out and placed a warm palm on the good side of her face.

See, I was right. He doesn't accept me as I am either. The only time he touches the damaged

120

side of my face is when he is being clinical.

'Anytime, Lucinda. You can see Charley or me any time you want.'

She smiled to cover her irritation at his invitation. The last thing she wanted was to get intimate with a grieving widower who was still in love with his wife – one who would always look at her damaged face on the pillow and wish Kathleen's perfect one were there. 'I won't forget. Thanks for loaning me Charley for the evening. Goodnight,' she said and quickly slipped out the door and hurried down the hall to the elevator.

Twenty-One

Feeling a little guilty for going out the night before and enjoying herself with Charley instead of working on the case, Lucinda got up early the next morning and headed down to her office. When she walked up to her desk she was surprised to find she wouldn't be working alone.

'Hey, Ted, didn't expect to see you here on a Sunday.'

'The Fleming case isn't letting me get much sleep. I thought I'd come in, look things over and see if it made any more sense to me.'

'Does it?'

'Not yet. At first, it seemed like such a slam-dunk – a husband, a boyfriend, or a jealous woman in love with one or the other. Then I thought an angry parent. But that didn't seem to go anywhere either. It seemed the more people I interviewed the less I understood. I was hoping to find the key by looking over my interview notes again. I fantasized about wrapping it all up and turning it over to you but no such luck.'

'It's not making a lot of sense to me either. I do have some suspects but not one that hits me as obvious. In fact, they all feel obscure and un-likely.'

'If you want to think out loud, I'm ready to listen.'

Lucinda laid out her suspect list. 'Superintendent Robert Irving is alibied by his wife, but you know how unreliable spouses can be so I can't scratch him off the list yet. Timmy Seifert is alibied by his mother and his grandmother – both biased, very biased. Then there's Monica Theismann, in HR. She's busy gossiping about the victim's alleged illicit affair with the superintendent. To be honest, I'd kinda like it to be her because she's so damned obnoxious. But no matter how hard I try, I just don't see it. She seems too busy playing games with Robert Irving to actually get around to serious direct action. Then, too, Doc Sam thinks we're looking for a man because of the force involved. I could argue that some women could do the deed but I would think it would have to be someone more athletic than that self-proclaimed sex kitten with her perfectly groomed claws.'

Ted grinned. 'Am I detecting a lack of respect for another professional woman?'

Lucinda rolled her eyes and continued. 'Then there's Steven Broderick. No one has seen him since the day of the murder. He came to work that day but not the next. And he hasn't been in since. Irving couldn't find anyone who had a clue about Broderick's whereabouts. He said that Broderick was married when he moved here just before the preceding school year began but his wife moved out of town shortly after they arrived and now he's divorced. Irving promised to pull the personnel file first thing Monday morning and look for next-of-kin information so we can follow up there. If that doesn't lead us

123

anywhere, we need to consider a forced entry into his home. But if he turns out to be the person we charge with the crime, that break-in could compromise any evidence on the scene.'

'Despite his suspicious disappearance, you seem to be lukewarm on him, too. Or are you just accepting the reality that actual coincidences exist?'

'Funny, Ted. Not hardly. I still don't like coincidence. And I don't think Broderick's disappearance is a coincidence. I think it is connected to the murder but I get the sense that although he is running from it, he probably had nothing to do with it. Still, why did he feel the need to run?'

'You've got four suspects; where do we go from here?'

'I hate even calling them that, Ted. I don't seriously suspect any of them. We're missing something. How are you with crime database searches?'

'Pretty good. What do you need?'

'First of all, can you check the parameters of the search that Kristi did for me the other day?'

'Should be able to,' Ted said as he signed on to the computer and then to the program. He pulled up a log of previous searches and found three relevant files. 'First she searched Central Atlantic – that's our region. Then she checked southern, then New England. She pretty thoroughly covered the whole east coast a couple of states deep.'

'Maybe we'll have to check the other regions, but first – how specific is the victimology?'

'We have age, occupation, marital status, physical descriptors, education and income level.'

'The physical descriptions – are they thorough?'

Ted scanned over the details. 'Looks like it. Can't see anything missing at all.'

'How about the occupation information – how specific is that?'

'"School district administrator" is all it says here.'

'OK. That's what I thought she was at first but that isn't exactly accurate. Let's narrow it down a lot further. If it's a bust, we can broaden it again. Input "Executive Director of Communities in Schools" and search that.'

Ted ran the revised data, finding no matches in two regions. The third search of the New England region, however, scored a hit – a homicide in Maine. Lucinda and Ted read together about the unsolved murder of another person, in the same position for the same organization, nearly two years ago. Lucinda jotted down the contact information, turned to Ted. He gave her a nod, confirming her unspoken suspicions. She grabbed a phone and placed a call.

A male voice answered. 'Violent Crimes Division. Officer Howe.'

'Officer Howe, this is Lieutenant Pierce. I'm with the homicide division in Greensboro, Virginia. I just got a national crime database match with a crime in your area and need to talk to your Lieutenant Mick Trivolli.'

'It's Sunday, Lieutenant. Trivolli doesn't sit on

125

a desk over the weekend.'

'How 'bout his home phone, Officer?'

'No, can do, Ma'am. But if you give me yours, I'll pass it along to him.'

Lucinda sighed, rattled off her phone numbers and sat back, expecting a long wait. The phone rang in two minutes. 'Lieutenant Pierce.'

'You have a database match to my Carney homicide?'

'Is this Lieutenant Trivolli?'

'Yes, sorry. But do you?'

'Is Carney your murdered Communities in Schools Executive Director?'

'Sure is. Are we looking at the same method?'

'No. Not that. I have a woman in that same job down here who is a homicide victim. Can you fill me in on the details from your crime scene?

'Bloodiest one I've ever seen, Lieutenant. The perp had to have been covered in it. He slit the victim's throat from side to side. But the positioning was so disturbing. The vic was flat on the floor with his hands folded on his chest. What bothered me the most were the vic's fingers. They stuck up in the air at unnatural angles.'

'Oh, man. The fingers? Were they broken?' Lucinda asked.

'Yep. Every one of them.'

'Post-mortem?'

'Yep. Yours, too?'

'Yeah, sure were,' Lucinda confirmed.

'Does that sound as significant to you as it does to me?' Trivolli asked.

'Certainly does.' Lucinda thought about the

note she'd found but hesitated to mention it. She didn't want to throw something distracting into the mix. *Then again,* she thought, *if he has a note just like it, that would answer my question, wouldn't it?* 'Tell me, Trivolli, did you find any notes at the scene?'

'I don't know, eh. I don't know if I did or not.'

'What are you telling me, Trivolli?'

'I found a note there. And I couldn't connect it to the victim or to anyone else. But I just don't know if it's relevant.'

'What did it say?' Lucinda asked. No matter what it said, she was amazed that his reaction to it was so much like her own.

'I found a little spiral notebook sitting on a desk in the room. It was folded open to a page where someone had printed out: "I was left behind."'

Lucinda didn't realize she was holding her breath until Trivolli said, 'Hey, Pierce, you still there?'

'Yeah. Yes, Trivolli. I hope you collected that note as evidence because I've got one just like it, right here.'

'Holy shit,' Trivolli whispered under his breath. 'Yep, I've got it. I just knew this guy would kill again. Damn, I wish I was wrong. You know what else, Pierce? I never thought my homicide was his first. The way he waited for the victim to die. Then broke his fingers and arranged his hands on his chest. It was a terrible scene with arterial blood spurting everywhere and this guy seems unaffected by it. He just waits till it's done and then moves in to finish

127

things up. This couldn't have been his first kill. But I found no other matches at all.'

'You were focused on the way the victim died, right?' Lucinda asked.

'Yes. The cut throat.'

'My victim was beaten to death. Yet, I have no doubt that our homicides are connected, do you? Lucinda asked.

'No. Their jobs.'

'Right.'

'Their fingers.'

'Right.'

'The note.'

'Right.'

'They have to be connected,' Trivolli said.

'We need to work on refining the searches in the database and see if we can find another way to locate more matches. It was the Communities in Schools link that brought your case to our attention. But yours was the only match we got. That detail is not what we need.'

'So it's not going to be as easy finding any others,' Trivolli acknowledged. 'We need to figure out what else the victims had in common.'

'It might help to compare the names of Communities in Schools staff as well as the school district employees. Maybe we've got some overlap – a person who was there and is now here,' Lucinda suggested. 'I've got detailed lists that include social security numbers. How about you? Do you have something we can compare?'

'Not at my fingertips but I know I can get hold of them first thing Monday morning. Can you email me your lists? When I get mine, I'll compare them and let you know what I find.'

'Sounds like a plan. You take care of that and we'll alter our search parameters and see if we find anything else on the database,' Lucinda said. She emailed her lists to Mick and stayed on the line to make sure he got them and could open the attachments before ending the call.

She felt satisfied and energized. She had a fresh, promising lead. But the far-reaching implications embodied in the connection to Maine roiled in her stomach, threatening the serious onset of heartburn. She chewed on an antacid and hoped Trivolli was wrong about the magnitude of the problem.

All we have now is two connected homicides. Nothing more. Not yet. Maybe not ever.

Twenty-Two

It was so easy to find him. The announcement for the Sunday afternoon Open House led him right to his target's door. He arrived before anyone else and hid behind the dumpster in the far corner of the parking lot and waited.

He didn't have a plan. In fact, he might not even make a move today. He'd just wait and see if any opportunity presented itself.

The skin on the top of his skull tingled when he spotted his target, the Executive Director of the local Big Brothers and Sisters chapter, Michael Agnew, stepping out of an SUV. He watched Agnew until he was out of sight, inside the building. The only window on the back wall was a small, high one – probably in a bathroom. The rest of the wall was blank. He smiled – he wouldn't have to sneak.

He strolled over to Agnew's car to peer in at its contents. The dark tint on the windows made that impossible. He could barely see a thing. But he did notice that the driver's door was not locked. He pulled on a pair of latex gloves and eased it open. He looked around and, seeing no one in the vicinity, he slipped behind the steering wheel, scooted over to the middle and climbed into the back seat.

He knew staying upright would tempt fate so he slid on to the floor in the space behind the driver's seat and pulled out his knife. He studied the blade then tested it on the upholstery. The feel of the edge slicing through the leather felt so much like cutting through skin, he shivered from head to toe in excitement.

Nestled in position, he wouldn't be able to see when Agnew approached. He needed a warning. He pulled himself up on to the seat, leaned forward over the front seat and clicked the lock. *Agnew will assume that he locked the car before he went inside. When he unlocks it, I will hear it and be ready.*

Satisfied, he settled back in place to wait. He listened as cars arrived, doors slammed, voices returned and cars pulled away. *Sounds like he's having a good turnout for his last event – ever.* He giggled at the thought. He knew, though, that he did not have time for levity. Now that he'd seized the opportunity, he needed to make a plan.

Should I kill him right here and leave him in his car in the parking lot? No. There's not enough space in here. I might get hurt. I might leave unintentional evidence. Even though the windows are tinted, someone might see something.

I have to make him drive. But where? The inner city where no one cares? Or out in the country where we could get lost in the wide, open spaces? He didn't really like rural settings but this new car in the worst part of town would draw unwanted attention. They had to head out.

He knew if the target was scared enough, he'd cooperate and get them where they needed to go. *And if he doesn't? I'll kill him, push him out of the way and drive myself.*

When the lock thunked open, the excitement was so intense he had to struggle to control himself. He turned forward, checked his grip on the knife and waited for Agnew to get settled into the vehicle.

Agnew tossed a leather portfolio on the passenger seat then climbed in and shut the door. From the back seat, the man sprang up and had the knife at Agnew's throat before he was even aware he was not alone.

'Start the car,' the man hissed into Agnew's ear. 'Drive out of the parking lot and to the beltway.'

'Whatever you want, man, you can have it. The car, my wallet, my watch, the contributions I collected today – it's mostly checks but still, it's all yours. Just let me get out of the car and you can be on your way,' Agnew offered.

'Shut up and start the car.'

Agnew started the engine and said, 'You know, man, it isn't a critical situation yet. How about if we talk about your options and figure out what you really need to get your life on track? I'll be glad to help. I mean, I work for a non-profit – that's what I do, help people.'

'Shut your damn pie hole. I don't need any of your psychologist-social-worker-love chatter. Drive.'

Agnew shifted the car into gear and eased forward. A flash of inspiration went through the

132

mind of the man in the back seat. 'Stop!' he shouted.

Agnew eased on the brake and shifted out of gear as he brought the SUV to a stop. Encouraged, Agnew said, 'See, there is a better solution for your problems.'

'I want a notepad and a pen.'

'Sure, sure you can make a list of your demands, your needs, and then we can go from there,' Agnew said.

A surge of anger welled up in the back seat. The man jerked the tip of the knife into Agnew's neck, nicking the skin and making the driver cry out. 'Shut the hell up. I am pulling the knife away but you will not move. You will not speak. Or I'll stab you so fast you'll be burning in the eternal fires before you even know you're dead.'

He eased the knife from Agnew's throat, grabbed the portfolio from the front seat, rummaged around in it and pulled out a pen and a steno pad. The man brandished the blade beneath Agnew's eyes to make sure he wasn't getting confident enough to make a move. The man flipped to a blank page in the pad and printed out in block letters: I WAS LEFT BEHIND.

He jerked the knife back to Agnew's throat. Agnew flinched, causing another small cut in the underside of his chin.

'Unroll the window.'

Agnew reached a finger to the button and pushed the electronic control. The man in the back seat tossed out the notepad into the parking lot. 'Roll up the window,' he ordered. 'And head for the highway.'

Agnew complied.

The man remained tense until he saw that Agnew was following the signs to the beltway. Once on that thoroughfare, the man knew he'd be able to find an exit that would take him into the countryside. He smiled. *What fun! A new way to play the game and it all came together like it was meant to be. All they have now is just a note. And now, we play hide and seek with the body.* He laughed out loud.

Agnew shuddered in revulsion, ignoring the small drips of blood that fell from his neck to the wheel as he steered the SUV on to the highway. After a few miles, he took the exit when the man instructed.

Twenty-Three

Lucinda and Ted brainstormed and searched the database for hours. Their hunt for any other cases with a note reading 'I was left behind' yielded nothing. Before today, though, they hadn't known it was a part of the crime scene and Trivolli in Maine didn't either. Someone else might have that note but not realize its relevance. They left the note as a descriptor on their case hoping it might jar something loose eventually.

They also did a thorough search through every region for post-mortem broken fingers. It led them to a lot of dismemberment cases and beating deaths with overkill but nothing that seemed to fit their case here and the one in Maine. After a number of fruitless hours at the computer, Lucinda said, 'What if we're narrowing details down too much?'

'But, Lucinda,' Ted objected, 'if we hadn't narrowed things down, we would have never found the case in Maine.'

'Yeah, I know, but it can work both ways. Look we had an error in our victimology at first, listing Fleming as a school district employee. Then we narrowed it down specifically to Communities in Schools. What if it is bigger than that one organization? What if it is related to non-profits?'

'Do you realize how many different non-profits there are?'

'Yeah, that may be too broad. But what if we tie the non-profit angle into something that narrows down the nature of the organizations? What if the note connects it all? What if it has something to do with that education slogan, "No Child Left Behind?"'

'So you think it's school related?'

'Maybe. Or maybe it's just kid related.'

'So how do we narrow that down?' Ted asked.

'Maybe we shouldn't.'

'What does that mean, Lucinda?'

'I'm thinking out loud here, Ted. Bear with me. Let's say we just entered a group that we know works in the schools or a group that we know works with kids and see if anything pops up.'

'OK. How about Reading is Fundamental?' Ted suggested.

'Try it,' Lucinda said.

He tapped away, entering the information, running the searches but finding nothing.

'Try the Make a Wish Foundation,' Lucinda suggested.

That input provided two matches. One in Jacksonville, Florida, just a week before Shari Fleming's murder and another nine months earlier in Philadelphia. Both looked like good leads.

'So what now?' Ted asked. 'Do we just start putting in one organization after another?'

'No. Do a global search looking for victims connected to any non-profit. We're less likely to miss something and we can start weeding out from there.'

That search created an avalanche. Some were easy to eliminate, others went on the list. When they were done with scratching off the cases that were obviously not connected, they still had more than thirty cases to review. Not one of those remaining mentioned the broken fingers or the note but still they were possible connections.

Outside the windows, the sun set without their noticing. The whole day dissolved in pursuit of their perpetrator and although they still did not know who it was, they had a wealth of leads to follow. 'It'll be easier to find the other detectives we need to contact on Monday,' Ted said.

'Besides that, Ted, my brain is totally fried. I'll think a lot more clearly in the morning.'

Lucinda dawdled, straightening up her desk, waiting for Ted to leave. When he moved in her direction, she escaped to the ladies' room. She stayed inside long enough to allow Ted time to leave the building but when she opened the door, there he was, leaning against the wall.

'Lucinda...'

'No, Ted,' she said, turning away and heading to her desk to pick up her things. She kept talking as she moved. 'I gave you my terms, Ted. I told you a year ago, if you want to pursue anything beyond a working relationship with me, you need to tend to your marriage first. You need to get Ellen back on track. Then, when she's dealt with her grief over your lost child, if the two of you decide the marriage is not worth saving, you get a mutually agreed upon divorce. Then, and only then, will I even entertain spending time with you outside of the job.'

Ted followed her around, trying but failing to interrupt her monologue.

She jerked to a stop. Ted stumbled as he tried not to run into her. 'Ted, is that clear? Do you understand?'

'Yes, but...'

'No buts, Ted. That is the way it is. I am leaving now. I'd appreciate it if you'd just wait inside for a few minutes and give me a chance to pull out of the parking lot. OK?' Without waiting for an answer she headed down the stairs and out of the building.

The last thing she wanted to see was another note on her car. But there it was. 'WHY WON'T YOU QUIT? WHY DO YOU IGNORE ME? STOP NOW. OR ELSE.'

'Damn it!' she shouted. She spun around, looking for a silver Honda, looking for anything suspicious. 'Who are you? What do you want from me? I can't stop if I don't know.'

She sighed when she got no response. Then she tossed that note in the back seat with the others and drove away.

Twenty-Four

At 6'4", Jake Lovett cast a long shadow down the alleyway as he walked to the back of the non-profit agency's offices. For the most part, he was attired in the typical uniform of any FBI agent – a dark suit, striped tie and a button-down shirt – but one thing set him apart. Poking out from under the hemline of his pants was the distinctive white rubber toe of a pair of black Chucks.

His hair was another focal point of bureau criticism. It ran a bit long by FBI standards, brushing the collar of his shirt at the back and flopping forward into his eyes at the front. Despite the obstruction, his color-shifting eyes did not miss a thing. He noted every cigarette butt, lost button and scrap of paper blown against the buildings on each side of the alleyway.

He stepped into the parking lot that Monday morning without any illusions. He knew the D.C. cops called the bureau for two reasons and two reasons only – the political heat was high, the odds for a happy ending were low. He had to admit he was impressed that they'd thought to preserve the scene here. Not every investigator would have observed this evidence and suspected abduction.

He disagreed, though, with their assumption that the notepad and donation checks were accidentally dropped by the victim when he was snatched. Jake thought both looked more like intentional messages. The victim had no reason to write 'I WAS LEFT BEHIND' because he wasn't; he was taken. He sensed the note was from the perpetrator. The perpetrator, on the other hand, had no reason to leave behind the checks because their presence here suggested foul play. He thought that they were a deliberate discard – a silent cry for help from the victim. And it worked – abandoned contributions from yesterday's fund-raising event were the only reason this parking lot was now considered a crime scene.

But who did it and why? And where were they now? Was Agnew still alive? The lab would run tests on the notepad and checks but that would take time. Time Jake did not have if there was any prayer of finding Agnew alive. He needed actively to seek leads and the best way he knew to do that was to find a match in the database.

He headed back to his Field Office on NW Fourth Street. He hung his highest hopes on the note and focused on that first. The match in Maine popped up on the screen. He called Trivolli.

'Listen, Special Agent Lovett, I don't think I can be much help to you. I've been sitting on this case and watching it turn colder every day for nearly two years. Heck, I didn't even know that note was part of the crime scene for sure until Pierce pointed it out to me.'

'Then can I speak to Pierce?'

'Nah. Pierce isn't one of ours. She works homicide down in Greensboro, Virginia.'

'What was that name again?'

'Pierce. Lieutenant Lucinda Pierce.'

Jake searched the database for crimes in Greensboro and found the one he wanted. He called the Greensboro Police Department, identified himself and asked for Lieutenant Pierce. He was put on hold and then was told she wasn't at her desk. He left a message.

Lucinda and Ted were plotting out the day when the front desk called. 'Hey, Lieutenant, I got a call here for you from a Special Agent Lovett, FBI.'

'Special Agent, my ass. Tell the Feeb to peddle his specialness elsewhere; we're not buying any today.'

'Aw, c'mon, Lieutenant, you know I can't tell him that.'

'I know. I know. Tell him I'm not here. And you don't know where I am. I never check in. I'm totally unreliable.'

'OK, Lieutenant, I'll take a message.'

'Don't bother; I won't return the call,' Lucinda said.

The only response she got was a sigh before the call disconnected.

She laughed. 'Damn Feebs.'

Lucinda and Ted and started making phone calls to the detectives in charge of the possible matching cases. A couple of hours later, they had significantly whittled down the list to a more manageable number of potential related homicides. A case in Atlanta last month looked very good and administrative staffs in Atlanta and Greensboro were busy scanning in reports and exchanging information. But most of the other remaining prospects were temporary dead ends. Detectives at other locales promised to call back after looking through evidence boxes and autopsy reports. While they were occupied with this endeavor, Special Agent Lovett called two more times but Lucinda continued to refuse to talk to him. She did accept the call from Lieutenant Trivolli in Maine.

'I've got one for you, Pierce.'

'Trivolli?' Lucinda asked.

'Yep. I compared the lists and found one person who was working here at the time of the Carney murder and is now working at your school district – Steve Broderick. You know him?'

'That figures. He's the one person we can't seem to find.'

'That's not good.'

'Tell me about it. Did you question him about your homicide before he moved down here?'

'More than once,' Trivolli admitted. 'His wife backed his alibi for the time that Carney was killed but I never knew if I should believe her or not. To the best of our knowledge, he was the last person to see our victim alive. But aside from that, there was nothing suspicious about him. He was kind of dull and ordinary. It was hard to imagine him getting worked up enough about anything to slit someone's throat like that.'

'Don't want to second guess you since I haven't even met the guy, Trivolli, but sometimes it's the cold, emotionless ones who are capable of the worst.'

'I hear you. You could be right. But somehow I just couldn't see him breaking the fingers of a victim. Boring 'em to death, maybe. Course, now that he's shown up on your turf with a related homicide, I'm beginning to think I read him all wrong.'

'Listen, Trivolli, it still might add up to nothing. But you've given me what I needed to get a search warrant to go into his place. We'll let you know what we find.'

'Oh by the way, Pierce, you'll probably be getting a call from an FBI agent. He called asking about the note at the scene.'

'He's called. Waste of time, Trivolli. The Feebs always are,' Lucinda said.

The other detective laughed. 'Don't need to convince me, Pierce. As you southerners would say, "you're preaching to the choir."'

With a forcible-entry team and a handful of crime scene techs, Lucinda entered the home of Steve Broderick. There was no sign of the home's resident, alive or dead. And no sign of a dog except for the two dishes on the floor near the back door. The techs went through each room in the house with a spray bottle of luminal and a portable long-wave UV light, squirting the chemical on spots and anything that looked recently cleaned as they sought out any signs of human blood.

In both the bathroom and the kitchen, they found what they were seeking but the small droplets and little smears appeared to be caused by tiny cuts or nicks; none were indicative of foul play.

Since the search warrant specified any computers in the home, Lucinda made sure her team included her favorite computer forensic geek, Alex Farina. It was his search that led to a Eureka moment.

'Lieutenant, could you come in here?' Alex hollered down the hall. 'I think I know where you'll find Broderick.'

Lucinda walked into the home office. 'What have you got, Alex?'

'Two likely locations. Broderick visited Map Quest and pulled down directions from here to a street in Jacksonville, Florida; directions from here to Baton Rouge, Louisiana; and directions from the Jacksonville address to Baton Rouge. I'd say he wasn't certain where he'd head first but wanted to go to both places. You want me to print them out?'

'Yeah. But no street address in Baton Rouge?' Lucinda asked.

'No, Ma'am. Not sure what that means,' he said with a shrug. 'Maybe he knows that city well enough that he doesn't need directions once he gets there.'

'I'll look into that,' Lucinda said. But her mind was already elsewhere. *His car is in the driveway. He wouldn't need driving directions unless he had a car.* 'Did he log on to any car-rental sites?'

'I didn't see any and didn't see any confirmations in his emails. But there's always a possibility that he deleted information. I'll have to get the PC down to the lab and clone the hard drive before I can dig for that.'

'Thanks, Alex,' she said and picked up her cell to call Ted. She asked him to contact the two police departments in the suspect cities to get them looking out for Steve Broderick and to get someone busy calling all the car-rental outlets looking for him as a customer in the days before or after the murder.

While she was talking, a tech pushed a cell-phone bill into her hand. 'And Ted, I've got a cell phone number. Get the D.A.'s office to set up a pen register so we ping his location if he uses the phone.'

'Will do. When do you think you'll be back in?'

'I'm not sure how much longer we'll be here. Why, Ted?'

'You really need to call back that Lovett guy from the FBI.'

'And why do I need to do that, Sergeant Branson?' Lucinda bristled.

'Don't get all bitchy on me, Lucinda. He's been calling here every fifteen or twenty minutes, driving the front desk crazy.'

'Tough,' Lucinda said as an incoming call beeped its signal in her ear. 'Gotta run, Ted.' She pushed the button, waited for the phone to click over, and then said, 'Pierce.'

'Do you ever return phone calls, Pierce?'

'Captain? I didn't know you called.'

145

'I haven't, Pierce. An FBI agent has been trying to reach you for hours. He must have left a dozen messages.'

'I've been busy, Captain. I'm in the middle of an active homicide investigation.'

'Yes, I know, Pierce. So is the FBI. I need you back here, in my office, now.' Captain Holland disconnected the call before she had a chance to object.

Twenty-Five

Lucinda jerked away from the curb, nearly sideswiping the police vehicle parked in front of her. She stopped the car. Already angry, Lucinda's outrage soared when she was forced to acknowledge that her monocular vision was even less reliable when she was ticked off. She knew, though, that she could not let her emotions overtake the lessons she'd learned in her visual therapy sessions. She suppressed the ire she felt at the FBI, her captain and her limitations for the time being.

She ignored the screaming voice in the back of her mind as she navigated the streets back to the station. But it was persistent. Echoes of creative scatological commentary made her grin as she imagined saying them out loud. At last, she was safely parked and able to give rein to her angry thoughts. When she was on foot, she could trust her subconscious mind to make the necessary depth adjustments to the flat aspect she perceived through her one eye.

She strode into Captain Holland's office, kicked the leg of a chair in front of his desk, angling it in her direction. The captain raised an eyebrow but did not acknowledge her presence. She threw herself into the seat, crossed her legs,

147

folded her arms and said, 'No.'

Holland looked at her, sighed and said, 'Yes.'

'Damn it, Captain, this is my case. I've got leads. I'm working them. Why do I need to make room for the Feebs?'

'Pierce, don't you think the FBI might have some information or assets that would help further your investigation?'

'Captain, the FBI doesn't share information; they take it.'

'You need to work with them on this, Pierce.'

'Oh, they want another joke task force?'

'Pierce, Joint Task Force.'

'Captain, you know it's a joke. Investigators from local jurisdictions do all the leg work. We're on the ground asking the questions, building the case, dealing with victims' families. Then the FBI butts in, takes all our work, and announces victory – their victory. And in the meantime, they usually alienate half our witnesses and make the D.A. crazy because they don't want to share with that office either.'

'Are you done, Pierce?'

Lucinda rolled her eyes, turned her face away from his and expelled a noisy blast of air.

Holland continued. 'You need to go home, pack your bags and head up to D.C. this afternoon.'

'Oh, no, Captain. You've got to be kidding.'

'They asked for you, Lieutenant. They want you, specifically.'

'Why? They need someone to blame and I have all the makings of a good fall guy?'

'No, Pierce. They heard about your work on

148

the Prescott case and were impressed with it.'

'Impressed? Oh sure. I did such a good job of following precise, book-delineated procedure on that one. You know how anal they are, Captain.'

'Strictly following procedure would have cost an innocent's life. You did what needed to be done. Period. And right now, you need to head to D.C.'

'I'm sure I'll make a pretty good scapegoat for the bureau, Captain, but I'm not so sure why *you* want to sacrifice me.'

'That's not it, Pierce. In fact, what I'm doing here is trying to save your ungrateful ass.'

'What does that mean?' Lucinda demanded.

'I wasn't going to mention this because I know how political games and inter-agency maneuvering make you bat shit, but here goes. Did you hear about the shooting down in Pulaski over the weekend?'

'The deputy who shot two innocent bystanders?'

'Yes. The deputy, who lost an eye a month earlier.'

'Listen, Captain. That is no reflection on me. I was a desk jockey for much longer than a month. I re-qualified on the shooting range. I've gotten so good now that the guys down there would start calling me "Dead Eye Pierce" again if they weren't afraid of pissing me off. What therapy did that deputy have? What work did he do on the range before going out in the field again? He might have been a risk but I am not.'

'You are completely right, Pierce. I know your ability. I know your skill. I trust you in the field.

But sometimes in the political world, none of the facts matter.'

'What are you telling me, Captain?'

'I really need you out of town right now, Pierce.'

'Why?'

'The mayor contacted the chief and the commissioners after the Pulaski story hit the news. They want a review of our department's monocular policies. The mayor doesn't think we should have any officers like you in the field.'

'Damn it, Captain. We've been through this before,' Lucinda objected.

'And this probably won't be the last time, Pierce. Hey, I'm on your side here. I want to keep you out there working cases. That's a big reason why I want you to go to D.C. When I talk to the mayor's exploratory panel, I want to be able to say that you are out on loan to the Federal Bureau of Investigation. I want to tell them that the federal government has you working in the field on their special request. I want to ask them, if the FBI thinks our monocular investigator is a valuable asset in the field, why, in heaven's name, wouldn't we want to keep her working here?'

Lucinda shook her head in disgust and defeat. 'Damn it, Captain.'

'I know, Pierce.'

'I hate the Feebs.'

'I know, Pierce.'

Lucinda sighed. 'OK, then. Why do they want me? And why do they want me up there? I've got a case down here.'

'They've got a note.'

Lucinda uncrossed her limbs and scooted forward in her chair. 'The same note?'

Captain Holland nodded. 'Someone used block letters to print out "I was left behind" on a notepad left at the scene of the abduction.'

'Abduction? He took the victim away from the scene? Where? Have they found the body? Gotten a ransom note?'

'Yes, he snatched the victim from a parking lot behind his office. They are hoping to find the victim still alive. That's why the urgency to have you on the team as soon as possible.'

'OK, that makes sense.' Lucinda said as she popped to her feet. 'Ted is up to date on the status of our local case. Have him call me if he gets stuck or needs to bounce something off of me. I'm outta here.'

'Wait, Lucinda. They don't want you at headquarters; here are the directions to the metropolitan office,' Captain Holland said as he stood and held out a sheet of paper. 'When you get there ask for Special Agent Jake Lovett.'

'Oh, I bet he's real special,' Lucinda sneered.

'Hey, Pierce, try not to alienate the guy on the first day.'

'I'll teach him the real meaning of "special".'

'C'mon, Pierce.'

Lucinda laughed. 'Lighten up, Captain. A little hostility can be very motivating.'

Twenty-Six

Lucinda made the three-hour drive up Interstate 95 toward the nation's capital. Even though she hit the city after normal business hours she knew the FBI agent would be waiting in his office for her arrival. *Special Agent Jake Lovett. Just why do they put 'special' at the front of their names? Insecurity? Arrogance? A combination of the two?* As she pulled into the downtown parking garage by the Judiciary Center, Lucinda vowed to focus on the missing man, not on her unfortunate choice of partners in the case.

When she entered the office, the secretary-receptionist did a double take when she looked up at Lucinda's face, causing the detective to sigh. *Another reason why I don't want to be here.* She smiled at the woman and asked for Jake Lovett.

'Special Agent Jake Lovett?' she asked.

The bureaucratic hang-up with titles made Lucinda want to sneer and make a smart-ass remark but she kept her expression blank as she nodded and said, 'Yes.'

Lovett emerged in less than a minute and escorted her back to his work area. Lucinda's first reaction was surprise at how young the agent looked. Her second one was relief that

Lovett had done his homework. He obviously did know who she was because he showed no sign of surprise when he looked at her face. And he looked her right in the eye without hesitation. *That's one point for the junior G-man.*

'I am really happy to have you on our team, Lieutenant Pierce.'

'So, tell me why I'm here.'

'Looks like a serial. While you were on the road, I spoke with Sergeant Ted Branson and he shared the information the two of you have found. By the way, a couple of the questionable cases you were considering have now developed into positive links. Right now, we're looking at five connected cases with more possibles. The uncertainty in some is that if a note was there, no one thought to collect it as evidence.'

'As you can tell from Branson's information, we were making good progress down there. So why am I here?'

'Because of Michael Agnew, our abduction victim. Because you're smart. You're intuitive. And you are willing to do what needs to be done to save an innocent person's life.'

'Ah. Got it. I'll break rules when necessary. So you call me in to do that so you won't have to. Smooooth. Special A-Gent Love-it.'

'Hey, come on, have a seat and let's talk this out,' Jake said, gesturing to a chair. 'For starters, call me Jake. Secondly, look at me. Do I look like a cut-from-the-mold-FBI-guy to you?' Jake held his arms straight out from his shoulders and crossed one Chuck-clad ankle over the other.

Lucinda took in his unorthodox hair length and

153

his bright red high-top Chucks and decided it just might be possible to work with this guy, after all. 'Like the shoes, Jake,' Lucinda said with a grin. 'But what's being done to locate Michael Agnew?'

Jake twisted an ankle coyly in the air. 'Got a closet full of them – every color you can imagine, except pink – I draw the line at pink.' He slid into a seat next to Lucinda. 'As for Agnew – we've issued a multi-state bulletin with photos and a description of the vehicle and of Agnew to all law enforcement jurisdictions. We've canvassed the area around the abduction site several times. A few people saw Agnew drive out of the parking lot in his vehicle but no one saw another passenger. Tomorrow morning, we're sending a helicopter up to do an aerial reconnaissance to see if we can locate his vehicle tucked away somewhere. Of course, if it's abandoned in the area, that doesn't bode well for Agnew.'

'What can I do?' Lucinda asked.

'I thought you might want to review my case file and ask questions. I'd appreciate insight or even stray thoughts on our two connected homicides – so feel free to think out loud. Any theories on the meaning of the note?'

'"I was left behind?"'

'Yeah, is he a military guy left behind enemy lines during some conflict or another? Our victim has a background with the Marines but the other linked crimes seem to be missing that kind of armed forces connection.'

'I hadn't thought of that angle but I rather thought it had something to do with the presi-

154

dential slogan, "No child left behind." I'm surprised that didn't pop up in your mind with you being here in D.C. and all. But every one of the victims we've identified worked for an agency that helps children.'

'So you think he's getting revenge because no one helped him as a kid.'

'No. That may be what he wants us to believe but I think he's a rage-filled sociopath who is using the excuse of a bad childhood to do what he wants to get his kicks. It's kind of ironic that this guy is killing off the very people that would be most likely to make excuses for his violent behavior.'

Jake nodded and grinned. 'Listen, I need to level with you about the politics here. If you're right, and this is a reflection on the administration's policy, even indirectly, there could be fallout. I am not the favorite agent of the Assistant Director in Charge and because of that you could get caught in the crossfire. I'll do what I can to shelter you from the bureau's bull crap, but you might find yourself suddenly jerked out of here and sent home through no fault of your own.'

'This doesn't surprise me, Lovett. I figured I was brought in here to take the fall when things go wrong. I'm sure I'll make a good scapegoat for you and save your career from disaster.'

'Wrong, Pierce. I didn't bring you here to serve as my fall guy. I did it because I think you'll be an asset to my investigation. I fought to have you here because I thought your involvement could make a difference.'

'Right, Lovett. Like how dumb do I look? I

know how you Feebs work and I have agreed to come up here and play sacrificial lamb.'

Jake popped to his feet and leaned down toward Lucinda. 'I don't want your sacrifice. I want your help. I need someone whose thinking is not shaped by the academy. I need an independent, intuitive thinker. I need you.'

Lucinda stood up in his face, her finger poking toward Jake's eyes. 'Right, right, right. You'll go along with any of my hare-brained theories. If you get lucky and I'm right, they'll suddenly become your theories. If I'm wrong, you can point to me and say, "Man, that woman was a real wack-job." Either way, you win. I'm willing to play that game because right now it fits into my purposes to be here.'

'And just why do you hate the bureau so much?'

'It's not the bureau. It's the people who work for it.'

'The bureau is its people. What's wrong with us? What's wrong with me?'

'You are a bunch of arrogant, self-righteous, spineless users.'

Jake slumped down into his chair, placed the fingertips of both hands on his chest. 'Me?' He gazed up at her with a forlorn expression, his hazel eyes turning nearly brown.

Lucinda put her hands on her hips and turned her back. She dared not speak until she calmed her breath and snuffed out the spark of unbidden attraction that arose, causing a lump to form in her throat when she looked into the warmth of his eyes. When she did open her mouth, her voice cracked. 'You can't help it. You're a Feeb.'

'Work with me, Lieutenant. Not for me. Not for the bureau. But for the victim who needs you. Help me bring Michael Agnew home.'

'Do you really think he is still alive?' Lucinda said without turning around.

'I don't know. But I do know that regardless of whether or not he survived the abduction, his family needs us to find him. Come, sit down, talk to me. Let's make a plan of action for tomorrow. Then I'll take you to your hotel room for a good night's sleep.'

She inhaled and exhaled deeply then made a slow turn and returned to the chair. 'OK, Jake. What do I need to know about your victim and your abduction scene?'

Jake outlined what he knew, answered her questions and then she ran down the Fleming homicide for him. 'I suppose you recovered no fingerprints?' he asked.

'Every one we got connected to a known employee or were too indistinct to be usable. How about you? Did you find any on the notepad or the checks?'

'I don't suspect that the perp ever touched those checks and all we found on the notepad were the victim's prints and a few smears over prints that indicated he wore gloves. Ted said that you've got a missing suspect.'

'Only if you use the word "suspect" loosely,' Lucinda said, then ran down the situation with Steve Broderick.

'That all sounds pretty suspicious to me,' Jake

said. 'Why are you so cool on the possibility that he's the perp?'

'It's a combination of things really. Nobody that knows him thinks he's capable of an act of violence – not even Trivolli up in Maine.'

'But...'

'Yeah, I know. Sometimes the worst socio-paths are the best are covering up their true identity.'

'Exactly...'

'But it was his house, Jake. That was the clincher. The man is a slob – clothing on the floor, dirty dishes in the sink, mail and other papers sprawled over every surface. And yet, in all that mess, no bloody clothes, no possible murder weapon, no signs that he washed off blood in the shower. Lots of dishevelment and dirt gathered in corners but no evidence of his involvement in a brutal crime. It doesn't fit.'

They sat in silent thought until a growl from Jake's stomach made both of them laugh. 'Are you as hungry as I am?' he asked.

'Obviously not! But I haven't had a bite since noon.'

'That was nine hours ago, Lieutenant. I think you need to refuel. We oughta check you in at the hotel; it's not far from here. Then we can walk a couple of blocks to a twenty-four-hour diner I know. Nothing fancy but their food is tasty. Sound good to you?'

'Just point the way.'

'There is one rule,' Jake said.

Lucinda rolled her eyes. 'Of course there is.

You're a Feeb. You can't function without a rule.'

Jake looked heavenward and sighed. 'The one rule is no talking about the case while we're having our belated dinner.'

At the restaurant, Jake maneuvered Lucinda to the side of the booth that put the damaged side of her face toward the wall and away from the waitress and the rest of the late-night diners. *Is he considerate? Or is he embarrassed to be seen with me?* Lucinda wondered.

After the waitress left with their order, Lucinda and Jake exchanged flickering smiles. Each one parted lips as if ready to begin conversation then shut them without uttering a word. Lucinda broke the silence with a nervous laugh. 'Looks like, unless we talk about the case, we have nothing to say.'

'Actually, Lucinda, I've got a lot of questions I'd like to ask you but I'm afraid I'll step into a landmine if I ask them and you'll hightail it out of here.'

'Like what?'

'I want to know more about your injury. I want to know about your shootings in the line of duty. I want to know what caused your resentment of the FBI. I'd like to know all about you.'

Lucinda's face flushed. She felt the stir of a strange sensation in her chest at the thought of his interest but she wasn't about to let her guard down. 'You don't want to go there,' she said with a grimace.

'OK. Nothing professional-related then. How

about your parents? Tell me about your mom and dad.'

'Dead. Both dead.'

'Oh,' Jake bit his lip. 'Ever married?'

'Yes.'

'Still married?'

'No.'

'What happened?'

'He left me, Jake.'

'Oh.'

'Without warning.'

'Oh.'

'Without even a note of explanation.'

'Oh,' Jake said again, hanging his head.

'My husband was a Feeb.'

'Uh-oh.'

'A special A-Gent man, Jake.'

'OK,' Jake said and exhaled forcibly. 'How 'bout we do talk about the case?'

Lucinda barked out a cold, brief laugh. 'My, my, Mr FBI. Jettisoning a rule already? Maybe our partnership does show some promise after all.'

Twenty-Seven

The next morning, Lucinda set out from her hotel on foot and walked the seven blocks to the field office of the FBI. She started out thinking about the Fleming case and the Agnew case but in less than two blocks, she was thinking about Jake. By three blocks, she was arguing with herself about Jake.

What is wrong with you? He is just a kid.

No, Lucinda, he is not a kid. He's very much a man.

But he's ten, twelve years younger than I am. And he sure looks good.

Stop it. He's FBI. He even looks FBI. Shoot, he looks so FBI, he could play one on TV.

Stop lying to yourself. He could be a TV FBI just because he doesn't look exactly like the cookie-cutter version the bureau prefers.

But it's not just the way he looks; it's the way he looks at me. All through dinner, he looked straight at me. He never flinched. He never grimaced. Except for that one almost-question about the injury, he never mentioned it. It's as if when he looked at me, he was blind to every flaw.

Snap out of it, girl, that good-looking virile young male is not interested in an older, scarred cop.

So why can't I stop thinking about him?

Lucinda tried to force Jake's image out of her mind but became so focused on that task that she walked half a block past the entrance to the office before realizing what she had done. She doubled back and went inside.

Jake had not yet arrived when she entered his work area. *He wanted to know a lot about me but he sure didn't volunteer any information about himself. Let's see what I can find out before he arrives.* She looked around for snapshots. There were a few pics hanging on the wall from his training days at Quantico. The similarity in backgrounds and activities to her ex-husband's old photos made her wince.

She spotted a pedestal trophy with a yo-yo on top. *There's got to be a story behind that.* That thought made her smile. It dropped from her face when she saw a picture of Jake with a woman. *An older woman. Older like me? No. Older than I am. Must be his mother. I hope it's his mother.* She picked up the frame as if holding it in her hands would answer the question. She was staring into the woman's eyes when Jake entered the room.

'That's my mother,' Jake said, startling her so badly she nearly dropped it.

'Oh, I'm sorry for being so nosy,' a blushing Lucinda said as she fumbled with the photograph, nearly dropping it to the floor. With shaky fingers, she set it back on the shelf.

'No need to be sorry. You're a detective. It comes with the territory. If you weren't curious, you wouldn't be worth a damn in this line of work,' Jake said. 'My mom was a wonderful, courageous woman.'

'Was?'

'Yeah. I lost her about a year and a half ago. Breast cancer. Fifty-two years old. No known risk factors. And she's gone. Seemed like it was overnight but really it was a couple of years of struggle against a particularly aggressive type.'

'I'm so sorry to hear that.'

Jake shrugged and pushed his hands in his pants pocket. They stood in awkward silence. Lucinda changed the subject. 'So what's the deal with the yo-yo trophy?'

It was Jake's turn to blush red. 'Don't we have a case to work on?' he asked, picking up a pile of faxed pages from his in-box.

They dug into files sent in to them from homicides in other jurisdictions that had the potential for being connected to theirs and soon fell into a rhythm of comfort in one another's company. Lucinda slid off the jacket of her pantsuit and hung it on the back of a chair. In minutes, Jake's was draped over the chair beside it. Jake leaned back and threw his feet up on the work table, causing Lucinda to snicker.

'What?' Jake said in a hurt voice.

'Lime-green shoes, Jake?'

'Hey, they're not pink.'

'No, they're not,' she said with a chuckle.

They shifted immediately back into work mode, asking questions, making comments, exchanging files. When Jake's cell rang, Lucinda barely noticed. But when he reached for his jacket, thrust in an arm, switched his cell to the other ear in order to slip in the other arm, Lucinda got to her feet and reached for hers. She didn't know what was going on but she knew they were on the move.

As soon as Jake disconnected, he said, 'They found the car.'

'Agnew's car?'

'Yeah. About thirty-five miles out of town by a falling down, abandoned farmhouse.'

'Any sign of Agnew?'

'Don't know. They spotted the car from the chopper. No one is on the ground yet.' They went down into the parking garage. To Lucinda's surprise, Jake approached a silvery blue older model convertible and slid a key into the door. He climbed in and leaned across the seat to unlock the passenger door.

'Close your mouth and hop in,' he said. 'I'll tell you about this baby while we drive.' Jake pulled into traffic and continued, 'Isn't she a beauty? Uses a bit more gas than is politically correct but she was my Dad's car and I can't bring myself to part with her. She's a 1966 Impala Super Sport and, man, can she rock and roll. She's got a 396 under the hood with 325 horses and a ride as smooth as glass.'

Lucinda leaned back in the spacious leather seats and luxuriated in the comfort of having enough room to stretch her long legs all the way out. She had to admit, it was a cool car but it took next to no time for her to regret the ride. In her opinion, Jake was a typical male driver – impetuous, impulsive and erratic. *Tomorrow, I'll drive to the office and walk back to the hotel.*

That way, my car will be at the office and available so I can do the driving the next time.

When they hit the highway, Jake's driving, in Lucinda's opinion, was even worse. She gritted her teeth and kept her mouth shut. Before long, they exited Loop 495 and headed away from the city. The sudden transition from crowded urban sprawl to bucolic countryside was jarring. Without warning, the congestion dissolved as one vehicle after another peeled off, leaving an empty roadway. The only noise was the hum of their tires on the asphalt.

Jake turned into a small blacktop lane and slowed his speed and the hum became nearly inaudible. After a few miles, they spotted police presence around a dirt drive off to the right. They turned in and Lucinda looked down the rocky, uneven surface and braced herself for a rough ride. But Jake was right, as they drove toward the farmhouse, she didn't feel a single bump. Jake stopped and parked outside the ribbon of yellow tape. As they stepped out of the vehicle, a uniform approached Jake and asked, 'Special Agent Lovett?'

'Yes,' Jake answered. 'And this is Lieutenant Pierce.'

'Sir, we cordoned off the area. Went in to check for a live hostage. When that search was negative, we retreated and have remained outside the perimeter as instructed.'

'Thank you, Officer,' Jake said as he lifted the tape and gestured for Lucinda to step inside.

Twenty yards ahead a farmhouse slumped in the middle of an overgrown yard. The white clapboards shed chips of paint. The Kelly green trim on the window frames was caked with road dirt. The once bright-red roof was faded and streaky as if a giant's tears had run down its slanted surface. The building was surrounded on three sides by a large porch with crooked banisters and broken steps. On one end, a porch swing hung drunkenly by one chain.

Lucinda squinted her eye and imagined the welcoming, wholesome image that once stood on that spot. She could almost see the smoke curling from the chimney. She nearly smelled the scent of fresh baked bread and could almost hear the thunk of the wood and the ring of the metal as an axe split wood. Then she opened her eye wide and the magic was gone; only a sorrowful and neglected facade remained.

They followed the path of flattened over-tall grass and weeds through the front yard and behind the house. Underfoot they heard the crunch and felt the sponginess of years of fallen, partially decomposed vegetation. They looked hard for any signs of another car moving out, away from the farmhouse, but the trampled undergrowth all pointed in one direction. It appeared as if whoever left the car must have departed from the immediate area on foot. They saw the vague indication of the kind of path a body would make through the tall weeds but although it could have been a person, it also could have been a wild animal or someone's dog.

The victim's SUV was parked on a bare patch of dirt at the back of the house. Jake and Lucinda circled around it watching where they stepped and taking care not to touch the sides. 'I've got a forensic team on the way out here. They should catch up with us soon,' Jake said.

Must be a woman who doesn't drive like a lunatic. Lucinda kept that thought to herself and just nodded at Jake.

In a few minutes, the techs tramped up through the weeds, hauling their gear. Lucinda and Jake stood back and watched them work. The team made a cursory survey of the car's interior – a more thorough job would happen back at the auto lab. The outside received an intense examination to capture any evidence that could possibly be lost in transport. A tech slid under the vehicle to take samples of any dirt, plant life or anything else caught up on the axles, struts or any other protrusion. When he finished with that, he took samples of the weeds and dirt from around the car. Then he headed down the dirt drive to pick up samples from there for comparison. If they could identify any material alien to this place when they were back in the lab, they could then extrapolate any other location the vehicle visited before coming to rest here.

Another tech focused on finding prints on the exterior of the car. After a few minutes, she turned to Jake and shook her head. 'None?' Jake hollered over to her.

'Looks like it's been wiped clean,' she shouted back.

What about the inside of the door handle? Lucinda thought but before she could say a word, the tech bent backwards in a seemingly impossible arc as she looked up at that spot. Lucinda couldn't imagine how she held that awkward position, let alone actually worked that way, but she did. When she finished she held up a fingerprint card and shot them both a big grin. 'Got one!' she said.

'How did she do that?' Lucinda asked.

'She's pretty amazing,' Jake said. 'Awesome, actually. I've never seen anyone that flexible. But, damn it, she's happily married.'

'Oh, please,' Lucinda said.

'It was a joke. Just a joke. Honest. In fact, I'm not sure if she's even married. I never asked.'

'Yeah, right.'

'Really. I did ask about how she manages all those gyrations when I've seen her do similar acrobatics. She says that it's genetics and yoga. If it were just yoga, I'd probably try it myself but there isn't much I can do about the klutzy genes I got.'

Hours later, with the area searched for any possibility of evidence, a truck pulled the vehicle on to a tow platform and they all headed back to the city. On the ride back, Lucinda asked, 'Why don't you fill me in on those klutzy genes?'

'Really? You really want to know?'

'Yeah, of course I do – unless it was just a throw-away line. If it was you don't have to make anything up to amuse me.'

'Well, the silly side of the klutzy gene pool is my mom,' Jake said. 'When she was six years old, she wanted to be a ballerina. My grandmother signed her up for ballet class. A couple of months later, the teacher approached my grandmother and said, "Elsa, I've never said this to a parent before, but save your money. Your daughter has the grace of an overweight elephant." A couple of years later, my grandmother realized how true that was and enrolled my mom in a special class so she could learn how to fall without hurting herself.'

'They have classes like that?'

'Oh yeah, for the truly, hopelessly clumsy.'

'That is funny. What about your dad's contribution to the gene pool?'

'Well, that isn't exactly funny. My dad tripped and fell in front of a city bus. He was dead before anyone realized what had happened. I was nine years old.'

'Wow! That explains your attachment to this car – it belonged to your dad,' Lucinda said.

'My mom kept it in a garage for me until I was old enough to drive. First time out, I crumpled a fender on a phone pole and it went back into the garage until I was old enough to appreciate it. I had to save up the money to restore the fender and get it fixed before she signed the title over to me. I've been driving it ever since. My only major expense was when I had to replace the convertible top a couple of years back – but still it's a lot cheaper than a monthly car payment.'

'And you have a piece of your dad with you everywhere you go.'

'Yeah,' he said with a sigh and a nod. A soft smile turned up his lips and his eyes filmed with moisture. 'Can't put a price tag on that.'

A mile further down the road, Lucinda said,

'Both of my parents are dead, too.'
'So we're both orphans,' Jake said.
'Yeah.'
'You wanna talk about it, Lucinda?'
'No. Not now.'

Twenty-Eight

It was one of those mornings designed to test an investigator's patience. A day of waiting for results from the search of the vehicle, for the processing of the fingerprint through the national database and living with the diminishing hope of finding the victim alive and the growing anticipation of recovering a body.

Teams of law enforcement, boy scouts and other volunteers spread out over the countryside in pursuit of the victim Michael Agnew. The dog search team with their handlers concentrated on finding the perpetrator starting at the spot of bare dirt where the vehicle was found and following scent from there. It led to the narrow path the investigators had spotted the day before, they plunged through the weeds following the canines' lead.

Jake and Lucinda chose to stay in town, close to the labs, while they reviewed the data and called around to other jurisdictions looking for information on the connected homicides. They focused on what they had in hand in a vain attempt to forget that they were waiting for others to provide a new puzzle piece they could use.

It was nearly lunchtime when a tech called up.

'We ran the door latch print through AFIS but didn't get a match.'

Jake and Lucinda slumped and stared into space. The intense disappointment over this news seemed to fill the air with a negativity they could taste with every inhalation.

'Maybe they've had better luck down in the auto lab,' Lucinda suggested.

Jake called down to where techs were still processing the victim's SUV. 'But it doesn't look good,' they were told. 'We've fumed the whole thing with superglue. This vehicle's been wiped down cleaner than any I've ever seen. And we haven't found any indications that it ever transported a body.'

Next they called the communications liaison in the field. The news he delivered was even worse. 'The victim search team has had no luck so far. The canines are still running, though. They've got the scent of something. But clouds are forming and getting thick. We're not sure they'll get where they want to go before the rain starts. If the weather forecasts are right about the intensity of the expected downpour, there won't be a scent trail left for them to follow any longer.'

'How about lunch?' Jake suggested.

'Let's go out there right now,' Lucinda urged.

'Aren't you hungry?'

'We can grab something along the way.'

'But it looks like rain.'

'Exactly. That's why we need to get out there. See exactly where the dogs are, see how far they've gotten, know first hand where they left off,' Lucinda said.

'Instead of reading about it in a report.'

'You got it.'

'Let's go,' Jake said, grabbing his keys off of his desk.

'You won't need those. I'm driving,' Lucinda said.

'I can drive.'

'I know but you're not. I am.'

'Just 'cause I drove out there yesterday doesn't mean you need to drive out today.'

'I know. I'm driving,' Lucinda insisted.

'Why?'

'You don't want to know.'

'Is there something wrong with my driving?'

'Yeah, but it's genetic, don't worry about it.'

'Genetic? What are you talking about?' he said, stopping and facing her with his arms on his hips.

'Keep moving, Jake. You really don't want to get into this.'

'Why not?'

'Because I'm right and you won't be able to acknowledge it and it'll screw up our working relationship. Stop lagging behind, Jake. Let's go.'

'OK. I'm coming but I still don't get it.'

'You don't need to,' Lucinda said.

They got into Lucinda's car and pulled out of the parking garage. Once they hit the highway, Jake said, 'No offense but your car is boring compared to mine.'

'You're right, Jake. You'll get no argument from me on that point. This is nothing but a box on wheels.'

173

'So why are we in this boring piece of crap that feels every little bump in the road instead of riding in comfort in my cool Chevy?'

'Jake, would you let me drive your car?'

'No. Absolutely not. I mean, no offense, Lucinda, but nobody drives my car but me.'

'Exactly. That is why we are in my car.'

'You like to drive that much?'

'Not really. It's just that I don't want to ride in any car with you driving.'

'What's wrong with my driving?'

'You drive like a man.'

'I am a man.'

'Exactly. And although there are a lot of things about men I simply love, the way you all drive is not one of them.'

'Then why are all the jokes about women drivers?'

'Two reasons, Jake. For one, men made up the jokes as a cover-up for their inadequacies. Secondly, there is nothing funny about how men drive – it's a scary, impulsive, roller-coaster kind of experience.'

'You don't like roller-coasters, either?'

'Although it's been years since I've been on one, I do like them. I just don't like it when that experience is artificially duplicated on the road.'

'Why haven't you been on one for years?'

'Haven't known anyone else who wanted to go, I guess.'

'Well, you do now. First chance we get, you and I are going to King's Dominion.'

A thrilling tingle surged through Lucinda from head to toe. *Is this a date? Is he asking me out?*

Or is it just partner recreation? How can I know? Ask him? No way. If I do and he says it's not a date, I'll be too embarrassed to go. Shoot, I'll be too embarrassed to look at him for the rest of the day.

'Well, Lucinda, is it a date?'

Oh, my, he used the word. But the word has two meanings. Just go with the flow and see where it takes you. Just say something. 'Sure, Jake, that sounds like fun.'

'What's this?' Jake asked.

Lucinda turned in his direction and saw he was looking in the back seat. 'What's what?'

'Those notes.' He unfastened his seat belt and reached into the back seat, grabbing the pile of paper that Lucinda had pulled from her windshield. 'It's all in block printing.'

'I don't know who wrote them. I found them on my windshield.'

'But they are all in block printing, Lucinda.'

'Yeah, so?'

'All the notes from the perpetrator are in block printing.'

'I don't think they're connected.'

'Why not?'

'I don't know. I just don't. It doesn't fit.'

'When did you start getting them?'

'I'm not sure. Let me think. I guess I found the first one the same day I went to the crime scene at the school district building.'

'And you don't think they're connected?'

'No. What do they have to do with anything we found at the crime scene? Or that anyone else has found at a crime scene?'

'The block printing,' Jake insisted, nearly shouting in his exasperation.

'Calm down, Jake. Jeez. Of course, I thought about a connection but how would a perpetrator know I'd be investigating the crime? And why me and not the others?'

'Did you ask any of the others if they found notes like this?'

'Not specifically. But I did ask about notes and a few of them told me about finding the same note at the scene as I did but none mentioned anything being left on the windshield.'

'So, maybe the perp is operating out of your area.'

'That's a leap, Jake.'

'Not really. Think about it. Where have we pinpointed linked homicides?'

'From Florida to Maine.'

'And you're in Virginia. Right in the middle of the geographic spread.'

'Well, yeah...'

'And, we've got that Steve Broderick guy missing in action and we know he was in the vicinity of two of the crime scenes. I'm going to get our geographic profilers on this when we get back to the office.'

'I don't know, Jake. It just doesn't feel right.'

'Gut feeling? Intuition?' I believe that both are valuable, Lucinda. But I also don't believe in coincidence.'

'I'm not real fond of it, either,' Lucinda admitted. 'I guess it is worth looking into it.'

'Got that right. In fact, these notes are going to be preserved as evidence. Anybody touched them besides you?'

Lucinda smirked and tried not to laugh out loud. 'Uh, you, Jake.'

Jake reddened and said, 'Yeah, well, yeah. OK, we'll have to eliminate both of our prints and see if there's anything else there. You should have bagged them.'

'Jake, if I bagged every silly, semi-threatening note I received in my career, the department would have to rent more storage space.'

'But still, Lucinda...'

'You win, Jake. Collect it as evidence. Keep it. Cherish it. But I still don't think it'll get you anywhere.'

'We'll see. Probably ought to have security for you when you go back to Greensboro.'

'Don't push it, Jake.'

Lucinda turned off the highway and on to the two-lane state road that led to the location where Michael Agnew's car was found. They'd only traveled a few yards when Jake's cell phone rang.

Lucinda listened to just one side of the conversation. It made no sense but it was clear that Jake was agitated by what he was hearing.

He hung up and said, 'When you get to the dirt lane we took yesterday, just keep driving.'

'What's up, Jake?'

'They think they found Michael Agnew.'

'He's not still alive, is he?'

'No. And I hope to God that they are exaggerating about what they found out here.'

The rain began with big, fat drops that fell slow and smooth as if they were dripping from an eave in the sky. The pace picked up until it was torrential and visibility was poor. Lucinda slowed the car to a crawl as they watched for the mail box marked with a yellow streamer of crime tape.

They turned in and crested a rise. The first thing they spotted were the florescent orange vests of the canine handlers, glowing in the dreary light from the front porch of another abandoned farm house where they went with their dogs for shelter from the storm. Although the house itself was in better shape than the one they saw yesterday, the gloom of the day made it appear sadder and more bereft.

They were led over to a small barn a hundred yards from the house. Deputies pulled open the large double doors as they approached. The sight took their breath away and then settled in their guts, roiled their stomachs and formed a hard lump inside their chests.

Michael Agnew looked like a marionette. He hung from a beam with a rope around his neck. Two other ropes extended down from above to tie around his wrists. His arms bent at the elbow stuck straight out. Every finger was broken and posed at an unnatural angle. Below his feet, in the dirt, lay a piece of yellow, lined paper held in place with a rock. Written across it in bold, block letters: I WAS LEFT BEHIND.

To the left of the body, on a bale of straw, Agnew's suit jacket was neatly draped, his tie stretched across it. A yellow folded clump of paper protruded from a pocket.

Was it a repeat of the message on the ground?

178

Or was it something more? Lucinda wondered. 'I want to look at that paper,' Lucinda said, pointing toward the jacket.

'Me too. The forensic team will be here as soon as they can. They were called right after we were. Once they photograph it in place, we'll snatch it up.'

Jake slumped over. He sighed as his shoulders heaved up then down.

'Jake?' Lucinda asked.

He shook his head.

She reached a hand toward him, hesitated, pulled back, then reached out her arm again, resting her palm on his shoulder. 'Jake, you didn't really think you'd find him alive, did you?'

'No, not really,' he said, raising his head. 'But I had hoped. I had hoped with all my heart.'

Their faces were inches away. Lucinda stifled a gasp as a rush of sympathy combined with desire flushed through her face. He looked at her with longing. Then they both backed away and hung their heads.

'We always hope, Jake. That's all that keeps us going,' Lucinda said. She wondered if he caught the double meaning behind her words.

Twenty-Nine

After a couple of hours of going in and out of the barn in the pouring rain as they released the dog search team, greeted the arriving forensic techs and consulted with the coroner and his staff, Jake and Lucinda were bedraggled and dripping. Lucinda stood in the corner of the barn waiting for the go-ahead to extract the note from the victim's jacket pocket.

Jake entered the barn carrying a couple of clean towels he'd managed to sweet-talk from a tech. He threw one over her head and they worked on getting dry enough that they didn't damage the note when they retrieved it.

They both donned latex gloves and approached the jacket. Lucinda eased the clump of paper out of the pocket and unfolded it with the tips of her fingers, trying to touch as little of the surface as possible. There were three sheets of yellow, lined paper torn from a legal pad. Jake held plastic sheet protectors open as she slid each individual page into a separate one. Once protected from moisture, they could read it without causing any further damage or contamination.

The missive was printed in block lettering that was a little smaller but otherwise looked identical to what they'd seen in the other crime scene notes. Halfway through the diatribe, though, the emotional state of the writer became clear as he applied the pen with increasing force, causing rips and gouges in the paper.

YOU CAN RUN BUT YOU CANNOT HIDE. I WAS LEFT BEHIND AND NOW YOU PAY. GOODIE GOODIE TWO SHOES TURN BLIND EYES. SEE ME BUT DON'T SEE ME.

NO CHILD LEFT BEHIND? ALL THEM GOODIE TWO SHOES ARE HYPOCRITES. THEY LOOKED AT ME. THEY LOOKED THROUGH ME.

NO CHILD LEFT BEHIND? HA! THEY LEFT ME BEHIND.

WHERE WAS THEM GOODIE TWO SHOES WHEN I WAS BEING USED?

I WAS LEFT BEHIND.

WHERE WAS THEY WHEN I WAS HUNGRY?

I WAS LEFT BEHIND.

WHERE WAS THEM GOODIE TWO SHOES WHEN I DIDN'T LEARN TO READ OR WRITE?

I WAS LEFT BEHIND.

WHERE WAS THEY THEN?

NOW I AM NOT BEHIND. I AM HERE. IN FRONT. IN THEIR FACE.

AND THE HYPOCRITES DIE. THE GOODIE TWO SHOES LOSE THEIR SOLES. (HA! HA!)

NO CHILD LEFT BEHIND?

I WAS LEFT BEHIND.

NO CHILD LEFT BEHIND?

I WAS LEFT TO DIE.

NO CHILD LET BEHIND?

I AM DEAD. THE WALKING DEAD.

181

NOW THEY ARE DEAD, TOO.

I LEFT THEM BEHIND.

THEY CANNOT WALK NOW.

THEM TWO SHOES DON'T DO THEM NO DAMN GOOD.

THE LEFT BEHIND WILL INHERIT THE EARTH.

SIGNED,

ONE OF THEM WHO WAS LEFT BEHIND.

P.S. WATCH OUT GOODIE TWO SHOES. NO GOOD DEED GOES UNPUNISHED.

The investigators stared at each other, initially too stunned to speak. 'He is very angry,' Jake said.

'And he might not have much formal education but he has a sharp mind. He played with words and wanted to make sure we knew it. He's laughing at us.'

'Do you see any indication of where he'll strike next?'

'I don't see it but that doesn't mean it's not there. You need to have a press conference. Let the public know what's going on here.'

'Lucinda, I'll be damned if I really know what's going on here.'

'Sure, you do, Jake. You know we have a perpetrator targeting heads of non-profit organizations. Those people who are potential victims need to be warned so that they can protect themselves.'

'You'll just create hysteria.'

'No, we'll create caution. Sure some people

will overreact. But for the vast majority know-ledge of an existing danger can lead to saved lives.'

'No. Informing the public will bring the loon-ies out of the woodwork.'

'Sure it will. But it will also bring out respon-sible citizens. Those who need to protect them-selves and those who want to help us nail this guy.'

Jake threw up both his hands. 'Hey, I'm not going to argue with you. It's simply out of the question.'

'Oh. I'm sorry. I forgot. I was thinking we were partners. I forgot for a moment that you are the mighty FBI. The keeper of the flame. The Holy Grail of law enforcement. We silly locals only communicate with the public because we are too stupid and incompetent to find the bad guys without their help. But you – you are miracle workers. So, tell me, oh great one. Where do we go to arrest our little psychopath before he kills again?'

'Man, you've got one hell of a pissy attitude.'

'Oh, so this is a surprise? I thought you researched me well before calling my captain. I thought "pissy attitude" was stamped on every page of my record. Did you slip up, oh mighty investigator?'

Jake threw his arms up in the air. 'I can't talk to you while you're in this frame of mind.' He turned and walked away.

'Well, I sure hope you can find a ride back to your office 'cause I am leaving here and heading back to Greensboro, right now,' Lucinda shouted after him. But she didn't move. She looked over at the techs who were staring at her. They quickly turned away. Lucinda sighed and plodded in Jake's direction.

Damn me and my pissy attitude. Michael Agnew matters. Shari Fleming matters. And you, Lieutenant Lucinda Pierce, you have lost track of your priorities.

'Jake, Jake!' she shouted after his retreating back.

Jake kept walking away as if he didn't hear, oblivious to the pesky light drizzle that continued to fall in the aftermath of the downpour.

'Jake, where are you going?' Lucinda asked and waited for a response. When none was forthcoming she hollered, 'Jake, Michael Agnew still needs you.'

Jake stopped but didn't turn around to face her. Lucinda splashed through puddles, catching up with him and stepping in front of him. Jake kept his eyes focused on the dirty muck that nearly obscured the bright yellow color of the Chucks he'd pulled on that morning.

'Jake, I'll give you a ride back to town. I'm not heading back home this afternoon. That was just bullshit.'

'Hey. No problem. I can catch a ride with the techs.'

'I know you can but I'm offering you a ride with me. I'm retracting my stupid threat. Damn it, Jake, I'm apologizing for being an ass and saying stupid crap I didn't mean.'

'Really?' he said, looking up at her at last. 'And just like that, you expect me to believe you didn't mean one insulting word.'

'No, Jake, I'm not going to lie to you. I think your agency sucks. I think your agents – present company excluded – are arrogant pricks.'

'Pricks? You know, we do have female agents these days.'

'Yes, Jake, but you and I both know that biological equipment is not required for someone to act like a prick.'

Jake grinned. 'Oh, that is certainly correct, Lieutenant Pierce.'

'Yeah, yeah, I asked for that,' she said, giving him a playful shove. 'Don't you smirk at me when you say that, Special Agent Lovett.'

'How come "Special Agent" sounds like a four-letter word when it passes through your lips?' Jake asked.

'You started it with that Lieutenant crap. How come we are still standing in the rain?'

'Shall we retire to the porch?'

'But, of course,' she said as they walked across the yard and took shelter under the overhang. 'Now, about our problem...' Lucinda began.

'What problem?'

'The press conference.'

'Do we have to go there again?'

'Yes. But listen, Jake, I have a compromise.'

'What? I shut up and do what you say?'

'Wonderful suggestion. Why didn't I think of that?

'Sarcasm noted,' Jake said with a sigh. 'Go ahead and explain.'

'OK, we have a basic conflict. I think we should go to the media and lay out the whole problem, complete with our suspicion of serial murders against people who work for non-profits. You want to stonewall the press and not give them an inkling of the problem until we make an arrest. Do you agree with that?'

'Essentially, for the time being, yes,' Jake acknowledged.

'OK, let's mix your theory into this situation. You think that the perp has a base of operations in or near my jurisdiction.'

'Well, base of operations is a bit too fancy for what I had in mind,' Jake objected. 'I'm thinking more like that's where he goes home to roost, lick his wounds, or whatever hokey phrase you want to use.'

Lucinda shrugged. 'Let's say you send out a press release with a profile of the person we want to identify in the Shari Fleming homicide. Throw in the suspect's interest in "No Child Left Behind". That might make someone remember something our unknown suspect said. Drop in Steve Broderick as a second person of interest and that would get maximum media coverage in my area. So if Broderick is still in town or a nameless perp is operating there, maybe some-one will call.'

Jake closed his eyes, lowered his head and placed a hand on his chin. In a moment, he was nodding. He looked up at Lucinda and said, 'That would work. But the release needs to be issued by the field office down there, not from my office in D.C.'

'Can you make that happen?' Lucinda asked.

'Should be able to if I go down there.'

'Now?'

'I really want to stick around for Agnew's autopsy in the morning. Then I'll go down. You want to ride together?'

'My car?'

'Yes, your boring car,' Jake said with a sigh. 'It would take a lot of gas for mine to drive down there. The mileage expense I get for travel hardly covers the cost anymore.'

'Great, I'll check out of the hotel first thing tomorrow and meet you at the morgue.'

'What are your plans for tonight?' Jake asked.

'All I want to do is peel off these wet clothes, soak in a hot tub, slide in between clean sheets and sleep until dawn.'

'Any room in your plans for dinner?' Jake asked.

'I might order something up from room service. Then again, I might just be too tired to bother.'

'Actually, I was asking you out to dinner.'

Nip this in the bud, girl. Bad idea in the middle of an investigation, she thought, but to Jake she said, 'Oh, gee, thanks, but by the time I get dry and warm again, I'm not going to want to get dressed to go anywhere. But I will take a rain check. OK?'

Jake stuck his hand out past the eaves of the porch. 'It's still raining.'

Despite the chill, Lucinda felt a warmth coursing through her skin. 'It most certainly is,' she said, drawing the warm blanket of her fantasy tightly around her as she plunged off the porch and ran back over to the barn.

187

Thirty

He worried about the long note. It seemed like a good idea at the time. In fact, it seemed brilliant. He smiled as he thought about writing it, retrieving the man's jacket from the car and draping it over the bale in the barn, sticking the folded pages in the pocket just like it was a suicide note even though it was not. It was visual mockery at its best.

His smile morphed into a creased brow and a frown as doubt flooded his thoughts. *Maybe I shouldn't have left it there. Maybe they can figure out who I am by reading it. But is that such a bad idea? Just 'cause they know who I am doesn't mean they can find me. Maybe I should have laid it all on the line. Maybe I should have sprawled a great big signature across the bottom of the page. Let them know who I am. Let them fear me and what society has made me.*

To him, society was an ugly word dressed in a pretty suit. It looked good on the outside but it was a mean, arbitrary place where the rules changed without warning and caught him by surprise. He hated prison but, at the same time, he felt safe there. He knew what to expect. He always knew where he stood. Out here, though, he found it confusing. People said one thing and did another. And simple survival required such monumental effort. Gathering food, finding shelter – it was almost impossible.

They made it so hard. They needed to be punished. His mind drifted back to the barn. He had been surprised at how well his first abduction had gone. *The stupid Goodie Goodie didn't even fight when I tied his hands behind his back before we left his car. All he wanted to do was talk. Talk about getting me help. Finding me services. Helping get me back on his feet.* 'I'm standing just fine on my own two feet, thank you. You're the one tied up and in trouble,' he told him. Then he kicked him from behind and sent Agnew sprawling on the ground. *Idiot. Hypocrite. Talk, talk, talk. In the end, he would have left me behind just like all the rest.*

He had no problem getting the rope over the beam and around Agnew's neck but then he encountered an obstacle when he attempted to finish the job. *The stupid goodie two shoes stopped his sweet talk, struggled and tried to run. I didn't want to hit him in the head with the shovel. He made me do that. Then it was easy to tug on the rope and pull him up. Easy to tie it off to a pole.*

He was especially proud of his innovative touch at the end. When he broke all of Agnew's fingers, the hands just dangled at the end of his arms. *So disappointing. No sense of drama at all.* The addition of the ropes to Agnew's wrist, pulling them upward, putting his fingers on display, made him laugh with joy when he did it

189

and made him smile now.

He had to admit, though, there just wasn't enough blood to satisfy him. He loved it when the deep red saturated every surface. There was some bleeding when he hit Agnew in the head but nothing like the torrent produced when he sliced a throat. Then it flew everywhere, drops fell on his face like rain warming him with their fresh spilled heat. Or that chaos of blood flying and oozing everywhere when he unleashed his fury in a good, long beating where time stood still. He let images from his bloodiest kills run through his mind as he drifted away into a peaceful sleep.

Thirty-One

Halfway between the house and the barn, the rain intensified again. Lucinda and Jake entered the shelter dripping and shivering. As a rule, Lucinda loved the sound of rain on a tin roof – one of the few pleasant memories from her childhood. But the pounding of the downpour above her head today sounded threatening and ominous. *Is it because I'm hearing it at the scene of someone's violent death? Nah. I'm not that complicated. I don't like the sound because I'm cold in this unheated barn and ever since I mentioned that nice warm bath to Jake, I'm having trouble thinking about anything else.*

'Whatcha got, Melanie?' Jake asked.

'The guy from the coroner's office said that it appeared as if there was blunt-force trauma to the vic's head prior to his hanging. And I thought you might want to look at this before I move it.'

She led them back into the corner of the barn where old hand tools hung neatly on rusted nails pounded into the wooden wall. 'See the shovel over on the left. I first noticed it because there were no cobwebs on it. Then I crouched down, put my cheek against the wall and looked up, like this,' Melanie said as she got into position, pounding on one knee with her fist as she did.

She flipped on her flashlight and shined its beam up the rough wood to the back of the metal blade. 'There I see something suspicious – like it might be hair and blood.'

Noticing the difficulty the tech had getting down on the floor like that, Lucinda asked, 'Why don't you just lift the shovel off the nails and look at it?'

'Well, excuse me for thinking about your case,' Melanie said, then turned to Jake. 'Although we took photos of the shovel in place, Jake, I thought you might want to see it there before I collected it as possible evidence.'

Lucinda winced under the rebuke. *Oh jeez, I did it again.*

'Thanks, Melanie, we both appreciate that. Go ahead and secure it for analysis at the lab.'

After the shovel was covered and stored in the crime scene truck, Lucinda approached Melanie. 'I don't think anyone told you my name; it's Lucinda Pierce. I want to apologize for my insensitivity. I saw the difficulty you were having and I just blurted out what I was thinking. I definitely should have known better.'

Melanie looked hard at the damaged side of Lucinda's face. 'Yeah, you should have. I'm sorry for snapping back at you like that, though. Melanie Handy,' she said, sticking out her hand.

Lucinda grabbed it and said, 'Apologies and forgiveness all around. Are you having difficulty with your leg, or hip or back or—?'

'Kick me in the shin,' Melanie said.

'Excuse me?'

'Go ahead, kick it, knock on it,' Melanie said,

rapping her leg with her knuckles. The sound reverberated in the air. 'See,' she said, pulling up her pants leg. 'It's not real. Sometimes in damp weather the joint moves slow and I get frustrated and hit on it a bit – that's what was going on back there in that corner.'

'What...?' Lucinda began. She shook her head and said, 'Never mind. None of my business.'

'I don't mind talking about it, particularly not with someone who's probably been through as much or more crap than I have. In fact, I'm surprised you're still out in the field after losing your eye.'

'It was a challenge pulling that one off. And there's no guarantee I'll stay here. The mayor's formed a panel to review policy about monocular officers. That's a big part of why I'm up here. The captain wanted me out of town and productive while he argued my case. But what about you? What's your story? You're in the field with a missing limb. That couldn't have been easy.'

'And it wasn't,' Melanie said. 'Talk about fighting on too many fronts for one lifetime – whoa. I was a patrol officer and I was in the National Guard. I got called up and went to Iraq. I hadn't been there too long before I had a fateful encounter with an I.E.D. While I was recovering from the loss of my leg and going through therapy to get used to my prosthetic device, I was an emotional basket case and pretty much did everything I was told to do. By the time I got my shit together, I was trained in forensics and working in a lab. It took a lot of badgering on my part to actually get out of the lab and out in the field again. I felt so disconnected from what matters when I couldn't get out and see it all first hand.'

'I know what you mean,' Lucinda said. 'People become statistics when you're stuck at a desk. I really want to stay out in the field, but sometimes I get so tired of people staring at me and asking me what happened.'

'That's where I'm lucky. If I'm wearing pants, no one can tell by looking at me. But this past summer, I actually got up the nerve to wear shorts a few times. I got a lot of stares. The ones I hate the most are the people who look away and pretend that they never were looking at you in the first place.'

'Oh, yeah, I get a lot of those.'

'So, what's your story, Lucinda?'

Lucinda tensed, as she usually did when asked, and then she let it all go. For the first time, she told someone of the horror of the shot to her face without embarrassment, anger or resentment. When she finished, she nearly cried with gratitude. It felt so good to talk to someone who understood what it was like to want to lead a normal existence in law enforcement with a disability that could, without a determination to fight, leave you on the sidelines.

Both women pulled out business cards and jotted personal contact information on the back, exchanged knowing smiles and firm handshakes.

Jake wanted to head back to town but he stayed occupied talking to the other techs while Lucinda and Melanie huddled together. He kept his distance, not knowing what was going on between the two women but sensing it was personal and important.

When Lucinda signaled that she was ready to leave, Jake gratefully slid into the passenger seat of her car.

As he headed down the road, he asked, 'So, was it a good bonding experience?'

'Oh, you know, girl stuff. Make-up, our favorite depilatory cream and, of course, guys.'

'Did you talk about me?'

'Oh, my, wouldn't you like to know.'

'You're not going to tell me?'

'Of course not. You can't share girl talk with a guy. Aren't you old enough to know that by now?'

'I'm not that young,' Jake objected.

'A lot younger than me,' Lucinda said. She knew she really said it for her own benefit, in an attempt to put emotional distance between herself and Jake.

'Not by a lot.'

'What? Ten, fifteen years?'

'Twelve, tops,' he argued.

'And that's not a lot?'

'It's nothing,' he said with a snap of his fingers.

Lucinda felt a tingling in her breasts and between her legs. Color rushed into her face as she tried to suppress her physical reaction. *Not now, Lucinda. We are in the middle of a case. Stow the hormones.*

Jake reached over and lightly touched the inside of her forearm. 'You sure you don't want to go out to dinner tonight?'

As the skin of his fingertip made contact with hers, an electric charge raced straight up her arm and into her head, making her scalp tingle. She swallowed hard and licked her lips. When she spoke her words sounded unconvincing to her own ears. 'Nah, Jake. I'm just too tired tonight. Some other time, OK?'

Thirty-Two

Lucinda and Jake stuck their arms into surgical gowns, pulling them over their clothing to protect them from incidental contamination, and took their positions near the autopsy table where the body of Michael Agnew rested. Lucinda found the sight of blackened tongue protruding from the victim's mouth unsettling. She had an urge to push it back in his mouth to restore the man's dignity in death.

Jake had worked with Doctor Angelo DiBlasio on other cases but it was Lucinda's first opportunity to meet the man. She was curious about forensic pathologists in general. Although her career brought her in close and frequent contact with death, those who performed autopsies seemed to have a darker, colder and yet more intimate relationship with it. It took years before she'd felt comfortable around Doc Sam.

She knew she should make allowances for her bias and her perceptions but still, when she looked at Doctor DiBlasio, she wanted to keep her distance. She even backed up half a step. His dark eyes appeared to have a matte finish as if a life lived in these corridors of the dead had robbed them of all light and humanity.

Then she saw the laugh lines around his eyes

and was embarrassed by her negative reaction. Despite his occupation, he had a life like anybody else – a life filled with the joys and sorrows that never seemed to be dished out in fair proportions.

He combed his black hair straight back from his forehead, dramatizing his natural widow's peak. Grayish-white streaks darted past his temples and nearly consumed his sideburns. A prominent, sharp nose added a harshness to his face that was softened a bit by the plumpness of his lower lip. She wouldn't classify him as a handsome man but she suspected that in a business suit or a tux, he'd probably cut a dashing figure despite his middle-aged paunch.

Doctor DiBlasio glanced briefly at her as he weighed and measured the victim, but either he didn't notice her injury or he had no more interest in her than he had in the box that held his surgical gloves. He began his external examination by carefully slipping the noose with its knot intact over the victim's head and securing it as evidence. 'I must admit, after the thousands of autopsies I've done, if you are correct, Lovett, this will be my first homicidal hanging. A lot of suicides by hanging, a few accidents, but murder doesn't happen that way too often. I'd be most likely to believe that the blunt trauma to the head caused his death but, at least at this point, it doesn't look like it did.'

The doctor noted the state of the victim's tongue, the thin line of crusty saliva running from the corner of his mouth, the small amount of pinkish fluid in his nostrils. He lifted the eyelids and observed no petechiae, the dots of blood normally present in a death by manual strangulation or smothering.

He put a finger under the chin on the table and lifted. There the distinctive groove pressed in deeply leaving the impression of the rope's surface embedded in the skin in the typical V-formation of a hanging. 'Well, we can eliminate the second most likely candidate as the cause of death. There definitely are no circular markings to indicate that ligature strangulation killed this guy before he was strung up. But the marks on his neck don't necessarily mean he was alive when he was hung.'

Removing the ropes from around the wrists proved more difficult. They were tied too tight to slip over his hand. DiBlasio cut them away, snipping the binding cord as far from the knot as possible. After removing them, he handed each one with delicate care to his assistant who taped the cut ends together before bagging the ropes as evidence.

'Now, I can't be one hundred per cent certain until I do an internal examination. But I'd say that those ropes were tied to the wrists post-mortem. Which is pretty odd.' He manipulated one of the hands and added, 'And I could be wrong but it looks like the breaks in these fingers happened after death, too.'

Lucinda spoke up. 'That, sir, would be consistent with a homicide in my jurisdiction as well as a few others we believe to be connected to the same perpetrator.'

Dr DiBlasio looked up over his mask. 'You got

others where the fingers were broken after death?'

Lucinda nodded.

'And no personal connections between the victims? No indications that they knew each other?'

'No, sir.'

'Humph.'

Doctor DiBlasio turned the victim's head and felt the area around the injury on the back of the skull. 'Doesn't seem severe enough to cause death. But, again, I'll have to look at the brain to be sure.'

The tech stepped up with fingerprinting ink and paper, recording the pattern on each of the victim's fingers and his palms. As soon as the ink dried on the document, another employee delivered it to the fingerprint analysis section.

Jake looked away when the doctor's scalpel bit into the flesh to make the classic Y-incision. For some reason, that had never bothered Lucinda. She had been present, though, when other seemingly tough detectives had keeled right over and hit the floor the first time they saw that cut. She braced herself for the moment that filled her with dread, when the autopsy tech snapped the breastbone. She never watched that procedure after her first autopsy observation, but even without seeing what was happening, she knew it by the sound. The snapping, the crunching of the bone as it cracked open to reveal the heart and the chest cavity made her skin crawl and her stomach lurch. She closed her eyes, held her ground, and winced when she heard the brutal noise.

DiBlasio removed the body's vital organs, weighing each one except for the adrenal glands and pancreas. They were both noted as unremarkable and set aside. Although it was unlikely that there would ever be a need for any microscopic investigation in this homicide case, samples of tissue from all major organs were saved on slides.

Lucinda felt Jake turn rigid by her side. She suspected it was his time for dread coming up. He flinched when the Stryker saw came out to cut off the top of the skull. Lucinda noticed that he swayed in place as if his knees were about to buckle, but despite that sign of weakness, he remained standing throughout.

She'd met other officers who were repulsed by the sight of the brain. They couldn't explain why. They admitted it wasn't logical. If anything other organs looked gorier but, for some reason, the contents of the skull always came closest to making them lose their lunch. It never much bothered her. It struck her as a bizarre curiosity that the convoluted mass controlled so much in life.

Doctor DiBlasio found no sign of fatal injury to the brain but preserved several tissue sections just the same. The pathologist next turned his attention to the dissection of the neck, looking for any internal signs of injury. As with most deaths by hanging, none were found – the thyroid cartilage was intact and the hyoid was not fractured.

When the procedure was complete, Doctor

DiBlasio pulled off his latex gloves and dropped them on the stainless-steel surface. 'I'll wait for the toxicology results before I file my official report, but here's what you need to do your job: the manner of death is homicide, the means of death is asphyxia, the cause of death is hanging by a rope – definitely not like a judicial hanging; I do not believe he dropped from a height to hang since there were no broken vertebrae.'

Doctor DiBlasio sloughed off his surgical gown and let it fall to the floor. He walked from the room, leaving the techs to clean up and prepare the body for delivery to the mortuary.

Once outside, Lucinda took her first deep breath of the morning. 'That's certainly not the best way to start your day.'

'You're telling me,' Jake said. 'Not in my list of career choices. I don't know how those guys get up and come to work knowing that's what's waiting for them.' He gave an exaggerated shiver and said, 'It's lunchtime. You up for it?'

Lucinda grimaced. 'How about we drive a few dozen miles and get the smell of that room out of my nose first?'

'Good idea,' Jake said as his cell phone rang. He listened and said, 'Well, that figures. Thanks anyway.' He turned to Lucinda. 'That was fingerprints. They've got a match. To our victim.'

'The fingerprint on the door latch?'

'Yeah. And I got word from the handwriting analyst this morning, too, about the notes at the scene and the notes found on your car.'

'Already?'

'Well, mostly she just gave me a lecture about how difficult it was to draw any conclusions from block printing and then said that the two samples could not be verified to be from the same source nor could the two samples be eliminated as being from the same source.'

'So, really, she said nothing?' Lucinda asked.

'That's what I said and that pretty much ticked her off. She snapped back, "The results are inconclusive. Next time bring me actual written, not printed, samples." I told her we'd put that request out to the public at our next news conference. She hung up.'

'I just don't see it, Jake. I just don't see a connection.'

'Exactly why it's good that I'm coming along with you. I can watch your back.'

Lucinda was torn. A part of Lucinda wanted to snap back that she was perfectly capable of taking care of herself and although she knew that was true, it was nice to find a man who was not intimated by her strength and tough exterior – a man who could look at her honestly and still want to offer protection. Ted Branson often acted protective but that was only because he still saw her as the young high school girl she had been when they had dated. He'd never completely acknowledged the woman she'd become. Jake, on the other hand, only knew the woman that stood before him. *He'd read the worst about me. He'd looked me full in the face. And still he cared. Or did he? Did he really? Watch out, girl, hope is a dangerous commodity when placed in the wrong hands.*

Thirty-Three

While Jake worked his cell phone, Lucinda drove towards home on a familiar route, seeing little of her surroundings as she plunged deep into her own troubled thoughts. She tried in vain to purge the image of Michael Agnew from her mind. But every time she shut her eye, she saw his mocking marionette hands with twisted, broken fingers, the blackness of his protruding tongue, the hopelessness of his limp, still body as it hung in mid-air. *Thank God, Agnew was a white man* skittered past her consciousness as a series of still-life black-and-white photos of racially motivated lynchings from the state's past history flashed through her mind.

She'd been to many crime scenes and seen many gruesome photos from others. Those sights were not alien – they were the stuff of her life. She could think and work as she looked on the gory remains of a brutal death. She could hash over the details with her fellow professionals without the slightest churn in her gut. She swore that none of it bothered her any longer. But then there were those images that burned into her brain. The visuals she wanted to forget but instead they hung on, haunting every blink of her eye and troubling her dreams. Michael

Agnew's body in the barn was one of them. He would be with her for a long time.

She was grateful when Jake clicked off his cell and turned his attention back to her, drawing her away from the unrelenting darkness in her head.

'Well, I got as much done by phone as I can for now,' Jake said. 'My techs are in touch with your Ted Branson. Ted told me that he'd already gathered information and created a spreadsheet on the different types of potential evidence found at each of the similar crime scenes up and down the coast.'

Lucinda laughed. 'Ted and his spreadsheets. I wouldn't want to take on a complicated case without them but his instinctive need to create them always makes me laugh.'

'The techs are loving it. They eat that stuff up. In Ted, they found a kindred spirit. Ted emailed the documents to them and they are in heaven reviewing data. They told me that he's out of place and under-appreciated in homicide; he should be working with them full time. I think they're looking into the possibility of stealing him away.'

'Did they bother to ask Ted if he was interested in moving to D.C.?'

'That's not how they operate. They prefer making offers that people can't refuse.'

'That sounds so *Godfather*.'

'They don't call it organized crime because it's devoid of bureaucracy,' Jake quipped. 'Somebody ought to do a doctoral thesis on the similarities between the mafia and the bureau.'

'I can't believe you're saying that,' Lucinda said.

'Hey, I'm not exactly your prototype federal employee. I annoy my supervisors on a regular basis. Anyway, the next step for the techs is to figure out what additional tests they can do on the material retrieved from other scenes and how to get it up to their lab.'

'Have they exhausted what they found in Agnew's car and at the murder scene?'

'Not at all. They completely vacuumed out the SUV. But it'll take days for the assigned tech to comb through that, pull out and categorize any bit of lint and strand of hair with potential significance. Then after figuring out what to test and how and cross reference it all with what's been found at the other scenes, the lab geeks will get busy. It's a mind-boggling amount of detail and I really don't know how they or Ted can spend hours in a lab and in front of the computer sifting it, collating it and coming up with something that actually makes sense when I look at it.'

'I know what you mean. I can pretty much do what I need to do on the computer but it takes me a lot more time than Ted to achieve the same results and I just don't have the creative flair that he has to organize it in a way that makes sense to others. It's a real talent.'

'Have you known him long?' Jake asked.

'Who, Ted? Yeah, we dated in high school.'

'Is there anything...' Jake stalled, looking for words.

'Between me and Ted? Ted is married and has

two kids.'

'And that makes him off limits for you?'

'Yeah,' Lucinda asked, giving him a quick sidelong glance, amused by his apparent discomfort. 'What are you getting at, Jake?'

'Well, I was trying to figure how the lay of the land – no, sorry, bad choice of words. Just trying to prepare for a new environment. Yeah, that's it.'

'Jake, are you trying to find out if I am involved with anyone back home?' A charged thrill rose from Lucinda's core and raced across the surface of her skin.

'Jeez. I didn't want to come right out and ask.'

'Why not?'

'It just didn't seem appropriate.'

'Why not?' Lucinda asked, knowing the answer but wanting him to squirm a bit.

'We're working together, on a case, you know, I didn't want you to think I was coming on too strong or being sexist or whatever.'

'Are you?' Lucinda teased.

Jake exhaled a noisy blast of air. 'About your crime scene again – could you run through the details before we get to town?'

Lucinda laughed and launched into a full description of the discovery of the homicide of Shari Fleming. She was still running down details when they pulled into the parking lot at the Justice Center. She shifted the car into park and cut the engine. 'By the way,' she said, 'I am not involved with anyone.' She got out of the car without waiting for a response.

* * *

After Ted Branson finished his telephone and email communications with the FBI techs and found the answers to a few questions raised by Jake, he allowed his thoughts to drift to questions he had about the agent that traveled his way in Lucinda's car. Ted envied Jake the forced companionship with Lucinda that the long drive required. *It's been a while since Lucinda and I spent any time together unless it was in the office or over a dead body. We used to meet up for coffee, lunch or a drink every now and then but I don't think we've done that once since Ellen and I separated.* That realization struck Ted as weird. *Why now that I am less encumbered have our encounters become less frequent?*

He didn't like where the line of thought led him so he switched his musings to Jake Lovett. *Is he the reason why Lucinda seems to have dropped her hostility toward the FBI? Is there something happening between the two of them? If so, how serious is it? Will he stay with her while he's in town?* Ted thought about Lucinda's apartment. As he recalled there was only one bedroom. *Would he sleep on the sofa or would he...?* Ted shook that thought out of his head and returned to his spreadsheets. There were always refinements possible. He didn't want anyone on the federal level to find any flaws in his databases.

Again, his mind slid away from the tasks at hand. *What does Lucinda see in him?*

Whoa, Ted, who says she sees anything?

Well, one, I have not heard her describe the agency as 'the Feebs' on any of the calls since she met Jake. Two, he is riding with her instead of taking his own car. Three, there's something in the way he says her name.

Isn't there? Or am I being paranoid?

They'll be here soon. I can judge their inter-actions face to face. Will I be able to see the truth?

The phone on Ted's desk buzzed and a bored voice announced, 'Line Two, Sergeant Branson.'

Ted picked up the phone. Ellen, his estranged wife was on the line asking if he'd like to come over for dinner that night.

'Tonight?' he asked and then listened for her response.

'Sorry, Ellen, wish I could but I've got an FBI agent on his way into town to meet with me.'

In response to her challenge, he said, 'Aw c'mon, Ellen. It's my job. And, no,' he lied, 'I'm not waiting for Lieutenant Pierce. I'm waiting for an agent from D.C.'

He returned the receiver to its cradle and sighed.

Thirty-Four

After a few minutes for introductions, the three investigators plunged into work on the case. Ted took Jake to review the computer data and Lucinda sat down with hard copies of reports and notes from interviews with investigators in other jurisdictions. When the phone rang, Lucinda answered it. 'Homicide. Pierce speaking.' On the other end, a receiver slammed down with force.

'Was that for me?' Ted asked.

'You better hope not, Ted. That caller disconnected that call with vengeance.'

Work continued as it was before the call until Jake asked, 'Where can I find a cup of coffee fit to drink?'

'The stuff in the break room on this floor comes in your choice of weak and watery or thick and charred. I'd recommend the ground-floor cafe,' Lucinda said. 'I could use a latte, if you're going down.'

'Bring back a cup for me and I promise to say something nice about the FBI at least once this month,' Ted added.

After Jake got directions and left in pursuit of caffeine, Ted stood in front of Lucinda with a hand on each hip.

Lucinda looked up at him with a smile. 'Good teamwork. We got the new guy to fetch the coffee.'

'Do you really think it's wise?'

'What? I'm sure he takes home a bigger paycheck than we do – he can afford to pay for our coffee. And the fetching part is a worthwhile lesson in humility for an FBI guy,' Lucinda said.

'Not the coffee. You know what I mean,' he said with a head jerk in the direction of the departing Jake.

'So far, he's been very helpful. He's not bad for a Fed.'

'A Fed? Not a Feeb? See. Just as I suspected, the looks you two exchanged were very telling. Pretty much gave it all away.'

'Ted, what are you talking about?'

'I'm talking about what's going on between you and the agent.'

'We're working together, Ted. That's it.'

'So, where's he spending the night?'

'I don't know. I'll find someplace to stow him.'

'I bet you will.'

'Ted, what is this shit? You are not my dad. Not my big brother. Not my boyfriend. What gives you the right to interrogate me like this? I plan to take Jake to a hotel but if I want to toss him in my bed instead, what business is it of yours?'

'I'm thinking about you, Lucinda. I want what's best for you.'

'Oh, and I guess you think that's you, Mr Married Man.'

'I'm married in name only, Lucinda. You know that.'

'Have you been to counseling with Ellen? Have you even sat down and talked with her face to face?'

'No. It's a waste of time.'

'If that's so, then why is she doing everything she can to drag out the legal process?'

'I don't care why. Maybe because she's a bitch. Maybe for some reason I don't understand. But I don't want our marriage to work. I want to be with you. I thought I made that clear.'

'That has to be a mutual decision, Ted. And I've told you before that you owe Ellen. You need to help her get past the death of her baby before you just walk out the door. You need to at least talk with her, heart-to-heart. She deserves to at least have closure on the relationship.'

'Oh, right, talking is the answer. I guess that's why you don't take any of your sister's calls.'

'That's different,' Lucinda said, her nostrils flaring.

'What's so different? You had a disagreement. You should talk.'

'You know it's different. You read the newspaper. You know she told that reporter after the accidental shooting of that little boy.' Lucinda saw the words as distinctly as if she were still holding the paper in front of her face. *My sister Lucinda has been one big ball of anger since our parents died. She tried to be a good sister but the bottom line was circumstances left her with a cold, cold heart. She became a police officer because she was hell bent on getting revenge.*

I'm surprised she hasn't shot more people. 'Ellen has never done anything like that to you. She may have said some mean things to your face. But she has never shredded you in public. Nothing like that. You owe her.'

Jake cleared his throat. 'Coffee anyone?'

Lucinda and Ted turned from each other toward Jake. They smiled in a futile attempt to pretend he had not interrupted a private conversation. They both took their coffee with downcast eyes and got back to work without comment.

The three sketched out the investigation battle plan for the next couple of days. Ted would work in the office coordinating with the FBI techs, inputting new data and keeping in touch with all the detectives and their local FBI agents on related cases in other jurisdictions. Jake would take care of any communication breakdown between his bureau and local investigations if Ted waved a red flag.

Lucinda would take Jake around to her crime scene in the morning and to follow-up interviews with the people who knew Shari Fleming best. Now that it was clear that her murder was not an isolated incident, a new line of questioning was in order, one that included new queries about Broderick and any comments he might have made about 'No Child Left Behind'.

When they called it a day, all three were beat but encouraged about the prospects for progress on the case in the coming days. They were also haunted by the possibility that their killer would strike again before they could identify him.

Lucinda approached her car and shouted, 'Shit. Not again.' She pulled the piece of paper of her windshield.

'What's the matter with you, Lucinda? Don't touch that. We need to collect it as evidence,' Jake admonished.

'It has nothing to do with this case, Jake.'

'You don't know that.'

'Come on, Jake. Does this sound like a serial killer?' Lucinda read from the paper, '"I've had it now. You just won't listen. I'll find you when you least expect it." That's personal, Jake, and this killer is not someone I know.'

'And what makes you so certain of that?' Jake asked in a disturbingly quiet voice.

'Because – because – because...' Lucinda stammered.

'Because you don't want to believe that possibility. It could even be someone you work with or someone you talk to every day. It could be the guy behind the counter at the cafe, it could be the man who delivers your mail, it could be Ted. He's been around every time you've gotten one of this notes, hasn't he? But you don't really know. Do you, Lucinda?'

Lucinda opened her mouth to object to his suggestion of Ted but then realized that, as unlikely as that possibility was, she didn't really know with certainty. She stared at Jake for a moment with a slack jaw and then she said, 'I don't know, do I?'

Thirty-Five

Lucinda snapped out of her sleep disoriented. For a second, she did not understand the weight on her stomach or the noise that popped her eyes open. She recognized that the familiar sensation of heaviness was Chester her cat first, then she identified the irritating sound as her telephone. She glared at the clock by her bed. *Four seventeen? Damn.*

She picked up the receiver and tried to sound alert when she muttered, 'Pierce.'

'Hey, Lieutenant, this is Officer Colter on patrol. You might remember me from the school district case? I kept the superintendent from coming in the side door.'

Does it matter who the hell she is at four a.m.?

'Yes, Officer. What do you want?'

'Uh, you ordered extra patrols past the Broderick residence?'

'Yeah.'

'It says we're, uh, supposed to call you if we noticed any signs of activity?'

'Yeah. Get to the point, Officer.'

'When I came by here a couple of hours ago, everything was the same as always. But right now, there are lights on and another car in the driveway.'

215

'You run the plates?'

'I thought you'd want me to do that,' she said, her smile apparent in her voice, 'so I did. The vehicle is registered to Angela Dromgoole who lives over on Parsons Drive. No priors. Not even minor traffic violations.'

'Thanks, Officer. Are you there alone?'

'Yes, ma'am.'

'Call for back-up. But stay away from the house. I'll be there as quickly as I can and I'll want some force there in case it's needed.'

Lucinda disconnected the call and pressed in the numbers to Jake's cell.

'Lovett,' a gravelly voice answered.

'Up and at 'em, Special Agent. We've got work to do.'

'What time is it?'

'Doesn't matter. Duty never sleeps. I'll be there in ten minutes or less. Be out in front of the hotel.'

'What's going on?'

'I'll explain it all when I pick you up. In about, oh, seven and a half minutes,' Lucinda said.

'Shit.'

Lucinda grinned as she hung up the phone.

At Broderick's house, Lucinda and Jake peered in windows hoping to get an idea of what to expect before they knocked on the front door. 'I think I hear two people talking in there,' Jake said.

'Are you sure there are two people?'

'No, not really. It could be a radio or television.'

216

'Look over there, does that look like the same guy that's in the driver's license photo of Broderick?' Jake said, pointing to the far side of the room.

Lucinda shifted her angle of vision and got a glimpse of a retreating back. 'Couldn't tell.'

They slipped to the back of the house to the sliding-glass door taking care to stay out of sight. 'There he is again,' Jake whispered.

'Yes, that is the guy. That's Broderick. But who is that woman?'

'Angela Dromgoole?'

'Yeah, probably. But who is she?' Lucinda asked.

A short tan dog with big ears rounded the kitchen counter. 'What is that?' Jake asked.

'That's the dog,' Lucinda said.

'Are you sure it's a dog? Ears of a bat and no sign of legs...'

'It has legs. They're kinda stumpy. It's a Corgi,' Lucinda whispered.

'A what?'

The dog's head jerked in their direction. His tail curled up, his ears stiffened, a low growl issued from his throat.

Lucinda and Jake sprinted for the front door as the first bark rang out. They hit the doorbell and tried to compose themselves before it was answered.

Although it was quite early in the morning, the man who answered the door appeared dressed for the day – yesterday. His clothing was rumpled and wrinkled. His sandy-haired head showed no signs of bedhead but didn't look like it had seen a comb for quite some time. His eyes were alert and squinted with suspicion.

Lucinda and Jake flipped open their badges in unison. 'Steve Broderick?' Lucinda asked.

The man's eyes shifted back and forth between the two investigators.

'You are Steve Broderick, aren't you?' Jake asked.

'Yes. What's it to you?'

'May we come in?' Lucinda said as she pushed forward, forcing the issue.

'Do you know what time it is?' Steve said as she walked across the room with the Corgi matching each of her steps with a fresh bark and a few inches of retreat.

'Steve, I can't find your computer,' a woman's voice sounded from down the hall.

Ignoring her, Steve turned to Lucinda and asked, 'Have you been here before?'

'Yes, we have. We had a search warrant.'

'You took my computer?'

'Yes, sir. There is a complete list of what was removed from your home on your kitchen counter along with a copy of the search warrant.'

'I didn't see anything like that.'

Lucinda walked across to the dining room and over to the bar stools beside the counter between that room and the kitchen. Pointing, she said, 'Right there, Mr Broderick. It was the only clean surface we could find.'

'Are you saying my house is dirty?'

'Cluttered, Mr Broderick. That's all, cluttered. Looks better than my place, actually,' Jake said. 'We do have some questions we need to ask you.'

'Do I need an attorney?'

'That's up to you, Mr Broderick. If you think you do, we can go down to the station and wait for your lawyer to arrive. It's your call,' Lucinda said.

A woman with long dark hair and a rail-thin body strode into the room. 'Steve, don't even say that. Everybody knows only guilty people get attorneys. You've done nothing. Nothing at all.' She turned to the officers and said, 'Please have a seat. We just got back in town. We were away visiting family.'

'Really?' Lucinda and Jake said and then grinned at each other in surprise.

'Why, yes,' the woman continued. 'Our relationship is getting serious so we thought it was time.'

'And you are?' Lucinda asked.

'Angela Dromgoole. Steve's fiancée.'

'So, Broderick,' Jake said, 'you just thought it was so urgent to meet this woman's family that you tore off from work without letting anyone know where you were going.'

'I called the district offices several times but at first I got a recording asking if I wanted to leave a message. Then, I got a message that the mailbox was full. Here,' he said as he pulled out his cell phone, 'you can check the list of calls I made on the log.'

'But why, Mr Broderick, did you find it so urgent to leave when you did?' Lucinda asked.

'Angela wanted me to,' he said as he stepped toward her and put an arm around her shoulders.

'And what Angela wants, I try to deliver.'

Angela giggled. Lucinda and Jake exchanged an eye roll.

'I imagine we'll find a whole list of missed phone calls from the school district in your menu, too, Mr Broderick. Why didn't you take their calls?'

'Because I was on vacation.'

'An unauthorized vacation,' Jake said.

'Well, yeah, but I didn't leave any loose ends around when I left.'

'No loose ends? Really, Mr Broderick?' Lucinda said. 'How about we try to get a truthful answer about the timing of your departure? We know about the Carney homicide in Maine.'

'See, see!' Steve said to Angela. 'I just knew it. I knew I'd be a suspect. I just couldn't face it again. That's why I left Maine in the first place.'

'But, Steve, I told you running away is no way to solve a problem.'

'Angela, let's not go into that now.'

'Excuse me, Mr Broderick. Could I please get an answer?' Lucinda interrupted.

'Yes. Yes. Yes. I decided to leave town when I heard about Shari's death. I just couldn't deal with it again. I was feeling like some sort of bad luck generating machine. I pop up and a Communities in Schools Executive Director dies.'

'So, where did you go, Mr Broderick?' Jake asked.

'We went to Jacksonville, Florida, to visit my parents, and to Baton Rouge, Louisiana, to visit his brother,' Angela said.

'Please, ma'am, let Mr Broderick answer for

himself,' Jake said.

'I was just trying to be helpful, Officer. Steve is a bit freaked out by all of this and not as quick with answers as he usually is.'

'Please, Ms Dromgoole. If you could have a seat at the dining-room table, we'll let you know if we have any questions for you,' Lucinda insisted.

Angela's mouth opened and shut.

'Please, Angela,' Steve said.

Angela plopped in a seat with enough noise to make her indignation clear to everyone.

Lucinda turned away from her. 'Mr Broderick, did you go anywhere else on this trip?'

'We stopped in New Orleans for a couple of hours but we didn't spend the night there or anything.'

'How about Washington, D.C.? Anywhere near there?' Jake asked.

'No. We've spent a lot of time on the road but our route didn't take us anywhere near there,' Steve said. 'What happened in D.C.? I thought you were here about Shari Fleming's murder.'

'Mr Broderick, if you had been at the school district offices on the day Ms Fleming's body was found, you would have been questioned along with everyone else. But because you disappeared for a few days, you've now become a person of interest in her murder as well as a few other homicides including one in D.C.,' Jake said.

'Man, I'm sorry. I just panicked. That's all. I left town just to get away.'

'Where were you on Wednesday evening, the

week before last?' Lucinda asked.

'Why are you pestering him? He just needed to get away for a while. What's wrong with that?' Angela interjected.

'Ms Dromgoole, you need to keep quiet. Or else we'll have to take everyone down to the station,' Lucinda threatened, then turned back to Steve. 'Mr Broderick, please answer my question.'

'I went to prayer meeting at church and then I went home,' Steve said.

Angela jumped to her feet. 'I went with him. I am his alibi.'

Steve turned a puzzled look to his girlfriend. 'Angela, you can't lie to the police.'

Angela thrust her chin out. 'I'm not lying, Steve. You don't need to protect my reputation.' She walked up to Lucinda and said, 'I went to church with Steve that night and then came home with him and committed fornication. Now that sure is a sin but I don't think it's a crime. So why don't you just take your ugly face and your uglier accusations and get out of here.'

Lucinda looked up at the ceiling and let out a big sigh. She looked at Jake and, after exchanging shrugs, they each pulled out a set of handcuffs. While Angela ranted about the outrage, Steve cooperated without saying a word and the little dog bounced around the room, barking and nipping at heels. Jake and Lucinda slapped the restraints on the couple's wrists and escorted them both out to the car.

Thirty-Six

Jake placed Steve Broderick into one interrogation room and Lucinda took Angela to another. While the couple sat on uncomfortable chairs, in separate rooms, looking at bare walls, Lucinda and Jake went down to the cafe to grab a cup of coffee and a bite to eat. They took their time eating breakfast biscuits and sipping on two cups of coffee each. Then they sauntered back upstairs to deal with Steve and Angela. By mutual agreement, Lucinda took Angela and Jake went into the room with Steve.

Jake started by asking about the couple's road trip. Steve went through more detail about meeting each other's family members than Jake ever wanted to hear but he let Steve ramble hoping at some point he would say something that actually mattered.

In the middle of an explanation about the interaction between Angela and Cousin Bertie, Steve took a sharp intake of air and said, 'I've got it. I've got proof.' He twisted his arm around to his back pants pocket. Then he jerked forward, held up both his hands and, 'Sorry. Sorry. No false moves, right? I'm not used to this stuff. Do you want to remove my wallet from my rear pocket?'

Jake shook his head. He had a juvenile urge to pull his gun out of his holster and see if the guy started begging for his life. Instead, he suppressed that baser impulse, squeezed the bridge of his nose between his thumb and index finger and said, 'No, no, Mr Broderick. You go right ahead and remove your wallet and show me what you've got.'

Steve moved with slow deliberation providing play-by-play commentary. 'I'm turning at the waist. I'm reaching my arm to my back pocket. I've got my fingers on my wallet. I'm sliding it out. I'm bringing it to the front of my body and setting it on the table. There!' He beamed at Jake.

In the most patient voice he could muster, Jake said, 'What's in the wallet, Mr Broderick?'

'Oh, yes, right.' Steve carefully folded down one side of the tri-fold and then the other. 'I'm going to remove the contents now,' he said.

'Fine, Mr Broderick.'

Steve spread apart the section that holds paper money, pulled out a modest wad of folded bills and set them on the table. Then he reached into the corner and pulled out a small bundle of white receipts folded together with symmetrical, crisp corners.

'Did you iron those?' Jake asked.

'Oh, of course not. I was on the road, Agent Lovett. But when I got each one, I laid it on a flat surface and smoothed it flat before putting it with the others.'

Observing the seriousness of the response, Jake nearly choked as he struggled to suppress laughter. He hunched over with a hand over his mouth until he regained control. Steve pushed the neat pile of receipts across the table. Jake glanced at each one for the location and date, more out of respect for the offering than because he felt a need to verify Steve's statement. 'Mr Broderick, I accept your story of your journey to Florida and Louisiana. I believe you are telling me the truth. Although it appears pretty impossible for you to have made a side trip to Washington, D.C. during this time frame, it still doesn't account for your whereabouts on the night that Shari Fleming was killed. And before you say it, I am sure lots of folks saw you at church that Wednesday night but what about after church? Was Miss Dromgoole with you as she said?'

Steve threw a hand over his mouth, closed his eyes and furrowed his brow. He took a deep breath, dropped his hand and looked at Jake. 'It pains me to have to say this, Agent Lovett, but Angela told a fib. She was trying to protect me but I know she should not have done that. It was wrong. And I am sorry. I was at home alone. No one but my dog saw me that night after the services. Angela is a good, God-fearing woman. I have not had ... uh ... uh ... carnal knowledge of her,' he said, his face burning bright red.

Jake looked down at the table and took a couple of breaths to prevent himself from losing it. Then he asked, 'Did you stop by the school district building before you went home?'

'Absolutely not.'

'Did you stop anywhere?'

'No, sir. I went straight home.'

'Did you go out that evening at all?'

'No. Scout's honor,' he said, raising his fingers in the pledge sign.

'OK,' Jake said as he pushed away from the table, 'you wait right here for a while. I'll be back.'

'Please don't arrest Angela.'

'Relax, Mr Broderick, I doubt we'll find a reason to do that.'

In the other interrogation room, Lucinda was not at all amused. Angela kept insisting she was with Steve all night long. After trying to coax the truth out of Angela, Lucinda was exasperated. 'Ms Dromgoole, please stop lying about Mr Broderick. You are not helping the situation.'

'I am not lying. We spent all night long in hot, steamy sex. Do you want the details?'

'Oh, please, no. I do not want to hear about your sexual fantasies. I just want you to admit to where you were that night.'

'I told you. I spent the night in Steve's bed with his arms around me. If he'd left even for a moment, I would have known. I would have felt the absence of his warm, passionate body the second he pulled away – before he even set his feet on the floor.'

Lucinda threw back her head and contemplated the ceiling. When she looked back at Angela, she said, 'Don't you want to go home? If you tell me the truth, I'll let you go home.'

'Oh, right. I know that cop trick. I've seen it on TV. You can't fool me. And you can't prove I wasn't with Steve.'

'I probably can, Ms Dromgoole. So why don't you save us both some time?'

'What did you run your face into anyway? It's a mess.'

'This is not about me, Ms Dromgoole.'

'Oh yes it is. You're jealous. You're jealous that I look good enough to catch a man and you don't. You're jealous that I can spend the night with a man and no one wants you. I know your type.'

Lucinda clenched her teeth, rose from her seat and walked to the door.

'Where are you going? You can't leave me in here,' Angela protested.

Lucinda left without comment. She went into the observation room just in time to see Jake stand and exchange a few last words with Steve. She met him in the hall.

'I sure can see why you and Trivolli eliminated him as a suspect,' Jake said. 'He's a boring, anal weenie. You should see how he folds his receipts.'

'The aged sex fiend in the other room is sticking with her story,' Lucinda said.

'Broderick is not sticking with it. He apologized for her behavior. And get this: he swears he has not had "carnal knowledge" of her.'

'Carnal knowledge?'

'His words, not mine. I swear,' Jake said with a laugh. 'I think we ought to find somebody to give them a ride back to Broderick's place.'

'It really irks me to let her go home while she's still lying to me.'

'OK, let's both go in and see if it'll help if I confront her with Broderick's words.'

When they entered, Jake slid into the seat across from Angela and Lucinda slouched against the wall.

'That woman,' Angela said, pointing at Lucinda, 'called me a liar.'

Jake turned to Lucinda, who shook her head. Then he looked at Angela and said, 'Really?'

'Yes, sir, Agent Lovett.'

'She actually used those words?'

'Yes, sir,' she said with a nod.

'I'll have to review the tape.'

Angela blanched, followed by the appearance of a bright red circle on each cheek. 'Tape?'

'Yeah, you knew it was all being recorded, didn't you?'

'Yes. I forgot. Maybe she didn't use those exact words but she implied them. She accused me of lying.'

'Did you tell her you were with Steve Broderick the night of Shari Fleming's death?'

'I certainly did,' Angela said, straightening her posture and jutting out her chin, 'because I was.'

'I don't think so.'

'What you think, young man, does not affect the truth.'

'Ma'am,' Jake said, leaning forward across the table, 'what you say doesn't change the truth, either.'

'Are you calling me a liar, too?' Angela said as she pressed back in her chair.

'Yes, ma'am. And so is Steve Broderick. On

his recorded statement, he apologized for your lie.'

'He's just trying to protect me and my reputation.'

'No, Ms Dromgoole.' Jake turned to Lucinda and said, 'Lieutenant, could you please give us some privacy.'

Lucinda squinted her eye, plastered both of the people at the table with a sneer and left the room.

Jake gave her enough time to get into her observation post on the other side of the glass before scooting his chair to the end of the table. He took one of Angela's hands between both of his. 'Angela, listen,' he said and paused, waiting for her full attention. When her eyes were firmly fixed on his, he smiled. She smiled in response. 'I am about to let Mr Broderick go home. I sure would like to let you go with him. But Lieutenant Pierce is a real tough ass – pardon my language, but I just don't know how else to describe her. I need you to tell me the truth. Then I can force her to let you go home.'

Angela looked down at the table then back up at Jake. 'You can do that?'

'Yes.'

'You're not going to arrest Steve?'

'No.'

'Honest?'

'Cross my heart,' Jake said as he removed one of his hands from hers and sketched an X on his chest.

She breathed in deeply, exhaled and said, 'I didn't even go to church that night. I had a headache.'

'So you didn't see Steve Broderick that night, did you?'

'No,' she said, shaking her head. 'I'm sorry. That woman just frightened me. She's so intimidating. If she hadn't been so mean, I never would have lied.'

'OK, Angela. You sit right here. I'll work things out.'

As he stood and pulled away his hand, she grabbed it tightly. She looked him in the eyes and in a breathy voice said, 'Thank you, Agent Lovett. I don't know how I'll ever repay you.'

He slid his hand out of her grip and said, 'No problem, ma'am. Just doing my job.'

Lucinda and Jake met out in the hall and looked at each other with clenched lips. They scurried away until they knew their distance was far enough that they would not be overheard. Then, they doubled over in laughter. 'Oh, jeez, Jake. "Just doing my job?" You were unbelievable. How did you keep a straight face?'

'It was not easy, not easy at all.'

'She might be holding out on Broderick but, I swear, if you asked, she would have given it up for you right there on the table.'

'Oh, please, that's a vision I don't need floating around in my head,' Jake begged.

'I'll go find a patrol officer to take them home,' Lucinda said.

They looked at each other and smiles faded from both of their faces. 'You know what I'm thinking, Lucinda?'

'Yeah, we just lost our only suspect.'

Thirty-Seven

He picked his next victim after seeing his photograph in the newspaper. He stood beaming, one arm raised high in the air, fingers arranged in a 'V' for victory. It was that symbolic gesture that aggravated him more than anything. He read about Frederick Lee's plan to end child abuse in his lifetime through 'Enough', a new program initiated by his organization, the Family Service Center. The story quoted Lee at length as it discussed the new total immersion approach that included intensive workshops, child-parent confrontation and guerrilla counseling. The whole project made him angry. Whether or not it was effective was irrelevant to his reaction. His irrational rage centered around one reality: *no one ever did this for me.*

He'd watched the offices of the Family Service Center for days and realized that the most effective way to get to his victim was from the inside. But to do that, he needed to clean up a bit, capture that presentable but humble look.

He scoped out a blue-collar neighborhood, seeking a home without a dog where the residents all left the house about the same time for work and school. From the handful of places that fit that requirement, he selected the one where the man's size most closely matched his own.

He returned early in the morning. He watched the Dad drive away in his car. He saw the kids walk off to school. Then he saw the Mom emerge and take her place at the bus stop on the corner. When she boarded and the transit system whisked her away, he slipped into the yard and found the most concealed window. Using the blade on his pocket knife, he forced the screen out of its track, twisted and pulled on the frame and set it behind a bush next to the house. He was pleased to notice the window latch was not engaged. His first attempts to push open the window, though, did not work. He ran the blade of his knife around the edges of the window frame, flaking away the paint that held if shut. He grunted as he shoved on it again. It gave just enough to create a slot for his fingers. He reached in and pushed up but the progress was slow; he struggled for every centimeter of elevation.

At last, the opening was wide enough that he could slide into the house. He looked around for any observers in the vicinity and, seeing none, threw one leg over the sill and edged his body into the room.

He stood in a bedroom – a little girl's bedroom from all appearances, ruffled pink bedspread, a mountain of stuffed animals and white painted furniture. He walked out into the hallway, looking for the master bedroom. When he found it, he slid open the closet door and selected a pair of pants, a shirt and a belt, taking care that each item he chose showed some signs of wear without appearing worn out.

In the chest of drawers, he picked out a T-shirt, a pair of boxer shorts and a rolled-up pair of socks. He transferred all of the clothing to the bed in the little girl's room. Just in case he had to make a quick exit, he wanted to be able to grab all of it on his way out the window.

In the bathroom, he turned on the shower to heat up the water while he undressed. The air was steamy by the time he pulled back the curtain and stepped inside. For a while he just stood there, head tossed back, water beating on his chest and sluicing down his legs. At first the rivulets ran dark, nearly black. It had been quite some time since he'd bathed. When the water finally ran clear again, he turned around and let it beat on his back and buttocks. It felt good to feel the water massaging his skin and the layer of grime dissolve in the stream and roll down the drain.

He grabbed a bar of soap and rubbed it between his hands, stirring up rich, foamy lather that he swabbed on his face and his neck, then in his armpits and every other nook and cranny of his body. Next, he poured a healthy dollop of shampoo into his palm and worked it into his hair. His dirt-encrusted strands felt liberated as the oils and caked-up residue washed away.

He smiled at the bottle of conditioner. It seemed kind of girly but why not? He put a handful of that on his scalp and worked it in. He hummed while he waited for two minutes to pass and then rinsed it out. Then he just stood there, shifting front and back under the shower, loving the sensation of the pellets of water pounding on his skin. He let it run until it began to cool.

He grabbed one towel off the bar and ran it all over his body, soaking up moisture. He tossed it on the floor of the shower. Then he grabbed another and used it to rub his head with vigor, pulling out as much moisture as he could, and tossed it aside. He grabbed a third towel and caressed his body as he savored the touch of clean cotton on his skin.

He picked up the electric razor off the counter and moved it across his beard and mustache areas until they were smooth. Then he ran it over the hair that sprouted on his neck at his collar line. When he was finished, he ran his hands over the freshly shaved places and grinned at his image in the mirror.

He walked naked down the hall, enjoying the feel of the carpet in his toes. He slid into the borrowed boxer shorts and sighed with pleasure. There are no words to describe how nice a clean pair of underwear felt after weeks without. When he finished dressing in the other man's clothing, he snatched a gym bag from the bedroom closet and stuffed his dirty pants, shirts and socks inside. He added a pad of paper and a couple of pens he found on a desk in the corner of the dining room. His used underwear were gross – too smelly and filthy to keep. He found a bag in the kitchen and stuffed them in there. He walked out the back door, gym bag in one hand, trash sack in the other. He dumped the latter into the first dumpster he encountered on his walk back to the Family Services Center.

He spent the rest of the morning spying on the center, estimating the number of people who worked there. For a while, he leaned against the back wall of the building writing a new note. When he finished it, he signed his full name with a huge flourish. The big, bold signature reminded him of the teacher who had taught him about John Hancock in American History class. The anger inside him rose up in a hot rage. *She left me behind, too. They all did. Maybe I should do a teacher sometime – they were goodie two shoes, too.*

He straightened up and struggled to wipe the emotion off his face. He didn't want to raise suspicion or give anyone cause for concern. It was time for the staff to leave for lunch. He watched the front door and drew a gender-specific stick figure for everyone who came outside. After twenty minutes, if he'd calculated correctly on previous days, there was now only one person inside: the receptionist. He tucked his gym bag behind a dumpster for safe keeping and walked into the office. He nodded in the receptionist's direction before taking a seat.

'May I help you, sir? Do you have an appointment?' the receptionist asked.

He stood and walked to her desk. 'I'm supposed to see a counselor.'

'They're all out to lunch now. Are you sure you've got the right time? Who are you supposed to see?'

'I don't know the counselor's name, ma'am. I'm supposed to meet my social worker here from the child welfare agency. She knows who we're supposed to see. I don't rightly know the time either. The social worker wrote it down for me but I lost it. All I remember was that it was this afternoon.'

'Well, maybe if you tell me why you're here, I can narrow it down.'

'Ma'am, I'm here on accounta my wife. She drinks and when she drinks, she beats on the kids something fierce. The social worker said you all had a program for people in denial about their problems and you might could help my family.'

'That sounds like the program with the guerilla-counseling component. You probably need to see Mr Lee. But I don't see any appointments on his calendar with any social worker this afternoon. Are you sure you have the right day?'

'Yes, ma'am. I'm sure of that. Is there someone else here you can ask?'

'No, everybody else has gone out to lunch,' she said and then swallowed hard with the knowledge that she'd just made herself vulnerable. She fiddled with items on her desk.

He picked up on her discomfort instantly. He entertained a momentary fantasy of taking advantage of her fear but reminded himself of his goal. *Tonight Frederick Lee will die. I don't have time for a side show.* He smiled softly at her and said, 'I'm sorry, ma'am. I didn't want to make you uncomfortable. I shouldn't have asked the question of a young woman like yourself. It was bound to make you nervous. I'll just wait outside.'

She blushed and responded, 'Oh no, sir. I am so sorry. Please have a seat.'

'That's mighty sweet of you, ma'am. But I grew up with a couple of sisters and I know just what you're feeling. I'll wait outside so you can relax.'

'It's really not necessary but thank you for your understanding, Mr...?'

'Gilbright,' he lied with automatic ease. 'Lucius Gilbright. Thank you for your trouble, ma'am,' he said as he turned and walked out the door.

He positioned himself with a clear view of the door and drew a diagonal line through the stick figure representing each person as they returned from lunch. Later, he'd add a line in the other direction making an 'X' over the staff as they left for the day – until only one remained, the person who was the last to leave every day: Frederick Lee.

The afternoon was sunny and comfortably warm. He brushed the dirt away from a patch of concrete at the base of the wall. He sat down with his back leaning against the brick and his legs stretched in front of him enjoying the warmth of the afternoon sun on his face. It made him feel drowsy and without knowing it, he dosed off and the pad of paper slipped from his hands.

He awoke with a rush of adrenalin. Sirens. Lots of sirens. Pulling up in front of the building. Pulling into the parking lot behind the building. People running inside the office. He didn't know what was happening. But he knew he had to get out of here. He cursed as he ducked behind parked cars. *Everything was ready. Everything in order. Tonight was the night. Damn. Damn. Damn.* He kept hidden behind cars and dumpsters as he made his way down behind the strip of office buildings. When he reached the end, he jumped up, darted to the side of the building and stood still. He calmed his breathing, listened for any sounds of pursuit, then sauntered away up the street. He was many blocks away before he remembered what he'd left behind – the gym bag of dirty clothes and the notepad with the signed letter.

Thirty-Eight

Even though there was a bit of a chill in the air, Lucinda and Jake chose to eat their dinner on the deck of the restaurant. It was quieter and easier to converse outside.

'So, now that we've pretty much eliminated every reasonable suspect, what now?' Lucinda asked.

'No other suspects at all?' Jake said.

'You checked up with the techs working your case in D.C., right?'

'Yes I did. Nothing from forensics or research points to anyone viable. We've got a couple of people that might have possibly committed the crime but none of them really add up.'

'Same thing here. I won't say all of their alibis are iron-clad but I really don't seriously think any one of them is the perpetrator. If they were available for Shari Fleming's murder, they weren't available for one of the others.'

'What about the others? Anyone standing out in those jurisdictions?'

'I talked to Ted. He is in contact with the investigators in all the identified jurisdictions on a daily basis, at the very least. Not one of them has a suspect. Some of them are following up leads or hotline tips but they all sound weak at this point. Ted said they're hoping we'll find something,' Lucinda said.

'Then we need to explore the connection between the notes at the crime scenes and the notes left on your car.'

'I still don't think they are connected, Jake. It doesn't make sense to me,' Lucinda objected.

'But it's all we've got.'

'That's pretty pathetic, then. I guess we do need to identify my little message leaver just to get that out of the way.'

'Your "little message leaver"? Lucinda, those notes were threatening. How can you be so cavalier about them?'

'Jake, I've seen a lot worse. I've gotten direct, graphic threats. These are lame in comparison.'

'You still shouldn't trivialize them.'

Lucinda shrugged.

'You are exasperating,' Jake said.

'It's just a gender thing, Jake. Men are bad drivers. Women are exasperating. It's a trade-off.'

Jake shook his head and chuckled. 'I'm not sure which trait is more dangerous. Tell you what, I'd like to continue this discussion over a drink but my teeth are starting to chatter out here. There's a nice bar in my hotel. How 'bout we go back there?'

'Why not?' Lucinda said.

When they reached the entrance to the hotel bar, Jake rested the palm of his hand in Lucinda's back and guided her to a booth back in a corner. His touch tingled at the base of her spine and sent a burst of electric impulse through her limbs. She was both disappointed and relieved when he removed his hand as they arrived at their destination and slid into their seats.

Lucinda ordered a glass of Merlot and Jake a bottle of Sam Adams. At first, they shared amusing stories from the lives in law enforcement. Then Jake switched to funny anecdotes from childhood. Without warning, the conversation turned serious and intense. Lucinda described the night her parents died and they talked about their shared fears and confusion over the childhood loss of their parents.

Lucinda nursed her solitary glass of wine for the entire two and a half hours. Jake, on the other hand, was working on his fifth beer. When Lucinda said it was time for her to head home, Jake said, 'Are you sure it's safe for you to drive?'

'Yes, Jake, I've only had one glass of wine all night.'

'Oh,' he said as he scratched a spot on his face for no reason. 'It still might not be safe. You can stay in my room. There are two beds. Honest.'

Lucinda sighed, her shoulders moving up and down with her breath. 'No, Jake. Not while we're working this case.'

'I'm serious about the two beds.'

'I know. I just have trust issues.'

'You don't trust me?' The forlorn tone of Jake's voice struck Lucinda as pretty pathetic, laughable and endearing.

'No, Jake. I don't trust me,' Lucinda said.

'You don't trust you? Oh, OK, I get it. And it

only took one glass of wine to get you to that point?'

Lucinda stood, resting her palms on the table. 'No, Jake, the wine wasn't even necessary.'

'Let me walk you to your car.'

'No, that's not necessary. In fact, it's not even wise.'

'That trust thing?'

'Yeah. See you in the morning, Special Agent Lovett,' she said as she spun on her heel and strode out of the bar.

Thirty-Nine

The next morning, Lucinda picked up the phone in her apartment and punched in Jake's cell number. When he answered, she said, 'Awake and ready?'

'Yep.'

'Alrighty then, I'll be there in ten minutes.'

'Not seven and a half?'

'Nah. This morning I plan to dawdle on the way to the car.'

When she exited the elevator in the garage, she stood still for a moment as usual, listening, looking, appraising the area. With the sun still low in the sky, the lighting was dim. The air she breathed was a faintly nauseating blend of gas fumes and carbon monoxide. From different corners of the garage, she heard the sounds of other residents, jingling keys, beeping locks, slamming car doors. Nothing seemed out of the ordinary. Two parking spaces away from her car, she heard a foot hit the concrete mere inches from where she stood. She started to turn in the direction of the sound but before she'd made any significant movement, she felt the cold metal circle of a gun barrel pressing hard into her neck just behind her ear. Adrenalin surged, bringing a tremble to her core, a tightness in her throat and a flush to her face. Her mind moved fast, seeking options.

'Drop the keys,' a woman's voice ordered.

From the other side of the garage, Lucinda heard running footsteps and hoped whoever was fleeing the scene understood the urgency and would call 9-1-1 or at least tell the security guard at the parking-lot entrance that something was amiss.

Without a word in response to the command, Lucinda clutched her keys even tighter. The hard edges of the metal keys pressed deep into her palm. She prepared to spin fast and jab her attacker in the eye. But the woman with the gun was a heartbeat ahead of her. Lucinda felt something hard slam into the small of her back, driving her forward. Sharp spikes of pain drove into her head as her face hit the trunk of someone's sedan.

'Don't try any crap on me. Ted taught me all of those self-defense tricks. Drop the damn keys.'

Ted? Ellen? No. It couldn't be. But who else?
'Ellen?' Lucinda asked. She felt the gun barrel jab hard and sharp and then press deeper into her flesh.

'Drop the damn keys now.'

Lucinda released her grip, allowing the keys to hit the trunk of the car and jangle as they tumbled down, clattering on the concrete. 'Ellen?' Lucinda asked again.

'Shut up! Lace the fingers of your hands behind your head.'

Lucinda hesitated.

'Now! Damn it!' Ellen said.

Lucinda felt the barrel pull away from her neck. Before she could register relief, she felt the impact of the butt of the gun just behind her temple. Her head spun in a familiar but uncomfortable sensation of vertigo. She felt both her real and artificial eye rattle around in their sockets. *Will my eye fall out?* Then the pain registered. Pounding, throbbing, solid pain mixed with spikes of sharpness that pierced her skull. *Am I bleeding?*

She put her hands behind her head and then said, 'Shit, Ellen, that hurt like hell. Just what the hell is your problem?'

'Oh, like you don't know. Give me a break.' Ellen grabbed one of Lucinda's arms and twisted it down.

Lucinda sensed the cold edge of metal encircle one wrist, listened to the clicking snap of a locking cuff. Then she felt a jerk on her other arm and heard the lock connected on the other wrist. She was effectively constrained. *I still have my feet*, she thought. 'Ellen, I swear to God, I do not know what is going on here. I do not know why you are angry with me.'

'You know what's going on. You just don't think *I* know.' Ellen's arm reached from behind Lucinda and snaked around the flap of her jacket. Ellen's fingers flipped the snap on Lucinda's holster and slid out her weapon. Lucinda listened, thinking she'd hear her gun hit the ground, but when she heard nothing she knew Ellen had kept it. *The risk to my personal safety has now doubled.*

'You've been trying to steal my husband for

quite some time and I am not going to allow that anymore. I tried to warn you to back off but you wouldn't listen. Now,' she barked, jerking on the cuffs, pulling Lucinda off the trunk, 'on your knees.'

Doubled in half at the waist, Lucinda stiffened her knees. 'Ellen, what warnings are you talking about?'

'The notes I left for you. Now, shut up and get down on your knees.'

Lucinda felt a downward tug on her cuffs at the same time a foot kicked the soft spot in the back of her leg. She hit the hard pavement and felt the jarring in her kneecaps on impact. She felt chunks of dirt and debris shred her pantyhose as it embedded in her skin.

'Ellen, you're not really going to shoot me, are you?'

'Shut up so I can pull the trigger.'

'Ellen, you shoot me and you are going to jail. Think about what will happen to your children, if you kill me.'

'You should have thought about those innocent kids before you started messing with another woman's husband. I tried and tried to warn you but you paid no attention to my notes. All I wanted you to do was leave my husband alone. That's all.'

'Ellen, what notes?'

'The ones I left on your car. I know you got them. I watched you read them.'

'Ellen, believe me, I didn't know those notes were from you. You should've signed them.' Lucinda heard surreptitious shuffling sounds in the distance. She suspected that a team was getting into place. She only hoped the noise was subtle enough not to alarm Ellen and that she could stall her until they made their move.

'You should've known.'

'Ellen, you never mentioned your husband in those notes.'

'Well, not in so many words, but I thought the message was pretty clear.'

'Ellen, it wasn't. My partner was convinced they were from the serial killer we're hunting.'

'Ted, said that?'

'No, Ellen, Ted is not my partner in this investigation. I'm working with a guy from the FBI.'

'I don't believe you.'

'It's true, Ellen.'

'Shut up. I can't focus when you run your mouth.'

A male voice shouted, 'Drop the gun. Drop the gun or we'll shoot.'

Ellen spun around, waving the gun in the air. The second that Lucinda felt the pressure of the barrel pull away from her head, she lashed out her legs. They connected with Ellen's calves, knocking her to the ground. The force of impact loosened Ellen's grip on the handgun and sent it skittering across the floor. A bullet fired at Ellen's head missed by a breath and plowed into the concrete wall.

Lying with her face pressed against the oil-stained floor, Lucinda shouted, 'She's got another gun!'

An officer grunted then said, 'We've got it,

Lieutenant.'

A pair of hands slid under Lucinda's arms and lifted her up. Then the officer unlocked her cuffs. Lucinda kneeled down beside Ellen who stared at the ceiling with a dazed expression. Lucinda slipped a hand under her head and felt blood. 'Was she shot?' she asked.

'No, Lieutenant. I had a good bead on her but when you knocked her down, the bullet sailed right over her head and hit the wall over there,' an officer said as he pointed. 'You ruined my batting average.'

'Be glad I did. This woman is the wife of a police officer. You don't want her death on your hands. Has someone called for an ambulance?'

Another voice shouted, 'It's on the way, Lieutenant. Should be here in two minutes or less.'

Lucinda's cell phone rang. It was Jake. 'Hey where are you?' he asked.

'I'm still in the parking garage.'

'That's some serious dawdling.'

'I guess you could call it that,' Lucinda shouted as the siren of the approaching emergency vehicle threatened to drown her out.

'What the hell is that, Lucinda? What's wrong? Are you OK?'

'Yeah. I'm fine. Somebody tried to shoot me and failed. I'll tell you all about it as soon as I can get out of here.'

'What?'

'And, oh yeah, Jake. The notes on my car? Forget them as a lead. Found out where they came from this morning.'

'What? How do you know they're not connected? I need to get over there right away. Can you send a patrol to pick me up or should I call a cab?'

'Everything's under control here, Jake.'

'I believe you, Lucinda. But I can't just wait here for you to show up. I need to come there.'

'Hey, Jake, relax. Have another cup of coffee. Read the paper.'

'You just don't get it, do you?'

'Get what?' Lucinda asked.

Jake sighed. 'You sending a patrol car?'

She thought about arguing but decided it would be a waste of time. It seemed obvious that he would not relent. 'Yeah,' she said. 'I'll have one in front of the hotel in a few minutes.'

Forty

Jake's arrival at the garage coincided with the departure of the ambulance carrying Ellen Branson to the hospital. He talked to a few officers on the sidelines of the taped-off crime scene, finding out the identity of Lucinda's assailant and everything they knew about what had gone down earlier. All the while, he kept a close watch on Lucinda as she answered questions and signed statements. When, at last, she looked up and caught his eye, he ducked under the tape. Standing in front of her, with a hand on each of her elbows, he asked, 'Are you OK?'

'Yeah, I'm fine,' she said, rubbing the spot on her head that had suffered a hit from the butt of the gun. 'I've got a lump here but Ellen got the worst of it. I can't help thinking I could have handled it better. I could have done something differently so that she wouldn't have been hurt.'

'From what I hear, you were cuffed, down on your knees and still managed to save her life.'

'Yeah, well...' Lucinda sighed. 'The only thing is that it just shouldn't have happened at all.'

'Can't blame yourself for that.' Jake stood back and looked her over, head to toe. 'You're kind of dusty and dirty.'

'Gee, thanks,' Lucinda said, taking a couple of

250

useless swipes at her skirt.

She stretched her wrists past the cuffs of her jacket, displaying light red rings caused by the cuffs. 'Cute, huh? I better go out and socialize with the S and M set before these marks fade away. I think my knees got the worst of it, though.' She pulled up the hem of her skirt to display run-filled hose and scraped up knees. 'I need to go back upstairs to change. You wanna come with me? I'll fix a fresh pot of coffee.'

'Sure, that sounds great,' he said.

In the elevator, Lucinda admitted, 'I'm not real eager to get into the station this morning. I don't know if anyone's told Ted yet and I don't want to be the one to do it.'

'Why? You think he'll blame you?'

'Not hardly. But I will blame him. I told him to take care of that woman and he just blew me off. If I see him this morning, I might well punch him in the nose.'

Lucinda's return to the apartment excited Chester. He dashed up and down the hall, skidding on the floor with each turn.

'Does he always greet you like that?' Jake asked.

'Nah, Chester is showing off. He does that when I come home with company.'

'Does that happen often?'

'Ha! Hardly ever. That's why Chester finds it so exciting. Have a seat, Jake. I'll get the coffee brewing.'

Jake walked past the kitchen counter over to the large living-room window. 'Nice view,' he said. 'What river is that?'

251

'It's the James. And it's the reason I picked this apartment and stayed here. I'd only move if I could afford one with a balcony overlooking the river but that's a bit beyond an investigator's salary.'

'Ever feel too cramped?'

'The place is pretty small but it's just me and Chester – plenty of room for the two of us. Why? Do you have a bigger place?'

'Yeah, I'm pretty lucky. When my grand-mother passed away, I got her townhouse in Georgetown, all paid for but the taxes and insur-ance each year. I'm a *bona fide* homeowner – the easy way.'

'Lucky guy. While this is brewing, I'm gonna go change out of these dirty clothes. Just make yourself at home. If Chester bothers you, clap your hands and he'll run off.'

Lucinda had slipped out of her suit and into a new one along with a fresh pair of panty hose by the time the coffee maker finished filling the carafe with coffee. When she walked down the hall, she saw Chester on his back with Jake bent over, stroking Chester's belly and chin. 'I guess he didn't bother you.'

'Nah,' Jake said. 'He's a nice cat.' Jake stood and Chester writhed on the floor hoping to entice Jake into continuing with the belly rub. Jake laughed, stepped over him and walked into the kitchen.

They carried their coffee cups over to the sofa and sat at opposite ends, turning to face each other as they did.

'So, Ted's wife wrote those notes on your car?'

Jake asked.

'Yes, her name is Ellen. Not at all who I suspected. I thought it was a family member of someone I'd arrested. Ellen never even crossed my mind.'

'That means we have no leads to follow at all.'

Lucinda sighed. 'We'll just have to start over and find something we missed.'

'I think it might be a better idea if we visit a couple of the other crime scenes. See what they missed. You guys here were thorough – very thorough. Not sure if that's true of all the jurisdictions. Some of them didn't even notice the note or weren't suspicious of it until we pointed it out to them.'

'You want me to go with you?' Lucinda said.

'Yeah, we're partners, remember? You are currently on loan to the FBI.'

'I should go into the station today and touch base with the folks working my local case and with my Captain.'

'No problem; I didn't plan on starting the road show until first thing in the morning anyway.'

Back at the station, Lucinda set Jake at a desk with a computer and a telephone and looked around for Ted. Then she walked down to Captain Holland's office. 'Hey, Captain. Didn't see Ted down the hall.'

'He went to the hospital as soon as he heard about his wife. You gave us all a serious scare but you look pretty good for almost dying this morning.'

Lucinda shrugged. 'Near-death experiences

are in the job description, Captain. How is Ellen Branson doing?'

'Pretty good. They're patching up her head injury and she will probably be processed into the jail before the day is over.'

'Why?'

'Why, what?'

'Why is Ellen Branson going to jail?'

The captain stood, put his hands on his hips and stared at her. 'Why? Pierce, you were there. Remember? She attempted to kill a police officer, namely you.'

'Yeah, I was there, Captain. She wouldn't have shot me.'

'Are you delusional? She had you down on your knees with the barrel of a loaded gun pressed against your skull. What about attempted murder don't you understand?'

'Captain, I want the charges dropped.'

'Dropped? You're nuts. She stole a police officer's gun—'

'That was her husband's gun. I don't see how that counts,' Lucinda interrupted.

'She stole a police officer's gun,' Captain Holland repeated. 'She lay in wait for another police officer. She assaulted a police officer. She abducted a police officer—'

'Abducted? She didn't move me more than a foot,' Lucinda objected.

'You were restrained, Pierce. Restrained and under her control. The D.A. can make an abduction charge stick. Then she confiscated your weapon – another gun theft from a police officer. These are serious charges.'

'When you put it that way, yes they are. But are they really necessary? That poor woman needs help, not imprisonment. And she has kids who need her, too.'

Captain Holland stepped around his desk and stood in front of her. 'Pierce, just get out of here. We are not dropping the charges.'

Lucinda stepped forward into his space. Her finger poked his chest. 'She held the gun to my head, Captain. This should be my call.'

Holland's jaw tensed and his nostrils flared. 'Back up, Pierce, or I'll stick you in the cell next to her.'

Lucinda started to snap back at him before regaining control of her emotions. Abashed, she looked down at the floor, stepped back and rested her hands at her side. 'Sorry, Captain.'

'You should be. You are an ingrate, Pierce. While you've been traipsing around with your FBI agent, I've been defending you in front of the mayor and his cronies and believe me that hasn't been fun.'

'Yes, sir. But I haven't been traipsing, sir. I've been working, sir. More hours than required, sir. Without a request for additional monetary compensation, sir. And I really appreciate what you are doing on my behalf and on the behalf of wounded officers everywhere, sir.'

'Jeez, cut the crap, Pierce. Get the hell out of here.'

'Yes, sir,' she said, snapping to attention and giving a smart salute.

'Pierce, you're trying my patience.'

'Yes, sir,' she said as she darted out of the

room. Holland barely had time to return to his seat before Lucinda popped her head around the corner and said, 'Sir, I hope you will reconsider the charges against Ellen Branson. I don't think they'd be good for the morale of my colleagues.'

The captain flung out his arm and pointed a beefy finger in her direction. 'Out, Pierce, out!'

Forty-One

Lucinda strode into the office where Jake pounded on a keyboard. 'That sure didn't go well.'

'What?'

'I tried to get the Captain to intervene on Ellen Branson's behalf and got tossed from his office.'

'Why would you do that?'

'Get tossed?'

'No, try to get your captain to give Ellen a break?'

'I do not want to press charges against that poor woman.'

'She held a gun to your head, Lucinda.'

'Oh, not you, too,' she moaned.

'She committed a serious crime. You could be dead. Not press charges? Are you nuts?'

'Don't get your boxers in a wad, Jake.'

'Who told you?'

'Who told me what?'

'That I wore boxers.'

'Nobody. It's just an expression. But you're changing the subject. Ellen would not have shot me.'

'Were you completely convinced of that while you were kneeling on the concrete?' Jake asked.

'That's beside the point,' Lucinda argued.

'No, it's not. Were you?'

'Yes,' she said but would not look him in the eye.

'Liar. If you were that sure, you wouldn't have kneeled in the first place.'

'OK. I admit it. I wasn't positive she wouldn't shoot me. I didn't *think* she'd shoot me but I didn't want to push my luck.'

'Fine. Then she committed a serious crime. Your life was at risk. End of story.'

'Oh, don't "end of story" me. You are not my captain, Mr Special Agent man.'

Jake raised his hands in front of his face as if warding off an attack. 'Sorry, sorry, that was out of line. I didn't mean it that way. I'm just arguing a point, not trying to tell you what to do. Friends?' he said with a grin as he stuck out his hand.

'Maybe,' she said as she took his hand in hers and gave it a shake. 'Maybe.'

The phone on Ted's desk rang and Jake reached for it. 'Branson's desk. Lovett speaking.'

He listened for a moment and said, 'Branson's out for the day. Hold on a second. Let me put you on speakerphone. I've got Lieutenant Pierce with me here.' Before pressing the button, he turned to Lucinda. 'This is my lab calling. They've got some results.'

'OK. We extracted DNA samples for the rope used to hang Michael Agnew. One profile fits the victim. The other profile does not. And we did not get a hit on the database.'

'Damn,' Lucinda said.

'The DNA database is still a work in progress.

Even though we didn't get a hit today, we could get one tomorrow. New profiles are uploaded every day. We'll put it on the high-priority list to double-check it until we have an identity.' The tech continued, 'Lieutenant, we did check the profile against those of your suspects and didn't get a match there either.'

'So you came up totally blank?' Jake asked.

'Not exactly. Branson got an investigator in Jacksonville, Florida, to forward a DNA profile they found on a crime scene down there. And it was a match. That's why I wanted to check with Branson to see if he'd dug up anything new.'

'I doubt if we'll see him today,' Jake said. 'But we'll dig on his computer and see if we can find anything and get back to you if we do.'

They navigated through Ted's database, amazed at the depth and breadth of the information he'd managed to organize and input in such a short period of time. 'I give up,' Jake said. 'I'm can't figure out what stuff is new and what stuff they already have.'

'Maybe we oughta shoot the new database up there and let them sort it out. They're probably more familiar with Ted's process than we are.'

'Good idea. I'll call and get the email address for whoever I need to send it up to.'

Lucinda sat in front of the keyboard, scrolling through the details of the unfolding case. Seven homicides had now been connected to the one at the school district building. Four more were being looked at as possible connections. The inconclusive finding there probably had more to do with sloppy crime-scene work than anything else. Jake was still talking to D.C. when the phone on Lucinda's desk rang. She walked over and answered, 'Pierce.'

'Hello, Lieutenant. This is Sergeant Blocker with the homicide department in Philadelphia. I want to apologize ahead of time if this is a stupid phone call – there are good odds that it is. But I couldn't get it out of my head without making sure.'

'Fine, Sergeant. What's on your mind?'

'We had this incident the other day. A 9-1-1 call, that really only required medical assistance, got a bit garbled and prompted dispatch to send out a couple of patrol cars. One team went inside the building. The other team secured the outside perimeter. The guys inside were finding out that there wasn't an assault in progress, after all. Some guy in the office was having a stroke or heart attack or something. Anyway, the guys outside found a notepad with a weird message written on it. The contents of it struck them as a little hinky so they figured it might be a good idea to look around and see if anything else looked suspicious. They had about given up and were approaching a dumpster to toss the notepad inside as just more litter. But then, they spotted a duffel bag tucked between the wall and the garbage bin. When they opened it up, there were dirty clothes inside. So, they bagged it as evidence and brought it all to me in homicide. They had no idea if it was connected to anything criminal but they didn't want to risk that it was clothing some perp dumped.

'Anyway, I figured that I just might have gotten lucky and the guys stumbled across some-thing I needed to close an open case so I sent it up to the lab for processing. Before I turned over the notepad, though, I made a copy of the note. I've read it over a few times and it just stuck with me.'

Jake had ended his call and stepped over to Lucinda's desk. He looked at her with raised brows. She raised a finger and mouthed, 'Just a minute.'

Sergeant Blocker continued with his story. 'So I checked the national crime database for any kind of match on the note's contents. I entered the phrase "I was left behind" and there you were. I still wasn't sure if I should call or not but then I noticed another coincidence. The event here occurred at the Family Services Center, a non-profit agency. And, well, I'm not real fond of coincidences. You think I might have any-thing here? Or am I just wasting your time?'

Lucinda's heart thudded in her chest and sweat oozed out of her palms. 'Can you fax that note to me, right away?'

'Sure can. Hold on,' he said.

Lucinda listened to the murmur of voices as the sergeant talked to someone else in the room with him. 'Jake, I'm going to turn this guy over to you when he comes back. They're processing some dirty clothes that might be connected to our cases.'

When Blocker returned to the phone, he said, 'OK, it's two pages and it's on its way.'

'Sergeant, did you say the bag and the dirty clothing are in your lab?' Lucinda asked.

'Sure did.'

'I need to get your lab in communication with the FBI lab. Special Agent Jake Lovett is here. He can give you the contact information.'

'A Feeb? You're working with a Feeb?'

'He's not bad for a Feeb, honest,' she said, with a grin in Jake's direction that caused him to roll his eyes. 'He'll need to get your lab co-ordinated with his lab in D.C. I'm going to go check on the incoming fax.'

'All right. But you owe me. I don't like Feebs.'

'Who does, Blocker?' she said with a laugh before handing off the phone and going across the hall to the fax machine. She picked up the first page as it hit the basket. One glimpse at the paper with its block printing and key words and she knew. 'It's our guy,' she shouted across the hall to Jake.

When he joined her by the fax, she handed him a sheet of paper. Lucinda tapped her finger on the machine, waiting for the next page to chug its way through the machine while Jake read the first page.

I WAS LEFT BEHIND.

WAITING FOR THE DAY TO END. FOR THE PEOPLE TO LEAVE. GOODIE TWO SHOES LEFT BEHIND.

BYE-BYE GOODIE TWO SHOES. GOODIE TWO SHOES POINTING HIS TOES TO THE SKY.

ARE YOU A GOODIE TWO SHOES, TOO? SOME COPS ARE.

MAYBE I'LL LEAVE A COP BEHIND NEXT. OR A TEACHER. GOODIE TWO SHOES COME IN

MANY SIZES, IN LOTS OF COLORS.
WHO'S NEXT? WHO KNOWS? I'M THINKING

Lucinda pulled out the second page and held it where they could read it together.

THAT MY WORK NEVER BE DONE. THEM THAT LEFT ME BEHIND SHOULD BE SHAKING IN THEIR GOODIE TWO SHOES. THEY SHOULD KNOW WHO I AM AND OWN THEIR FEAR.
TONIGHT, I'M COMING FOR FREDERICK LEE. HERE'S A NAME FOR YOUR FEAR, GOODIE TWO SHOES.

Across the bottom of the page, a large, blowsy signature: *Charles Sinclair Murphy*.

Lucinda and Jake looked at each other. 'Sure, but is that his real name?' Jake asked.

'I betcha it is,' Lucinda said. 'Let's see what we can find out.' In two minutes, they had enough information to confirm their suspicions. They sent out a mug shot and criminal record of Charles Sinclair Murphy to the dispatcher at the FBI to issue a 'Be On the Look Out' alert to law enforcement offices across the country. Now came the part of the investigation that filled them both with dread – the waiting. Waiting for someone, somewhere, to locate their suspect.

Forty-Two

The two investigators got busy learning all they could about Charles Sinclair Murphy. They sat back to back pulling up data on computers. The suspect had a lengthy rap sheet going back to a drunk and disorderly charge when he was eleven years old.

His most recent incarceration had ended with his release on parole four years and a couple of months ago. After that, he seemed to disappear from the face of the earth. There was a warrant out for his arrest in North Carolina for violation of parole.

It appeared as if the medical emergency in Philadelphia had derailed his plans for another victim. Who knew when or where he would strike again. In light of his recent frustration, though, both of them believed it would be soon.

Lucinda and Jake got busy calling around to prisons, jails and jurisdictions that had inter-faced with their suspect in the past. Within a couple of hours, they had a wealth of anecdotal information and a pile of documents faxed and emailed for their perusal. The ugliest part of his life story was revealed in reports filed by prison psychologists. One officer summed it all up when he said, 'Every time Murphy got a glimpse of life outside of the gutter, someone kicked him in the face and knocked him down in the muck again.'

Murphy's mother, Cynthia, a bitter and self-destructive woman, dumped him with his grandmother when he was only thirteen months old. Granny Ren had a long history of serious chronic depression, and as a result wasn't the best surrogate mother in the world but she offered him affection when she could, kept a roof over his head, clothes on his back and food in his stomach. He lived with her until his fifth birthday. Right after Granny Ren sang 'Happy Birthday' and Charles blew out the candles on his cake, there was a knock on the door and Cynthia had breezed in with John Langern. Jake and Lucinda studied photographs of them both. Cynthia had a brassy smile, too much make-up and hair like straw. John was a greasy-looking man with slicked-back hair and a crooked, leering smile.

Cynthia announced that she and John were married and now wanted to pick up their son and live like a family. Cynthia and her mother argued over Charles's fate, but in the end Cynthia left with her son in tow.

For a few years, the little boy lived a vagabond life with his mother and her husband. He'd go to school for a couple of months, then suddenly, when the couple's current scam went bad, they'd be on the move again. The presence of a young boy was just what they needed to get shelter, food and other necessities from various non-profit agencies and churches along the way until they found a place to set up shop again and start bringing in the ill-gotten cash. Charles would go back to school for a few more months and the furtive pattern of life on the run would start up again.

One morning, Charles awoke and his mother was gone. For days, he kept waiting for her return. He finally had to accept that it was just him and John. At first, nine-year-old Charles was nothing more than the target of John's physical abuse, taking the blows that used to fall on his mother every time John was drinking. Charles was miserable and lonely, aching for his pathetic excuse of a mother, longing for a return to his grandmother. But when he asked John to take him back to Granny Ren, John backhanded him and laughed when he cried.

Charles didn't think his life could get any worse but then John decided Charles made an appropriate sexual surrogate for his missing wife. John called Charles 'Cynthia' and battered him until he would respond. John raped him roughly and when he'd had his pleasure, he left Charles curled up in a fetal position where the little boy cried himself to sleep.

That was when Charles started sneaking sips from John's bottle. He developed a great fondness for alcoholic oblivion. He only stopped drinking when he was arrested. Every time he got out of a juvenile facility, a prison or a jail, he'd pick up his habit of drinking and taking drugs to excess. The substance abuse landed him behind bars over and over, until the last time. He went to prison in North Carolina for car theft.

There, he learned to read and write during his five years of incarceration. When he walked out a free man, he seemed more self-assured, more confident and definitely craftier.

On parole, he no longer got intoxicated – at least not enough to get in trouble – and he came up clean on his mandated drug tests until the day he simply did not show up.

Now, years later, a menacing note bearing his name had appeared in the parking lot of a non-profit agency and seemed to tie to several homicides. But North Carolina did not have his DNA profile on file to confirm. 'So where are you now, Charles Sinclair Murphy?' Lucinda muttered.

'It felt great for a few minutes to know who we were looking for, but now, how can you feel good when you don't know where to look?' Jake complained.

'Are we sure it's really him?'

As if on cue, the phone rang. Lucinda answered. It was Sergeant Blocker with additional information. 'They found a fingerprint on the duffel bag. We got a hit on AFIS. The owner of the bag is Charles Sinclair Murphy.'

Forty-Three

Lucinda slept fitfully the night after her confrontation with Ellen. She tossed and turned so many times that Chester lost his patience with her and abandoned the bed to sleep on the sofa. In the morning, he mewed incessantly, issuing an incredible range of sounds; some Lucinda didn't think she'd ever heard from him before. His tone and persistence, though, made his message clear to Lucinda. He was not happy that he'd had to spend the night away from her body heat. She gave him an extra scoop of tuna feast along with her apologies before she left for work.

She picked up Jake at his hotel and just listened as he threw out ideas about the direction of the investigation. The ride was short enough that he didn't notice her lack of response. She walked into her office feeling drained before she even started working. When she saw Ted sitting at his computer, she wanted to turn tail and run.

When he saw her, Ted jumped to his feet and rushed to her side. 'Lucinda, I am so sorry for what happened...'

'Don't apologize to me, Ted,' she said, taking a step back away from him.

He stepped toward her. 'Lucinda, I know you

are upset and I don't blame you. I am very sorry.'

'Ted, I am emotionally drained and physically exhausted. I really do not want to discuss this right now.'

'I understand. I just wanted you to know that I am here for you and I am very remorseful about what happened to you.'

'As I said, Ted, you may need to apologize but you don't need to apologize to me.' Lucinda turned her back to him and sat down in front of her computer busying her fingers on the keyboard.

Jake hadn't known Lucinda long, but he instinctively knew trouble was brewing. He stood back from both of them, eyes bouncing back and forth.

Ted leaned over her desk. 'I think now you can understand why I didn't think there was any hope for my marriage. Now you know what I was up against.'

Lucinda clenched her jaw and jerked to her feet. Spinning around, she punched an index finger into Ted's chest. 'You still don't get it, do you? You are a Neanderthal. A cretin. Is it just you or are all men this stupid?' She kept poking him with every pause in her speech. Ted backed up with every poke. Now he was up against his desk. Lucinda flashed her eye in Jake's direction. He put both palms in the air and shook his head. She almost grinned at him before turning back to Ted. 'What do you think I've been telling you for months? Did you ever listen to a word I said?'

269

'I did, but I ... I...'

'You just thought it was woman-babble, didn't you?'

'Uh, well...'

'You thought it was meaningless woman-babble.'

'Not exactly...'

'Blah, blah, blah, just another woman running her mouth. You should have listened. I told you that woman needed help. I told you she needed you. I told you that she needed help to heal from the loss of her child. And what did you do?'

'I ... I ... I...'

'You did nothing. You made no allowances for her. You just used anything she did as a reason for you to do nothing. You disgust me.'

'Gee, Lucinda, I didn't realize that she was this...'

'Then why the hell didn't you listen to me? I *told* you.'

'Well, sometimes you women just don't make any sense to us, Lucinda,' Ted said with a nervous laugh and turned to the other man in the room. 'Do they, Jake?'

Jake raised both palms in the air again. 'Look at me. Not involved. Innocent third party here. Just a bystander.'

Lucinda now turned to Jake. 'You could tell him I'm right.'

'Aw, man,' Jake moaned. 'Cut me some slack, Lucinda. Even though I know what happened yesterday, I'm still not sure what you two are arguing about. Just pretend I'm Switzerland. Or pretend I'm not here. Or better yet, I'll leave,'

Jake said, making a step toward the door.

'Don't you dare, Special Agent Lovett! We have work to do,' Lucinda snapped. She turned back to Ted. 'And what the hell are you doing here? You have a wife. In jail. She needs you. She needs a lawyer. She needs to get out on bail. And you need to assure her attorney that Ellen's so-called victim does not want charges brought against her and, in fact, I promise you when Lieutenant Lucinda Pierce takes the stand she will be a crappy witness for the state.'

'OK,' Ted said in a tone of voice he usually reserved for potential jumpers on the edge of a bridge.

'So what are you waiting for, Sergeant Branson? Move it. Get her out of jail. Every minute Ellen is behind bars is a travesty of justice and a mockery of our mental-health system. Go!' Lucinda said, raising an arm to point to the doorway. 'Go now!'

Ted nodded and sidled across the room, keeping as much distance between himself and Lucinda as possible as he slipped out into the hall.

Lucinda turned her still-angry visage over to Jake.

Jake smiled weakly. 'Hey,' he said.

'Oh, please,' Lucinda said.

'Remind me to never piss you off.'

'Oh, you already have. More than once. You survived.'

'How did I piss you off?'

'Oh, c'mon. You know this. Your employer pisses me off on principle. Your title, Special

271

Agent man, ticks me off whenever I think about it.'

'So, dare I ask why you haven't dressed me down like that?'

'Simple, Jake. You've pissed me off but you've never pissed me off because you hurt another person. You start pulling that shit and I'll be all over you like a duck on a June bug.'

'Being a city boy, I'm not sure if I totally get all the nuances of that analogy. But I do believe I get the gist. Is that sufficient?'

'You are such an ass, Lovett. Let's get to work. We've got a suspect to find.'

Forty-Four

Officer Rodney Sykes never regretted his decision to sign up at Big Brothers and Sisters. He enjoyed being a big brother to a fatherless boy. Nonetheless, he was not looking forward to this afternoon. He had agreed to take Derek in for his dental check-up so that his mom wouldn't have to take time off from work. Rodney wasn't wild about going to the dental office but Derek flat out hated the idea. Like kids everywhere, when Derek was miserable, he wanted everyone around him to be miserable, too.

Rodney picked up a couple of new comic books to distract Derek while they sat in the waiting room at the pediatric dental clinic. The non-profit facility offered inexpensive or free dental care for the working poor in the city, which meant they were always busy and the waits were never short. Rodney also promised Derek an after-appointment trip to the mall for an ice-cream cone and a visit to the toy store if he behaved.

He met Derek in front of his school. When Rodney first spotted the ten-year-old boy, he was with a couple of friends, laughing and appearing to be in a good mood. As soon as Derek saw Rodney, though, his laughter faded, his shoulders slumped and a petulant look, complete with thrusting lower lip, transformed his face into an unwelcome expression. Derek was going to make Rodney pay for this loathsome, unwanted excursion.

Rodney sighed and waved his arm in the air. 'C'mon, Derek. We don't want to be late.'

Derek mumbled, 'Sez who?' With slow, plodding steps that allowed the toes of each shoe to drag across the ground, he moved forward with all the energy of a sleeping slug. When Derek got close, Rodney threw an arm around the boy's shoulder and applied a little pressure to try to speed up his forward momentum. That was the wrong move. It provoked an escalation of resistance. Derek planted his feet in the pavement and turned rigid. Rodney pulled back his arm. 'OK, OK. I give. Move at your own pace, Derek. If we're late, it's on you. I'm not going to worry about it.' Rodney climbed into the car behind the steering wheel and waited patiently for Derek to drag himself into the passenger seat, close the door and fasten his seat belt.

Derek remained sullen and silent throughout the short drive over to the office. The large waiting room, decorated in early garage-sale, was a cheerful although mismatched place. About every style of chair created in the last five decades was represented for seating. On the walls, staff had framed and hung artwork from patients – from multicolored scribbles of the pre-school set to carefully rendered pencil sketches of eagles, deer and people by teenagers. Behind the counter, the comfy chaos disappeared in a world of white and stainless steel – every inch sparkling and smelling of antiseptic.

When Rodney and Derek walked inside, Rodney exchanged nods with a few people he knew from around the community and found a pair of empty chairs up against the far wall. Most adults had a child by their sides just as he did. He assumed that those sitting alone were waiting for a young one in the back getting treatment.

Minutes after their arrival, a single man entered through the outside door and took a seat on the opposite side of the room from Rodney and Derek. The man's clothing was worn but tidy. His sandy hair was tousled and either he had fast growing facial hair or he hadn't shaved that day. In short, he looked like a normal blue-collar worker down on his luck. But something about him jiggled the suspicion switch in Rodney's mind – and it was more than the fact that he'd arrived alone.

The man had an edgy, nervous energy. He crossed his leg and jiggled his foot. He switched legs and twitched the other foot. He folded and unfolded his arms. He looked all around the room, staring often at the front desk. But he never met anyone's eye. The longer Rodney sat across from the man, the more uneasy he felt about him.

Rodney turned his attention back to Derek, looking over his shoulder at the comic book. 'Is it good?' he asked.

'Yeah,' Derek said, looking up at him with a grin. 'It's real good.' He flipped back through the pages, pointing to panels and giving a synopsis of the plot line complete with sound effects.

Rodney nodded and made mouth noises in response, amused at the boy's excitement and how easy it was to divert him from his earlier foul mood. Busy with Derek, Rodney didn't notice right away when the man who'd captured his attention earlier rose from his seat and went to the restroom.

Rodney kept his eye on the door until the man re-emerged. When he did, he turned his face in Rodney's direction. The officer knew he'd seen those features before. While Derek continued his monologue, Rodney focused on excavating the memory remnant from his mind. The vague image of a mug shot floated just beyond his reach. No matter how hard he tried he could not resurrect sufficient detail. He pulled out his cell phone and typed a text message to a friend in the police dispatchdepartment.

'Hey, guy! Look 2day's mugs. 5'8", sandy hair, wh, 160–170 lbs?'

In a couple of minutes, he got a response. '2 fit.'

'Send plz,' he responded. He waited while the mug shots loaded into his cell. The man across the room was definitely not a match for the guy in the first shot, but he was a dead ringer for the second one – Charles Sinclair Murphy, wanted for questioning in a murder case. Rodney knew that 'Person of Interest' usually meant far more. Odds were that the man across the room was a killer.

Rodney's big thumbs got busy on the tiny

keyboard again. 'He's here,' he noted, then typed in the address of his location. He added, 'Send back-up. No lights. No sirens.'

Forty-Five

Charles Sinclair Murphy opened the door of the clinic and walked into the waiting room. The weight of the gun wedged in the small of his back pulled down on the waistband of his pants. Although he was at no risk of actually losing his pants, it felt that way to Charles. Every few steps, he'd tug on them to make sure they stayed in place.

Having a gun both excited and frightened him. He was practiced in their use but disdained those who liked blowing people away. He preferred to strangle, beat, cut or slice a person to death. As he'd recently discovered, even hanging can be an intimate act. Firing a bullet into someone's head or chest seemed so impersonal. He didn't plan on using his gun as a murder weapon, though. He brought it along for the power it gave him over others – the kind that makes people do what you want them to do without a struggle.

He knew the police were looking for him. They knew his name now. It no longer mattered if someone recognized him. He could boldly go where he wanted to go with his revolver leading the way. He planned to case out the rhythm of the office and, at the correct time, to remove the Goodie Two Shoes from the premises at the

278

point of a gun.

The big question in his mind was: which Goodie Two Shoes should he choose? Normally he preferred the head honcho, the Executive Director. But from studying news clippings, that person seemed more like a behind the scenes yes-man rather than the seat of power. The do-gooder that really hogged the spotlight was the Director of Program, Dr Alan Hirschman, a dentist who worked here and shone his shiny white teeth at any camera he could find.

The number of people coming in and out of the busy clinic made him nervous – not because he feared being caught but because he simply didn't like to be around people. Still, he sat in his seat observing the movements of patients, analyzing the patterns of the staff and planning his moves.

No one appeared to be paying any attention to him except a man across the room. The kid with him kept his nose buried in a comic book but the man kept looking over his way. Charles didn't like that, no matter what the man's motivation. Charles got up and went to the restroom so he could get a closer look at him.

Charles caught the man staring at him when he stepped out of the lavatory. He suppressed a rising sensation of panic. *People stare in the direction of opening doors all the time*, he told himself. But he kept an eye on the man across the room. Charles did not like it when that man suddenly got busy with the keypad on his cell phone. *Coincidence? Maybe.*

Then that man whispered to the boy, pressed

car keys in his hand and gave him a push toward the door. The boy went outside. *Going to fetch something for the man? Maybe.*

A couple of minutes passed. The boy had not returned. *What's up with that?* Charles wondered. *Now, that man was whispering to a woman. What is he doing?* The woman looked at Charles and quickly looked away. She rose and wrapped an arm around a little girl. Keeping her eyes on the floor, the woman hurried the child outside. That man moved on to a woman with a little boy and whispered to her. The woman gasped. *Something's up. What?*

Charles got to his feet and went to the front door and looked outside. He saw nothing out of the ordinary. He started to walk towards that man to eavesdrop when he heard a tire screech on the pavement. He went back to the doors and looked out again. Cars were filling the parking lot. Some looked like ordinary cars but others were marked cop cars. Uniforms jumped out and pulled their weapons.

Shit! Charles spun around and grabbed a little girl with stringy blonde hair and Kool-Aid red lips. He jerked her up to his chest and held his gun to her temple.

The other man pulled a gun and leveled it on Charles. *Bastard. He's a cop.* Charles pulled the squirming little girl up a little higher to protect his head from a fatal shot. He stepped backwards toward the door to the examination rooms. He didn't have a hand free to open the door and didn't dare drop his grip on the girl for a second. He waited beside the doorway. A staff member

280

would be out of there soon.

'Drop the gun, Murphy,' the cop said to him. 'You don't want to hurt any of these children.'

'Why don't I want to hurt them? So that you guys can leave them behind? So that you and the damned system can screw them kids over at your leisure?'

'Just set the little girl down, Murphy.'

'The second I do, you'll put a bullet in my head. Thanks, but no thanks.'

The girl in his arms started kicking. He put his nose right in her face and hissed, 'Listen, you little brat. You kick me again and I'll put a bullet in your head and you'll never see your mommy or daddy again. You got that?'

The child made a feeble, testing kick at the man's chest. He grabbed her foot and twisted it hard. The girl screamed. 'See. I'm not playing with you. Shut up and do what I say.'

At the sound of the scream, a couple of kids in the waiting room erupted into sniffling tears, a few others began whining, but one child topped them all by letting out an ear-shattering shriek. Charles turned the gun from his hostage's temple to point at the screaming child. 'You want that kid to live, asshole?' Murphy said to the police officer. 'Then get it out of here. Get every one of them out of here.'

'Just set down the little girl...'

'No!' Charles shouted. 'I'm keeping her. You can have the rest. But move them out right away. I'll start shooting at the count of ten.'

'OK, just give me some time here, Murphy.'

'One. Two. Three,' Charles said as he watched

the fearful parents. First, they looked like enchanted statues, terror and confusion carved into their faces, frozen in place by a wicked witch. Then, they all animated at once, most of them racing for the door. A handful of parents shifted their weight but didn't move toward the exit. 'Four. Get out of here,' he said, pointing his gun at the stragglers. 'Five. Six.'

Still those adults did not budge. Charles eyeballed the cop as he stepped up to the remaining adults.

'Seven. Eight. Get them out of here, asshole.'

'Murphy, you gotta understand. All their kids are in the back. Except for him,' he said, pointing to a man whose expression alternated between anger and fear. 'His daughter is in your arms.'

Charles jerked the barrel of the gun into his tiny hostage's head, making her cry out. 'Get them all out of here now or she dies and you can take her corpse with you.'

Just then the door to the back opened and a blue-smocked woman, with a big smile on her face and a patient file in her hand, opened her mouth to call out a patient's name. Before she made a sound, bewilderment raced across her face. As she scanned the room with a furrowed brow, Murphy knocked her away from the doorway and on to the floor. He darted through the opening and latched it when it shut.

Forty-Six

Lucinda and Jake began the next day with a stop at the school district building. Instead of going straight to the break room, the scene of Shari Fleming's murder, they walked further down the hall to make a courtesy visit to the school district superintendent. 'Hello, Mr Irving, this is—'

'You, again? Do I need an attorney?' Robert Irving asked immediately.

'Now why would you need an attorney?' Lucinda responded.

'Why? You told me I was a suspect.'

Lucinda sighed. *Why do innocent people assume we're out to frame them for a crime they didn't commit?* 'I told you that you were one of hundreds of suspects, Superintendent. And at the moment, every one of you has taken a back seat to the person we think committed the homicide.'

'Well, if that's true, why did you need to bring along back-up?'

'Special Agent Jake Lovett is not back-up. He is with the FBI and is my partner in this investigation.'

Jake stepped forward and stuck out his hand. 'Pleasure to meet you, Superintendent.'

Irving absent-mindedly held out his hand and shook the other man's but his focus was still on

Lucinda. 'You've brought in the FBI and you tell me I don't need to worry. You tell me that I don't need an attorney. I think I'd better give him a call.' He lifted the receiver on his telephone.

'Do what you want, Mr Irving. We just want to ask you about our suspect and I wanted to show Agent Lovett the scene of the crime.'

'Is your suspect one of the district's employees?'

'No.'

'A member of our school board?'

'No.'

'Someone I know?'

By this time, exasperated by his attitude, Lucinda's hands were on her hips, her elbows jutting out. 'I don't know until I ask you, Superintendent. Do I need to talk to the chairman of the school board or are you going to sit down and talk to us?'

Robert Irving stared at Lucinda, darted a glance over to Jake, then returned the receiver to the cradle and sat back down in his chair. 'OK, I'm sorry. The media's been tearing me up over the murder and the drug bust of a department head on the same day. It's all made me a bit paranoid. What can I do for you?'

'We're not here to cause problems for you, Mr Irving. We are here to solve a crime, find a perpetrator and secure justice for someone who worked with you every day,' Lucinda told him.

'Again, Lieutenant, my apologies.'

Lucinda doubted his sincerity but continued just the same. She pulled out a photo of Charles Sinclair Murphy and slid it across the superintendent's desk. 'Does this man look familiar?'

Irving studied the picture for a moment, shook his head and said, 'I certainly can't recall ever seeing him.'

'Does the name Charles Sinclair Murphy or Chuck Murphy or Cheese Sinclair or Gas Pump Murphy mean anything to you?'

Irving looked sideways and then up before shaking his head. 'No, can't say that they do. Are those all aliases for that guy?' he asked, pointing to the photograph.

'Yeah,' Lucinda nodded.

Jake asked, 'So to the best of your knowledge, this man would not have a key to this building.'

'No he would not and I think that if I don't recognize him it's impossible that he had a key.'

'But the building's been here longer than you have, sir,' Jake objected.

'Oh yeah – by a long shot. But part of our safety and security protocol is to change the locks at a minimum of once every two years and I've been here a lot longer than that.'

'So how else could a person get in here without leaving signs of a break-in?' Jake asked.

'It's a public building. Anyone can get in here during the day.'

'And possibly hide away until the building was locked up for the night?'

'Sure. Might get caught. Might not. But like I told Lieutenant Pierce, Shari often met here with parents when they got off work. If she thought that he was the father of a student, she would have let him in the building.'

Lucinda and Jake exchanged a glance and rose

to their feet. 'Thank you, Mr Irving. I'll just take Agent Lovett over to the break room now. The only other person we'd like to talk to again is Sammy Nguyen. But I'm sure we can find him on our own.'

'Well, I'm not going anywhere till lunch time so just stop back in if I can help you with anything else.'

As they walked away, Jake asked, 'Who's Sammy Nguyen?'

'The custodian who found the body.'

'Why do we need to talk to him?'

'We may not need to. But it gives us a good excuse to roam around the building if you think of any reason why you'd want to do that.'

Lucinda pointed out where the body had lain on the floor, where the blood spatter hit the walls and cabinets and where the custodian had dropped the mugs. Several school district staff members stepped into the room while they were there. Every one of them recognized Lucinda and backtracked out of the room without saying a word.

Lucinda took Jake on a tour of the building, drawing his attention to all the entrance ways and the many places to hide throughout the two floors and the basement. When Jake was satisfied that he had a good understanding of the building's layout and the physical limitations of the crime scene, they went to the station to plan their next steps.

The call they wanted but did not expect came in on Jake's cell. At the time, he was down in the café in the basement of the Justice Center picking up a couple of coffees to carry upstairs. He'd set them down on an empty table to answer the phone. He abandoned the hot, steaming cups after he got the word. He couldn't bear to wait for the elevator. He hit the stairway, bounding up the steps two at a time, until he reached the third floor.

'They found him,' he blurted out as he stepped into the office. He bent forward with his hands on his knees as he struggled to catch his breath.

'Charles Sinclair Murphy?' Lucinda asked as she spun around to face him.

'Yes.'

Lucinda jerked to her feet. 'Where?'

'In a pediatric dental clinic in Roanoke.'

'Damn. All the excitement will be over before we can get there.'

'Naw. It won't take us more than half an hour.'

'Nobody can drive it that fast, Jake.'

'The state cops are sending a helicopter. Due here in two minutes. We need to get up on the roof to the helipad.'

Lucinda slipped her jacket on over her holster, made sure her badge was in her pocket and said, 'Let's go.' They raced up three more flights of stairs. As they opened the door to the rooftop, they heard the unmistakable noise of the rotor blades approaching the building.

The force of the wind generated by the landing copter knocked them both back a step. A man in a flight suit stepped out of the hatch, bent over and ran to where they stood. 'I need to see I.D.,' he shouted.

287

Lucinda and Jake didn't understand him over all the noise. They both pointed to an ear and shook their heads. The man pulled his badge out and flashed it. Lucinda and Jake nodded and pulled out theirs. He looked at both of them and swept his arm in a follow-me gesture. They ducked down as he did, went over to the hatch and stepped into the chopper.

At first, Jake and Lucinda made a couple of stabs at conversation. When neither could hear the other, they gave up and watched the scenery pass, occasionally pointing out sights down below. In a shorter time than Lucinda believed possible, the helicopter began its descent to a helipad atop a brick building. Soon, she would confront Charles Sinclair Murphy. She prayed there would not be a repeat of her last encounter with a serial killer.

Forty-Seven

Shannon Witzer left her home that morning in total disgust. She was burned out over the same old argument with her husband Ben. She knew Ben was right: she could be making a higher salary working as a dental hygienist in a private office than she made at the clinic. But no matter how she tried, she could not make him understand why she wanted to stay where she was. He could not comprehend that the fulfillment she got from working at a non-profit agency with these children and these families far outweighed anything a paycheck could offer.

Maybe if he got a job, he'd understand. Ha! As long as I'm paying the bills, he isn't ever going to get a job – at least not one that lasts more than a month. Maybe it's time to move on. The constant bickering is depressing – and love? Well, he loves the way I support him but I think that's about it. And now, that's not even good enough for him.

As she backed out of the driveway in her ratty old Nissan Sentra, she glared at his shiny new midnight-blue car. It wasn't right that she brought home most of the income and yet she was the one that drove the old beater.

He told her he had to have a new, reliable car

for a sales position. He had a multi-state territory and needed to be prompt with all his appointments. He got a decent salary plus commission. He'd worked the job for a month, raising Shannon's hopes. *Maybe he has changed*, she'd thought.

On the Monday morning of the sixth week, he simply rolled over in bed and went back to sleep. He never quit. But he did not work a notice either. He never called his employer. He just stopped going to work and refused to answer the telephone. Shannon was stuck, again, with making excuses for him.

When she suggested that, since he wasn't working, they should switch cars, he shoved her into the wall so hard it made her teeth rattle. On this morning, she drove up the street already dreading the end of the day when she'd have to return home. *Why do I come home? Why do I need to come home? Why don't I just treat him like he treats his jobs and just not bother to show up? It would be so nice to not have to deal with him ever again.*

Once she arrived at the clinic, she banished thoughts of home. She glanced at her list of patients for the day. Most of them were repeat visits. That was good. She had less fear to confront and defuse with the kids who'd seen her before. She picked up a clipboard, opened the door to the lobby and called for her first child.

Except for one little girl who cried the whole time she was in the chair, the morning was rather uneventful for Shannon. She'd cleaned many little mouths, provided at-home dental hygiene lessons and traded lots of hugs. The afternoon began as more of the same. Every time her mind started to drift to her home life, she focused on concentrating more on the child in front of her. If anything, she was more attentive to the children than usual. Seven-year-old Ricky Turpin swaggered into the room. His tough-little-boy act didn't fool her. She knew he was a little scared but now, on his fourth visit, he trusted her. Examining the inside of his mouth, she said, 'You haven't been flossing every day, have you, Ricky?'

'I ran out of floss,' he said. 'But I did brush every day.'

'I'll give you extra floss in your goodie bag today. But I can tell you've been brushing. No sign of cavities. So, I'll let you pick an extra toy from the barrel, OK?'

'Thank you, Ms Shannon.'

Shannon jumped at the slamming of a door down the hall. No one slammed doors here. No one. No matter how angry they were. She patted Ricky on the shoulder and said, 'Back in a sec.'

She stuck her head out of the examination room and looked down the hall. She saw the back of a man holding a wiggling little girl in a hard embrace. The little girl's face was tensed tight in distress. She'd seen that look many times before on the faces of patients getting their first tooth cleaning or cavity filling. That didn't bother Shannon but the noise the child was making was troublesome. A low-volume, high-pitched squealing that brought the word 'terror' into Shannon's mind. Shannon was not alarmed yet –

291

she'd dealt with panicking children many times. Then the man turned around and she saw the gun.

For a moment, the weapon didn't register. Then it seemed to be a bizarre hallucination. Finally, the reality sunk into her perception. Shannon ducked her head back into the examination room.

Her first concern was for her patient. She stood in front of Ricky and put an erect index finger in front of her lips. He aped her movement and nodded his head. She unfastened the oversized bib from around his neck and reached out her hand to help him out of the chair. She crooked her finger and led him behind the panel where she went for protection during X-rays. She opened a cabinet and pointed. Ricky nodded his head and climbed inside. She knelt down and looked at him, holding her finger before her lips again. He waved goodbye. She gave him a big smile and shut the door.

She crept to the doorway and peered around the jamb. The man was only a few feet away now. He turned to look at her. Shannon summoned the courage to stand still and not waver. She looked him in the eye and said, 'I can take her now,' and reached out her arms to the child.

Murphy jerked back, slamming into the wall, making the little girl squeak in surprise. 'Shut up,' he said as he shook her. The little girl whined in response. He whacked the back of her head into the wall and screamed 'Shut up!' into her ear. The child whimpered.

Shannon took a step forward, her arms outstretched. 'Please let me have her. I can quiet her down.'

'Get away from me,' he said, sidling down the hall. 'I was left behind. I have nothing to lose.'

Shannon persisted, arms reaching toward the child as she matched each of his steps with one of her own. 'C'mon, let me quiet her down then we can talk about your problem and look for solutions.'

'Don't you listen?' he screamed. 'I was left behind!'

Heads popped out of examination rooms all along the corridor.

'I was left behind!' he yelled out again.

Shannon lowered her arms and spread them in a wide welcome like a statue of the Madonna. 'Please, let me help you.'

Murphy took the muzzle of the gun away from the child's head, bringing a smile to Shannon's lips. Then he swung it around, pointing it at Shannon's head. He pulled the trigger quickly before she was aware of her personal peril.

Splattering blood landed on the little girl's legs. She screamed as if each drop was boiling water. Murphy sneered as Shannon collapsed to the floor. 'Die, Goodie Two Shoes, die.'

Forty-Eight

The helicopter touched down on the roof of a hospital near the dental clinic. Uniformed patrolmen escorted Lucinda and Jake down the stairs and out to a waiting patrol car, whisking them to the location six blocks away. In the parking lot they were briefed on the situation and issued bulletproof vests.

'You said just one shot?' Lucinda asked.

'Yes, Lieutenant. Only one.'

'You have no idea who was shot?'

'No. For all we know, the shot went into the ceiling and there is no victim.'

'You've had no communication with the inside?'

'Just what we got from Officer Sykes before he evacuated the people in the lobby.'

'Where is he?' Jake asked.

'Over that way, with the other clinic patients.'

Rodney Sykes was crouched down in front of Derek, talking in earnest. 'Excuse us, Officer Sykes,' Jake said. 'I'm Special Agent Lovett and this is Lieutenant Pierce. We'd like to ask you a few questions.'

Rodney turned back to Derek. 'You wait right here and don't wander off. I'll be back as soon as I can.' He stood and the three of them stepped away from the others before beginning their conversation.

'There's nothing about his physical appearance that doesn't jive with the mug shot and description,' Rodney said.

'What about his mannerisms, his state of mind?' Lucinda asked.

'When I last saw him, he was very angry – very agitated. I think that's my fault,' Rodney answered.

'Your fault?' Jake asked.

'Yeah. He was fine until I recognized him. A little edgy, nervous-like, but not angry. When he spotted me trying to get folks to slip outside, he lost it.'

'Did the shot happen before or after you left the building?'

'After. I hope to God he didn't shoot that little girl,' Rodney said.

'The one he grabbed in the lobby?'

'Yeah,' Rodney said, hanging his head. 'I keep thinking I could have, should have, done something to prevent her abduction.'

'Hey, the should'ves will drive you crazy, Officer,' Lucinda said. 'You've got to let them go and concentrate on the lives you saved with your quick action.'

'Like it's that easy,' he said.

Lucinda's laugh contained no humor. 'Yeah, tell me about it. Do you know how many people are in the back?'

'Not directly. But I did talk to the dental hygienist that he knocked to the floor in the lobby. She estimated there were seven kids in the back. As far as staff goes, she says there were two dentists, three hygienists, and four administrative staff: the receptionist, billing clerk, administrative assistant and the executive director.'

'Nine adults. Seven kids. Adds up to sixteen hostages,' Jake said.

'That many will be difficult for him to control,' Lucinda said. 'He'll probably be willing to get rid of some of them.'

'Maybe that's what he was doing when we heard the gun shot.'

'I'd rather think he shot it into the ceiling to try to shut up the kids 'cause they're driving him nuts. If they're all whining, he may want an excuse to give them up.'

The door to the clinic opened a crack. All officers not already behind a barricade now dropped behind vehicles, drew their guns and pointed the barrels at the opening door. A white sheet flapped up and down through the crack.

Rodney Sykes rushed away from the two investigators. He went through the line of blue that stretched between the folks rescued from the building and the gathered force around the entrance. Lucinda and Jake moved closer to the door with their backs flat against the brick wall.

The commanding officer shouted through a megaphone, 'Drop your weapons.'

'I don't have any! I'm a dentist! I'm Dr Hirschman,' the person at the door shouted.

'Come out the door with your hands on your head.'

'I can't. If I don't return, he'll shoot that little girl.'

'What do you want?'

'I have a message.'

'What is it?'

'He is leaving something for you in the lobby. He had me drag it out here for you. Thirty seconds after I leave this door, you may come and get it. You will have one minute to get it and get out of the building or the little girl will be next.'

'What do you mean, "next"?'

'I can't say any more.'

'What are you leaving for us?'

'I can't tell you. Just come and get it. If you don't, he'll kill that little girl.'

'Dr. Hirschman?'

'I have to go now.' The white sheet pulled back inside.

The commander barked orders and men from the bomb squad approached the door in a squat walk holding metal high-impact shields. An officer jerked the door open and the men went inside.

'It's a body,' came a shout from inside.

'Bring it out.'

Rodney and other officers encouraged the parents to turn the children's eyes away from the door. He pressed Derek's face into his chest and held him tight.

The bomb squad backed out. Two emergency medical technicians rushed inside. One grabbed the ankles, the other grabbed the shoulders and they carried the dental hygienist out to the parking lot. The ambulance driver raced up with a gurney. The crew got busy making a futile but necessary assessment of the woman's non-existent vital signs. A shrill scream erupted from the staff member sequestered on the side with the patients and their parents. She struggled to get past the blue line but she was rebuffed.

Lucinda and Jake made a brief reconnaissance of the lobby area. Lucinda reached over the counter and grabbed a piece of paper and a pen off the receptionist's desk. She wrote, 'Call me, Charles,' and added her cell phone number.

'Out now!' the commander shouted over the megaphone. 'Five, four, three...'

Lucinda and Jake emerged, shouting, 'All clear.' They went back to their positions up against the wall.

The commanding operations officer waved an arm in the air, indicating that he wanted them to come over to his location. Lucinda and Jake crouched and ran across the pavement to the shelter of the armored truck to brief the commander.

'We saw no one,' Jake said.

'I heard some crying in the back when I wrote the note,' Lucinda said.

'What note?' the commander asked.

Lucinda described it and said, 'I think he'll see it when he comes out to make sure we all left the building.'

'Look around you. We have snipers on every rooftop. I've got an entry team on high alert. And you think we should wait for him to respond to your message?' the commander asked.

Lucinda stepped into his space. She used her two-inch height advantage to attempt to intimidate him. 'Oh, I see, you're a maximum force for any occasion kind of guy.'

Jake pushed in between them before the situation escalated. 'Listen, Commander, we have sixteen hostages in there. Seven of them are children. We need to do everything we can to make sure that we don't pick up the morning paper and read, "Seven Kids Dead". We need to try to negotiate those children out of there first.'

'So how long do you want to wait?' the commander asked.

'I don't know,' Jake said. 'We just need some time. We'll reassess in an hour, OK?'

The commander looked him over. 'An hour? I don't know.'

'Do you want me to call my supervisor in D.C.?'

'Hell, no. Having one Feeb at the scene is more than I need. OK. You've got an hour.'

Jake nodded and with a signal to Lucinda, they both jogged back to their position by the entrance. 'You're an out-of-towner here, Lucinda. Why are you trying to aggravate the local cops?'

'SWAT guys piss me off with their shoot first, ask questions later mentality.'

'Is that it or is it more personal?' Jake asked.

'Damn you, Jake. You know it is,' Lucinda said as the image of the tiny body of a dead little boy pressed its way to the front of her mind. 'I don't want to be connected to another child's death. Please God, don't let another child die.'

Forty-Nine

A half-hour later, the strain of prolonged high alert began to manifest its presence on Lucinda's body. She felt the ache of tensed shoulder blades, the uncomfortable tightness in the back of her neck, the slight pain caused by the twist of dread that settled in her lower spine. Lucinda disliked waiting for any reason. But when the stakes were this high, she loathed every passing second.

She looked over at Jake who nodded toward the logistics vehicle. The commander stood outside the truck staring in their direction. When he saw they were both looking his way, he made a pointed glance at his wristwatch.

'Damn him,' Lucinda said.

'Just doing his job, Lucinda.'

'His definition of doing his job interferes with our need to do *our* job, Jake. And I don't like that one little bit.'

They both sighed and slumped against the wall, trying to find a spot of comfort against the hard bricks and mortar.

Fifteen more fretful minutes passed before Lucinda's cell phone rang. She fumbled with it in her pocket before getting it out and flipping it on. 'Lieutenant Pierce.'

'I was left behind, Lieutenant.'

'I know that, Charles. And it wasn't right.'

'Don't patronize me, Lieutenant.'

'Sorry, Charles.' She closed her eyes and put a hand over the opposite ear to better hear what he was saying and the tone of his voice as well as to get better cues from the background noises on his end of the line.

'No you're not. You're just sorry that I didn't fall for it.'

Lucinda accepted the rebuke and remained silent, waiting for him to continue.

'I see you picked up the delivery I left for you,' Murphy said.

'Yes, Charles, we did. We weren't pleased with that. We do not want anyone else to die. I see you got my note.'

'Yes, I got your note. And no, I didn't expect you to be pleased, Lieutenant. But it was just another Goodie Two Shoes. There's too many of them in the world, acting important, acting like they make a difference. You think their deaths matter. You think it's disturbing. On the other hand, I don't think it would bother you at all if I were to die.'

'Every human being is capable of making a positive difference in the lives of others, Charles – even you.'

'You can't con me, Lieutenant. And no one made a positive difference in my damn life. Not one. No, ma'am. Those damn Goodie Two Shoes knew what was happening to me but did they do anything about it? No. And now they're paying. But the one this morning – she wasn't part of the plan. She forced me to shoot her.'

'What can we do to make sure no one else forces your hand, Charles?'

'Go away and leave me alone.'

'You know that's not going to happen. So what do you really want?'

'This whole thing was not supposed to happen. I was just minding my own business till that asshole cop called in the storm troopers. What the hell was that about? I didn't do nothin' to him.'

'He recognized you, Charles. He knew that law enforcement was looking for you.'

'Law enforcement. What a stupid name. You don't do that. You don't make people obey the law. You all show up after the law is broken. You all are avengers. That's all. You don't enforce nothing. And it was you. Not "law enforcement". It was you that was looking for me. You.'

'Yes, Charles. I wanted to ask you some questions.'

'Yeah. That's all you wanted. Right. Sell me a farm in Manhattan.'

'I certainly would have taken you into custody, Charles. But I did want to talk to you. I did want to ask you a few questions.'

'About the details. That's what you wanted to know, right? You murder police are just like me and all the folks you hunt. You get off on the details, dontcha? You get a big-ass thrill when we tell you about what we've done. You wanted to ask me how I did it. How it felt. What I felt. I know you. You're just like me.'

'Well, yes, someone will have to talk to you

about all of that, Charles, to make sure you are telling the truth when you confess to the crimes. But that's not what I wanted to ask you about. I wanted to ask you about your notes. I wanted to understand your notes. But, Charles, things are so confusing right now. I want to make sure that none of the kids die while we sort out this mess.'

'I'm not killing no damn kids unless you make me.'

'Charles, I can hear some of them whining and crying. I know how that can get on anyone's nerves. Let me take them off of your hands. Send them out.' She waited but got no response. 'Charles?' she asked. 'Charles?'

'I heard you. There are a couple of them that are making me nuts. They just won't shut up. I might let you have them two. You'll have to come into the lobby. Just you. No weapons. You come with weapons I kill kids. You come with anybody else, I kill kids. That work for you?'

'Yes, Charles. That's not a problem.'

'I'll call you back.'

'Charles, wait—' Lucinda began but stopped when she heard the dial tone.

303

Fifty

Murphy herded everyone back into Dr Hirschman's office where he ripped the phone cord from the wall outlet near the baseboard and attempted to collect a cell phone from every adult. Three of them claimed to have left theirs in another part of the building. He held a knife to the stringy blonde girl's throat and sent them out to retrieve their cells one at a time. He loudly counted down the thirty seconds of allowed time as each one scrambled for a device and returned with it.

He turned to Dr Hirschman. 'Pick them all up,' he ordered. As the dentist complied, Murphy shifted the child's body around, wrapping the crook of his arm around her stomach. She hung there trembling, facing the floor.

'Follow me.' He led him into the closest examination room. 'Drop them into the sink and turn on the water.'

'That'll ruin them.'

'No shit, Sherlock. Do it or I slice the girl.' He poked her with the tip of the knife hard enough to draw blood and cause her to squeal in fear.

Hirschman turned on the faucet full strength and blocked the sink with wadded up paper towels as instructed.

Murphy heard a quiet thump and stepped into the hall. He pulled his gun and pointed it at a door. 'Open it,' he ordered.

Hirschman pulled on the knob of a utility closet. A hygienist stood back in a corner. Murphy waved the gun and ordered her to come out in the hall. When she didn't move, he noticed the smaller legs hiding behind hers. 'Don't play hero. Your friend is dead because she did. Come out here with the kid or you and the kid will die in that corner.'

She hesitated for a moment and then reached down, took the girl's hand and walked out to the hall. As she walked past Murphy, he asked, 'Where's your cell phone?'

Her mouth was so dry he could hear the click of her tongue pulling away from the roof of her mouth. 'At the front desk,' she said.

He grabbed the shoulder of the girl, pulling her small hand out of the hygienist's hand. He jerked her to his side and he said, 'Go get it.'

Her nostrils flared. She swallowed hard. Turned and walked up the hall. She returned immediately. She dropped the phone into his hand and lifted the girl into her arms and glared at him.

He laughed in her face and stuck the cell in the waistband of his pants. Murphy then moved everyone down the hall and into the office with the others. A couple of children were whining and one was sobbing. 'Shut them up,' he said. They tried but despite the shushing and coaxing, the irritating noises still grated on Murphy's ears. He tried to ignore it as he spoke.

'We have a mess. A big mess. Most of you were not supposed to be involved. You can blame your predicament on that nosy cop in the lobby. He blew it. Now instead of coming in here and taking care of Chief Goodie Two Shoes here,' he said, pointing to Dr Hirschman, 'I've had to take all of you hostage. It was not my choice. And it's not my damn fault. I don't want to kill the whole lot of you but I will if I have to. So pay attention and do what you're told.

'Right now, I need you all to shut up 'cause I'm making a call. Anyone tries to get smart and I'll kill a kid and then kill you.' He laid the note Lucinda left on the desk and pulled out the last phone he confiscated. After talking to Lucinda, he pointed and said, 'I want that kid and that kid.'

A woman stepped in front of each child and said, 'No!'

Murphy fired a shot into the shoulder of one of the adults, making her stagger to the side. He pointed at the other woman. 'You want me to shoot you, too? I will. But I'll aim at your head. Do you want these kids to see that?'

'I am not going to let you hurt this child,' she said, her eyes wide and wet with unfallen tears.

'I'm not going to kill them damned kids. I'm giving them to the cop, you stupid bitch. Get out of the way or I'll shoot,' Murphy yelled as he leveled the gun just four inches away from her skull.

Frozen with fear, she still did not move.

'Please, sir,' Hirschman said. 'We're all a bit overwrought. Did you say you wanted to give two children to the police?'

'Yes,' Murphy shouted.

'Dee, please step away from that child and let him go with that man.'

'But how can we trust him, Doctor?'

'Dee, please...'

Dee's eyes slid back and forth between the dentist and the man with the gun. Fear furrowed her brow and made her teeth chatter.

'I'm giving you to the count of five, Dee,' Murphy screamed. 'One. Two.'

Dee stepped sideways. The little boy, who'd been behind her, screamed.

'You,' Murphy ordered Hirschman. 'Grab the brat. Pick him up. Then get that whiny little girl. Hurry up.'

Hirschman hoisted a child up into each arm. The children struggled against him but he held them tight.

'Go. Toward the lobby. Now. When you get to the door, sit on the floor in the hallway.'

Hirschman followed instructions, sitting with his back against the wall, holding the squirming children as firmly as he could. He whispered to them, trying to soothe and quiet them without much success.

'The cop is coming in for the kids; you try to leave with the cop, Doctor Goodie Two Shoes and you'll die where you stand,' Murphy warned. 'And then the kids'll all die, too. You understand that?'

'Yes,' he said with a nod. 'Yes, I do.'

'All right. Don't move. And you can smack those kids around to get 'em to shut up if you want.'

The two children squirmed and squealed even more, despite the dentist's assurances that he had no intention of hitting them.

Murphy called Lucinda again. When she answered, he said, 'Come in and get these two kids. But remember, I'll be watching every second. You try anything and the kids will die.'

Fifty-One

Ricky fought to suppress giggles. He wasn't sure what game he was playing but it seemed to be something like hide and seek. Inside the cabinet, it was dark and a little scary.

He sniffed the air, seeking something familiar there. One of the smells reminded him of the sawdust in his grandpa's workshop. That was nice. It made him smile. The other smell was damp and wet like a basement. That odor caused his brow to furrow and made him think of spiders and snakes and nasty little mice. In less than a minute, though, Ricky's eyes adjusted and he could see some of his surroundings, causing his fear to fade.

On one end, there was a sink above him. He saw the bowl curve down and the drainpipe go down through the floor. He touched the copper pipe for the incoming water. It was cold and damp.

He wondered when the lady was coming back. He wasn't all that good at keeping still and now he was getting restless.

Ricky heard a loud noise. He threw both of his hands over his mouth to muffle his spontaneous outcry. He recognized the sound of a gun firing. He'd heard it before, in Mr Franklin's store below his apartment the day it was robbed by a bad man and Mr Franklin's son was shot. And he died. And for days, he heard the sounds of Mrs Franklin's sobs drifting up through the floor. He knew that sound the second it echoed outside of his hiding place. He knew it and he hated it.

It wasn't a game anymore. He heard the little girl scream and thought the bad man must have shot her. He had no idea that the woman who hid him away now lay lifeless on the hallway floor.

Even without that knowledge, he was scared. He wanted to run. He wanted to throw the door open, jump out and get as far away from here as he could. Fear froze his limbs, locked his joints. He could not coax his body into motion.

He heard loud voices. He couldn't hear the words but he could hear the anger in one voice. That terrified him and created an intense urge to pee. He grabbed hold of himself and held tight. He couldn't pee in there. And he couldn't get to the bathroom.

He started bouncing in place but banged the top of his head and stopped. He held his breath, fearful that someone had overheard the small noise he made.

He heard something in the hallway – scraping, rubbing, slipping sounds – as if something was being dragged across the floor. A man made grunting noises. A door slammed. He heard the murmur of several voices. Should he shout for help? Or were they bad men, too?

In his indecision, he made the choice to remain silent. Noises he couldn't identify mingled with those that issued from human throats. Doors slammed shut. Then footsteps went back up the hall.

He was alone now. Should he run? Could he make it to the door? He didn't know. Tears formed in his eyes. He pressed his lips together to keep from crying out loud.

He sought refuge in withdrawal. He pulled inside of himself. The shaking stopped. The tears ended. Soon he breathed deeply, softly. He was asleep. The peaceful sleep of innocence in the face of fear.

A loud noise jarred him from his slumber. *What was it? Another gun shot? Where was it?* He sobbed in silence – lips pressed together, body rocking in place. *I wanna go home. I want my mom.* He rubbed his eyes and searched for the courage to break out of the cabinet and run.

Fifty-Two

Lucinda jogged over to brief the commander on the conversation. Jake leaned against the wall awaiting her return. When he saw the escalation of her hand movements, he knew it was not going well. He jogged over to give her support.

'Isn't that good news, Commander?' he asked as soon as he got in audible distance.

'I was just telling the Lieutenant that time was running out. About ten minutes before the hour's up.'

'Damn it to hell,' Lucinda blurted out.

Jake laid a hand on her forearm and said, 'Commander, the situation has changed. We need to give this a bit more time to work its way out.'

The commanding officer puffed out his chest and squinted his eyes at Jake. 'Why is it every time you say something, it sounds like a threat?'

Jake sighed, 'Commander, that's your problem. Not mine. I have never threatened you. I've merely stated the facts.'

'So you think we should let that asshole pull all the strings. And we just sit out here biding our time, waiting for him to do whatever it is he's gonna do?'

'Pretty much,' Jake said as he stuck his hands

on his hips and glared.

'Whatever,' the commander said with a shrug. 'But it ain't on my head.'

'No, sir,' Jake said. 'Neither one of us want you to take any responsibility for our decisions.'

'That's good on paper but you two get to leave town and I'll be the one they kick. You know that and I know that.'

Lucinda jumped back into the conversation. 'So, what's your point? I'm local. I've carried baggage that wasn't mine. But it's part of the job.'

Before the commander could respond, the muffled sound of a shot rang through the air. They all turned to the men by the building. One of them shouted, 'Gun shot. Inside.'

'Shit!' the commanding officer shouted. 'Damn me for listening to you. We're going in.' The commander got on the communications line and ordered the SWAT team into position.

As Lucinda and Jake watched the black-clad, helmet-wearing gladiators move around the building and prepare for an assault, Lucinda said, 'This is so wrong, Jake. Wrong. Wrong. Wrong. We need more time.'

'I know but we're not going to get it.'

Lucinda's cell rang. 'It's him,' she hissed before answering.

'Nobody got killed,' he said.

'We can't exactly take you on your word about that, Charles.'

'I know. But I'm still sending those kids out. They'll tell you. I did shoot somebody. But she's not going to die. Not unless you do something

313

stupid.'

'If she's shot, Charles, why don't you just send her out with the kids?'

Murphy did not respond.

'C'mon, Charles, if she by chance dies from losing blood while you're holding her in there, she's gonna be a big problem for you. Send her out with the kids. It'll give ya one less thing to worry about.'

'OK. I don't need her. But don't trying anything stupid. Just come into the lobby – just you – nobody else. And tell those storm troopers gathering around the building to back off or I'll get edgy and someone will die.'

When he disconnected the call, Lucinda turned to Jake. 'Go tell the commander. I'm going in to get those kids and I'm going in now.'

She pulled one gun out of her shoulder holster and her back-up from her ankle. She carried one in each hand as she walked to the door prepared to hand them off to the officer there. Before she made it, a SWAT team member stepped in front of her. 'You can't go in there, Lieutenant. We're ready to roll.'

'Put on the brakes and let me through.'

'Sorry, Lieutenant. No can do. I have my orders.'

'You also have my gun in your ribs. I will save those two kids. And you will not stand in my way.'

'You wouldn't dare.'

'Don't tempt me. Those kids are far more important to me than you, my career and even my life. Back off.' When he didn't move, she

314

added, 'Look at my face. You look hard and then answer this question: Do I have the face of a woman who takes risks? Huh? What do you think?'

He backed up a step and called into command central.

Lucinda wasted no time; she strode the remaining steps to the clinic, pulled open the door and handed her weapons to the nearest officer. Then she stepped inside. 'I'm here, Charles. No weapons. No problems.'

From some place eerily close, Murphy said, 'I hope you won't be offended, Lieutenant, but I don't really trust you. Dr Hirschman will come out first and see if you're telling me the truth. And he won't play any games with you or hide any of your secrets. So don't try. He sees me holding the knife to this child's throat. He knows she'll die.'

'No tricks from me, Charles. I'm just here for the kids.'

The dentist stepped out into the waiting room. 'Sorry, Lieutenant,' he said as he placed his hands on her.

'Not a problem, sir. I understand the situation. Is anyone else dead?'

'No. But I'm not sure how long that will last.'

'Do you think we can get more people out if we keep negotiating?'

'I think he'll probably let everyone go but me.'

'You're the target?'

'Yes. I think that's all that really matters to him. I'm going to die no matter what happens here. But try to get as many others out as you

315

can first.'

A voice boomed from the back. 'What you doing out there, Dentist Man? You want to get back here now or do you want me to kill a kid?'

'I'm coming,' Hirschman shouted. To Lucinda he said, 'I'm trying to protect the others. I don't know what else I can do.'

He walked through the door and into the back. Lucinda stood still waiting. Listening. Ready to move if she heard anything that indicated the level of danger to the children had increased. One minute passed. Anxiety formed beads of perspiration on her forehead and her palms. She wiped her hands on her pants. Another minute passed. Cold, clammy sweat gathered on the back of her neck, giving her chills.

Another minute passed. She heard a child's squeak of protest and her muscles tensed for action. The door opened. Two little kids ran through it, followed by a woman in scrubs with her arm in a makeshift sling.

Lucinda hustled them all out the front door and into the arms of waiting paramedics. Then she strode across the lot to face the wrath of the man she'd defied. *I sure hope he's not expecting me to be remorseful.*

Fifty-Three

From a distance, Lucinda could tell the commander was angry. Very angry. A clip of Elmer Fudd with a red face and smoke pouring out of his ears crossed her mind. She lowered her head to keep her amusement hidden. She stopped in front of the commander and raised her head to face him.

'Who the hell do you think you are?' he asked.

'Lieutenant Lucinda Pierce, sir.'

'Don't get smart with me, Pierce. Just what the hell do you think you are doing?'

'I safely recovered two children and a wounded adult from an ongoing hostage situation, sir.'

'You drew a gun on one of my officers, Pierce.'

'Not exactly...'

'You interfered with a police operation.'

'But we did ensure the safety of three individuals because of my actions.'

'In spite of your actions, Pierce. I want you outta here.'

'This is my case, sir.'

'This is my town, Pierce.'

'And I just saved the lives of three people in your stinkin' town.'

'I've already called your captain.'

'You what?'

'After you pulled a gun on my officer, I called him to find out what the hell I was dealing with.'

'And?' Lucinda snarled.

'He told me you don't play well with others. He told me you don't take orders well.'

It stung Lucinda to know that the Captain had said these things – sure, he'd said them to her face before, but it hurt to know he'd say it to someone outside of their immediate circle. 'He seems to be able to work with me just fine.'

'I asked him about that,' the commander continued. 'I asked him why he kept you around. You know what he told me?'

Lucinda wasn't sure if she wanted to hear this or not. 'I have no idea, sir.'

'He told me that you are usually right. That your instincts are good. So I asked him, what if she's wrong? And you know what he said?'

'No, sir, I don't.'

'He says when she's wrong, she's so spectacularly wrong that you won't have a problem pinning the blame on her. Just stick her under a spotlight with a "Kick me" sign on her back and the media will shred her to pieces.'

Lucinda clenched her jaw to stop the threat of a tear that wanted to form in her eye. She couldn't even figure out why she wanted to cry. Was she hurt? Was she angry? Was she a little bit of both? She stood rigid and stared straight ahead over the commander's head.

'It's a tempting thought, Pierce. But we don't do things like that over in these parts. We have rules and we follow rules. But since you're not fixing to follow the rules, you can just get the hell out of my way.'

Lucinda fought the urge to spit out names and insults. She stood still as if she hadn't heard a word.

'Now, Pierce. Out of here. Gone. Vacate the premises. Off my scene. Out of my town. Now!' he shouted.

Lucinda spun around on her heel, seeing a sea of faces flash in her view – jeering faces, shocked faces, empathetic faces – all staring in her direction. She marched back to the front of the building, passing Jake on the way. He reached out and grabbed her arm.

'Lucinda, what's going on?'

'He ordered me off the scene.'

'You just saved three lives.'

'Ah, but I broke rules, Jake. As a Feeb, you should know rules are more important than people.'

'Hey, Lucinda, c'mon. Gimme a break. I'm on your side here. And I don't want you leaving the scene.'

'I'm not leaving, Jake. Not unless he cuffs me and drags me out of here.'

'I'll go talk to him.'

Lucinda barked a laugh without any humor. 'Good luck with that.' She continued across the parking lot up to the wall beside the front door.

Another shot drew everyone's attention away from Lucinda. Then the outside door to the clinic flew open and a little boy burst into the parking lot. All around the building, voices rang out, 'Hold your fire! Hold your fire!'

Lucinda took three long steps toward the child, scooped Ricky into her arms and ran toward the paramedics. From the side of the building she heard a woman's voice shriek, 'Ricky! Ricky! Oh, thank God! Ricky!'

The little boy wriggled in Lucinda's arms and shouted for his mother but Lucinda kept moving toward the ambulance. She sat him down in between the open doors.

'Mommy. I want my mommy!' Ricky sobbed.

Lucinda crouched down to his level. 'Ricky? Ricky!'

He turned a tear-stained face to hers and with a quivering lower lip said, 'I want my mommy.' Then he looked away, trying to catch sight of her.

'Ricky. Ricky. Look at me.'

'Mommy...'

'Ricky, please, I need to talk to you. Look at me.'

Ricky turned and saw her for the first time. He yipped like a puppy. 'Did the bad man do that to you?'

'Not this bad man, Ricky. I'm OK but we need to make sure you're OK.'

'I'm scared,' he cried as his shoulders shook.

'We'll get your mommy over her in just a minute, Ricky. Did the bad man hurt you?'

Ricky shook his head. 'The lady hid me.'

'Did the bad man let you leave?'

'No. He yelled at me. He told me to come back. I didn't. And he shot his gun at me. But I ran. And he missed. I didn't stop running. But I want my mommy, now.'

Lucinda looked over to the side lot where a woman strained to get away from a uniformed officer. She waved over and the woman was released and ran towards the ambulance. 'There, Ricky, see. It's your mommy. She's coming. I'll talk to you a little later, OK?'

'OK,' he nodded with a smile.

The woman reached Lucinda and said, 'My boy. That's my boy.'

Lucinda nodded and stepped away as the distraught mother wrapped her arms around Ricky, kissing the top of his head and saying his name over and over again.

Fifty-Four

Profanities screamed in his head. Over and over and over. Blocking out thought. He choked out an inarticulate scream in hopes of shutting up the internal noise. Around him, the hostages cringed. Even that ticked him off. He hadn't hurt any of them. *What's their problem?*

'Stop it,' he yelled. 'Where did that boy come from? Huh?'

No one answered. A scream of outrage ricocheted in his head. He grabbed a lamp off the dentist's desk and threw it into the wall. A loud smash and then bits of glass and ceramic tinkled as they hit the floor. 'Where did that boy come from?'

Dr Hirschman stepped in front of his staff and said, 'He was Shannon's patient.'

'Which one of you is Shannon?' Murphy growled, casting his eyes across the huddled group.

'None of us,' Hirschman continued. 'She's the woman you shot and killed.'

'Damn it,' Murphy shouted as he swung his arm across the desk sending piles of paperwork flying through the air. 'Where was he?'

'I'm not sure,' Hirschman said. 'But I suspect she'd hidden him somewhere before she encountered you in the hallway.'

'Come with me. And bring one of them kids,' he said to Hirschman. Then he turned to the frightened group. 'You try anything and your boss dies and the kid dies.' He turned back to Hirschman and laughed. 'Need the kid just in case some of your employees hate your guts. Now, move. We need to check hiding places for anyone else.'

They went room to room looking in closets and cabinets. Murphy focused on quieting the shaking anxiety in his gut. *I need to think. I need to plan.* A couple of the cabinets were deep and Murphy could not penetrate the darkness. He ordered the child climb into a cabinet to check in the back corners. *The kid's scared of the dark but even more frightened of me. Good. That'll keep him honest.*

In the room where Ricky had hidden, the location was obvious. A cabinet door hung open in the wake of his flight. 'Little bastard,' Murphy muttered.

After checking the final room, Murphy asked, 'Is that it?'

'Yes,' Hirschman said.

Murphy grabbed the child and jerked him up against his body and placed the barrel of the gun to his temple. 'You better be telling the truth or I'll blow a hole in this kid's head.'

The child trembled against Murphy's leg, then his head dropped back, his eyes rolled back and he crumpled to the floor. 'What the hell is his problem?' Murphy said as he pushed against the child's body with the toe of his shoe.

'May I approach?' Hirschman asked.

'I don't know how you can answer my question if you don't. Idiot,' Murphy said, backing away.

'He's just so terrified, he passed out,' Hirschman said, scooping the child up in his arms.

'Damn. Damn. Damn. This is such a meeesss! It wasn't supposed to be this way. It wasn't supposed to happen like this. I just came here to kill you, not to get caught up in some drama with kids and women and cops. Damn. Damn. Damn. What the hell can I do?'

'What matters to you more? Getting out alive? Or killing me?'

'Killing you,' Murphy answered in an eerie flat tone. 'But I'd rather do both.'

'Why? Never mind. That doesn't matter. I've got a plan.'

'That's a good one. You've got a plan to help me kill you?'

'Listen, that cop you're talking with?'

'Yeah?'

'She wants the hostages out. You should negotiate with her, give her a few at a time. When I'm the only one left, it'll take them a while to account for everybody and figure that out. You can do away with me as you please during that down time.'

'This has to be a trick,' Murphy said.

'No,' Hirschman said. 'What did you call me earlier? A Goodie Two Shoes?'

'Yes.'

'That's what my wife – rather my ex-wife – called me. She said I'd give up anything for a

good cause. She wasn't happy to see me working in this clinic, earning a fraction of what I'd
earn in a regular practice. So she left. She said I
sacrificed our marriage on the altar of good
deeds. But she blamed it all on my ego. Said I
only did what I did so that I would look good in
the eyes of others. Maybe she was right. I don't
know. But I've lived doing the right thing for
whatever reason; I might as well die doing the
right thing.'

'You are so full of crap.'

'Maybe so. Maybe I ought to hook you up with
my ex-wife. I think she'd understand you better
than I would.'

'Shut up. Just shut your damned pie hole.
You're not living long enough to do any match-
making.' Murphy poked the gun in Hirschman's
side. 'Move it. Go back to the back. And shut up.
I have to think.'

'Think hard. You can have what you want if
you play it right.'

'I said, shut up!' Murphy screamed and
slammed the barrel of the gun into the side of
Hirschman's head. The dentist fell forward,
twisting his body on the way down, in order to
land on his back and not crush the little boy in
his arms.

'Charles!' rang out loud and clear, echoing in
the hallway.

'That's her,' Hirschman said.

'Shut up,' Murphy replied as he kicked at the
dentist's legs. 'Get up. Get into the back room.
Get up. Now. Hurry.'

'Charles!'

Hirschman struggled to his feet, leaning against the wall to give him the leverage to rise with the child in his arms. Murphy pushed at him, nearly making him lose his balance. He shoved him into the office with the others and shut the door. *Is the dentist right about this cop? Can I play her and get what I want?*

'Charles!'

'What?' Murphy finally responded.

Fifty-Five

Lucinda headed back to her post by the front door. She was only a few steps away when the commander stepped in front of her. Two uniformed officers stood behind him.

'I thought I told you to leave the premises, Pierce.'

'You did, sir.'

'Here, Pierce, you obey orders or you are made to obey orders. These two officers are going to take you back to the station.' He stepped away, heading back to the command truck without looking back.

Two, young, red-faced cops stood in front of her. 'Ma'am,' one said, 'I need to secure your weapons, if you don't mind.'

'I do mind,' Lucinda said.

'Ma'am, please...'

'I know, I know, you're just doing your jobs,' she said, removing both of her guns and turning them over to the officer to her right. 'Take care of them, OK. I want to get them back in good shape.'

'Yes, ma'am,' he said and headed for the patrol car to secure them.

The other officer said, 'Ma'am, it sure would be nice if you'd come with me to the car without raising a fuss. I sure don't want to have to hand-cuff you.'

'No, you wouldn't. It would look really bad to that TV camera that's zooming in on you right now,' she said, pointing behind him.

He spun around and when he did, she took off at a gallop for the front door, pulled it open, closed it behind her and ran into the center of the waiting room. 'Charles!' she hollered.

Jake opened the outside door.

'Go away, Jake.'

'You need help.'

'Yes. Stand outside the door and don't let anyone in here.'

'You need help in here.'

'No, I don't. Just watch my back.'

'Well at least you need a gun.'

'No, I don't.'

'Yes, you do,' Jake said and slid the weapon from his ankle holster across the floor. 'Pick it up,' he hissed.

She bent her knees, grabbed the revolver and tucked in into the small of her back. 'Now get out of here.'

As the door shut behind Jake, she shifted her attention back to the situation down the hall. She listened, hearing the mumble of voices and some scuffling noises. 'Charles!'

She flipped open her cell phone and called Jake. Before he could say a syllable, she said, 'Listen, I'm leaving this phone on when I slip it in my pocket so you can monitor. Please don't let anyone come in unless I ask for help.'

'Lucinda...'

'No time, Jake.' She slid the device into the pocket of her jacket and shouted again, 'Charles!'

'What?'

At last, a response. 'I need to talk to you before we all die.'

'Do you want me to kill these people?' he screamed as he ran down the hall towards her.

'No, Charles, but I've got to talk to you. They've run out of patience.'

'Sounds like a cop trick to me.'

'Damn it, Charles, I wish it was. We're both in deep.'

'Oh, good. Trying to relate to me. Where is that? Page two of the manual?'

'Charles, I'm in trouble, too. I swear to you. They ordered me to leave. But I knew I couldn't. I had to help you.'

'You had to help me? That's a laugh.'

'C'mon, Charles. You do want to be called Charles, don't you? Or is it something else, Charlie? Mr Murphy? What?'

'Cheese, my friends call me Cheese.'

'Cheese, you don't want to die before your work is done. You don't want to die until they understand why you are doing this. If you do, it will be just like being left behind again. You don't want that. I don't want that. It's not fair. You've been left behind all your life.' *Please, dear God, let him buy this line I'm peddling. If he doesn't, I don't know what I'll do.* Lucinda's heart pounded and her tongue stuck on the roof of her mouth.

'What do you want?' Murphy asked.

'Take me in exchange for the kids.'

'What good will that do me?'

'It'll take off some of the pressure. Get the kids out of here and the – what did you call them? The storm troopers. That's it. The storm troopers won't be so intense.' Lucinda allowed a minute of silence to pass before speaking again. 'Cheese, we're short on time here. What's it gonna be?'

'You got any weapons?'

'No, Cheese.'

'Show me.'

Lucinda removed her jacket, taking care not to turn her back in any direction that would be visible to Murphy. She unfastened her shoulder holster and placed it on the counter. She slid her jacket back on and bent over. Pulling up a pants leg, she removed the empty holster on her ankle and laid it beside the other one. 'See?' she said, spreading her arms wide. *If he frisks me, I'm dead.*

'Yes. Wait a minute. I'll get the kids.'

Oh, thank God. She tried to still the tension that created a vibration in her chest. She breathed deeply in and out all the while listening to the noises from the back. She tensed a few times when Murphy's voice sounded hostile but she held her position. The door creaked open. *One, two, three, four children.* Lucinda fought back the urge to shout out in victory. 'Cheese, I'm going to open the outside door and send the kids outside.'

'Don't you go with them or everyone else in here dies.'

330

'I know, Cheese. I'll send them out and then I'll come through the door to you.'

'You'd better. The people back here won't get a second chance.'

Lucinda shepherded the frightened children to the door. She pushed it open, ramming Jake in the back. 'What?' he said.

'Four kids. I made a trade.'

'Them for you? No way.'

'Yes. Get these kids away from here.'

She stepped away, letting the door slam shut, and walked into the hallway. 'Cheese, I'm coming in.' She steeled herself and put all her senses on high alert. If things went bad, it was unlikely she could get the gun out in time but she sure would try.

Fifty-Six

Lucinda went a third of the way down the hall before Murphy shouted, 'Stop! Hold up your hands.'

She did as she was asked, all the while pivoting her head around looking for Murphy.

'Lace your fingers on the top of your head.'

Again, Lucinda obeyed, hoping that her jacket was long enough in the back to cover the handgun concealed in her waistband.

'Don't turn around. Start moving.'

Lucinda realized he was behind her in the hallway. *Can he see my gun? Will he remove it? Will he shoot me for having it? Or is it still hidden?* She slumped her shoulders, attempting to give the jacket more length. She wasn't sure if it did any good. She tried to feel any sensation that would indicate whether or not the weapon had been revealed but could only stir up exaggerated images from her imagination. She kept walking.

'Stop!' he said again, resurrecting Lucinda's fear that he could see her weapon. 'Turn around,' he ordered. He stared at her. 'What the hell happened to you?'

'It's kind of a long story. Is there someplace where we can sit and talk?'

'Cute. Oh sure. We'll just sit down and have a cup of coffee and chat. Get real.' He leaned toward her, looking at her face. 'That eye ain't real, is it?'

'What do you mean by real? As in, is it a figment of your imagination? That kind of real? If that's the question, yes it is real.'

'Stop jerking my chain. You know what I mean. It's a glass eye, isn't it?' He leaned even closer. 'Yes it is. A glass eye. They sent a one-eyed cop after me. What a trip. Start walking. Don't turn around. Walk backwards.'

When Lucinda's back bumped into the end of the hall, she was standing by a door with a key ring hanging from the knob. 'Open the door,' Murphy ordered.

She did and stood facing the remaining hostages. Quickly she counted them – eight.

'Get in the room. Hirschman, you come with me.'

'Cheese, why do you need Hirschman?' Lucinda objected.

'Because he's the Goodie Two Shoes I came for.'

'But Cheese, I'm a cop. The ultimate symbol of authority. I should be the focal point. I represent everyone who left you behind.'

'Good try. But no. I need a Goodie Two Shoes. It's the Goodie Two Shoes who gotta die.'

'Cheese, c'mon. I'm a cop. That makes me a Goodie Two Shoes. You don't need the dentist.'

Murphy laughed at her. 'Goodie Two Shoes? You? Not hardly. You're more the avenging angel type.' Murphy jerked on Hirschman's elbow, forcing him into the hall. 'One Eye, you keep these people quiet in here and maybe they can live. Anybody comes out in this hallway and they're dead. I'll be back before you know it.' He shut the door.

Lucinda listened as the footsteps went down the hall. She heard another door open. *Was that descending footsteps?* 'Is there a basement in here?' she asked.

'Yes,' one of the two remaining hygienists said.

'What's down there?'

The executive director of the program spoke up. 'Old office furniture, old dental equipment, file cabinets full of old files, the water heater, furnace, Christmas decorations, that sort of thing.'

'Lots of places to hide, then?' Lucinda asked.

'Yes, there sure are.'

'Damn.' Lucinda went to the far side of the office where there was another door. 'Does this lead to the outside?'

'Yes, but it's solid metal and the lock can only be opened with a key.'

'Damn,' Lucinda said again. 'What about this window?'

'We tried. It's painted shut and won't budge,' the executive director said.

Lucinda tugged up on it without any success. She thought about sending them down the hall and out of the building but discarded that idea. Murphy would be sure to hear all those footsteps over his head and she couldn't predict what he'd do. She had to get them to safety before she confronted Murphy.

'Duck down behind the desk or file cabinet. We could have some flying glass.' She threw a visitor's chair through the window then grabbed the coat tree and used it to clear away the worst of the jagged edges. 'OK, c'mon. Hurry, Hurry! Out the window. Don't cut yourself. Watch where you put your hands. Run around that side and to the front.' She pulled the cell out of her pocket. 'Jake?'

'Yes. What is it? What was that noise?'

'I busted out a window. Hostages coming your way.'

'Holy crap. They sure are. Is that all of them?'

'No. He's still got Hirschman. I'm going after him.'

'I'm coming in.'

'No. Don't. This is a solo operation. More than that won't work.'

'Lucinda...'

'I don't have time to argue, Jake. Trust me. Gotta go.'

Lucinda crept down the hall, turned into the office side of the reception area and crossed it to the administrative wing. She took stealthy steps down to the end of that hall to the open basement door. She leaned against the wall, her gun straight-armed by her side. She took a deep breath, lifted her weapon and swung around into the stairway. She cringed. Stairways are the worst. She knew if he was looking in her direction, he had a better view of her than she could possibly have of him.

She descended, taking each step with care, peering under the wall and into the basement.

335

On the landing, she froze in place to listen. There was a small amount of sound over in the left corner. She rushed from the stairway to a large vertical file cabinet. She peered over it. In the distance she saw Murphy and his victim. Murphy had a large, fixed-blade hunting knife up against Hirschman's throat. Even from this far away, she could see that he'd already drawn some blood – it glistened on the blade and smeared on the dentist's white jacket. Murphy whispered something she couldn't hear into Hirschman's ear. Hirschman flinched. Murphy laughed.

'Cheese!' she hollered.

He turned his head to look in her direction.

'Drop the knife, Cheese.'

'Or what?' Murphy said, digging the knife a little deeper into Hirschman's throat.

'Cheese, don't make me kill you.' *Dear God, not this again*, Lucinda thought as the image of another victim in another sociopath's hands floated to the surface of her thoughts. *Please don't make me kill again. Please let him drop the knife.*

Murphy stood up straighter, pulling Hirschman up with him. He held the blade in his right hand, his elbow jutting out at a sharp angle. His chest was blocked by Hirschman but Murphy's head stood clear. It would be a good shot.

'Drop the knife, Cheese,' she repeated.

'You only got one eye. There's no way you can make this shot from that distance. Give me a break, bitch,' he laughed.

Lucinda pulled the trigger.

Fifty-Seven

The knife flew out of Murphy's hand, nearly hitting the bare light bulb before it dropped and clattered on the concrete floor. The dentist slumped down like an empty duffel bag, grunting on impact. Murphy's scream pierced Lucinda's ears. Then he fell to the floor, writhing.

Lucinda ran first for the hunting knife Murphy had held to Hirschman's throat and kicked it out of the way. She reached into Murphy's pockets, turning them inside out and recovering a handgun and a phone. She knelt by Hirschman and pulled out her cell. She could hear Jake shouting her name before she got the device to the side of her face. 'Jake. Paramedics. To the basement. Quick.'

'Are you injured?'

'No. The hostage is. The perp is. I'm fine.'

She slid her cell back into her pocket. 'Dr Hirschman?'

'Yes, ma'am,' the dentist said. He looked up at her but his eyes didn't focus. Lucinda wasn't sure if he really saw her at all.

'You're going to be fine. You've got a nasty slice on your neck that is bleeding quite a bit. But he didn't cut anything vital. I'm going to put some pressure on your neck now, please lay still.

Help is on the way. Do you know where you are, Dr Hirschman?'

'Yes. I'm ... no, no, where am I?'

'Hush, Dr Hirschman, it doesn't matter. It's over now. Everything's going to be all right. Hear those footsteps above our heads? Paramedics are almost here.'

The emergency medical technicians clattered down the steps. Lucinda rose, pointing to Hirschman and said, 'Him first.'

Murphy continued to writhe on the floor, alternating between screams and whimpers.

Jake grabbed both of Lucinda's forearms with his hands and pulled her close. 'You're OK? You're really OK?'

'Yeah. I'm fine. It was tense for a while but I'm fine.'

'You've got a lot of blood on your clothes.'

'Hirschman's. Not mine.'

Two more paramedics brushed past them on the way to care for Murphy. Jake nodded his head in the wounded man's direction and said, 'Where did you hit him?'

'I was aiming for the knob on his raised elbow but I'm not sure if I got it.'

A paramedic turned and looked up at her. 'Got it? You nailed it. I don't think they can put the pieces all together again.'

A smug grin flashed across Lucinda's face. *Damn, I'm good.* She stepped over to look down at Murphy. 'Sorry about that, Cheese. I know it hurts like hell but my only alternative was a bullet to your head and I just didn't want to do that.'

Murphy glared up at her. She turned to walk away but before she could take a step, she dropped to the floor.

'Oh, damn, that burns!' she cried out. Jake stepped down hard on Murphy's hand, where a small knife glistened red.

'You asshole,' he said through clenched teeth, bent down and took the switchblade away from Murphy. To the paramedics, he said, 'Take care of the Lieutenant. I'll frisk this bastard and get him out of your way.'

Lucinda used her hands to try to push herself back to her feet but fell again. She heard the paramedics telling her to stay still but their voices sounded as if they were coming from far away buried under a mountain of snow. Suddenly she felt cold, very cold. The only thing that spoke to her loud and clear was the pain. It tore through her body and felt like it blasted the top off of her skull. It burned. It ached. It stung. It throbbed. *What did he do? Why did I fall?* She wanted to ask those questions out loud but couldn't form any words. Her lips moved but nothing intelligible passed her lips.

'Agent, looks like he severed the Lieutenant's Achilles tendon.'

Achilles tendon? Achilles tendon? Lucinda wondered. *What is that? Where is that? In my leg? My foot? Yes. That's it. It connects the two. Damn, it hurts.*

Murphy shrieked as Jake twisted his arms back to cuff them together.

'Uh, Agent, that man is seriously injured,' a paramedic objected. 'You shouldn't be putting him in cuffs. You could cause more damage.'

'I don't give a shit! Take care of the Lieutenant. I'll get this jerkwad out of here.'

Going up each step, Murphy's body thumped against the riser. He screamed and Jake yelled, 'Shut up!' The rhythm of their departure filled the evening air with a revolting rhapsody. Lucinda heard the noise but could not understand it – bass, soprano, tenor, over and again. She felt the urge to snap her fingers but found she couldn't get her thumb to connect with her middle finger.

Fifty-Eight

Over the objections of medical personnel, Jake listened to Lucinda. She begged him not to send her into surgery that far from home. She wanted to be in familiar territory with a doctor she knew and trusted. Paramedics loaded her into the same state trooper helicopter that had originally brought them to the scene. While medical personnel bandaged her up and filled her with painkillers, Lucinda feverishly explained to Jake what needed to be done upon their return.

She kept talking as the helicopter rose into the air but soon she was lost in a pharmaceutical fog. When she slipped away, Jake made sure that Dr Rambo Burns would be waiting when they landed on a heliport of a hospital just seven blocks from Lucinda's apartment.

As soon as Lucinda rolled safely into surgery, Jake hailed a cab and headed for Lucinda's apartment to check on Chester. Lucinda's gray tabby was stand-offish at first but when Jake opened a can of tuna feast, Chester became an instant friend, rubbing on his shins and purring loudly.

Jake then traveled to the Justice Center where he updated Captain Holland on Lucinda's condition. Holland said, 'The mayor's called a meeting for the vote on the monocular-vision policy this morning. No matter how successful Pierce's surgery, she may end up permanently on desk duty.'

'That's not right, Captain. I'll see what I can do. But before I go, what's the situation with Ellen Branson?'

'After her husband and I sat down with the District Attorney, we made arrangements for her care. She left lock-up last night to go to a mental-health facility for an evaluation.'

'What about the charges? Lucinda was adamant that they be dropped.'

'They are, sort of. The D.A. agreed to drop them but retained the option of reinstating them at a later date pending the outcome of her treatment.'

'Good. Lucinda will be pleased. She was chastising herself for forgetting about Ellen's situation yesterday.'

'But she was in the middle of a hostage negotiation yesterday,' Captain Holland objected.

'And your point is?'

The captain sighed. 'Right, we are talking about Pierce. How am I going to keep her at home resting until she heals?'

'I'll try to help. I'll be spending a lot of time around here. We'll be forming a task force to coordinate all of the investigations and make decisions about which jurisdiction gets a piece of Charles Sinclair Murphy first. I'll bring Lucinda into the loop via conference call. That should keep her off her feet for a little while.'

'Probably not long enough. It's a shame she

didn't put a bullet in his head,' Holland said.

'It would make the job easier but that's not a burden I'd want her to bear. The thought of killing another person really gnawed at her.'

'I know. I didn't really mean that. But you know...'

'Yes, I do. See you later, Captain. It's time for me to annoy the mayor.' Jake walked up the street to City Hall. He breezed past the mayor's secretary and into his conference room, flashing his badge every step of the way. He opened a door to a dozen startled faces. 'Monocular-vision policy task force meeting?' he asked.

'Yes,' said the mayor from the head of the table. 'Who are you?'

'Special Agent Jake Lovett, Federal Bureau of Investigation.'

'And you are interrupting our meeting, because...?' the Mayor asked incredulously.

'As someone who works in Washington, D.C., the most policy- and rule-laden capital of the free world, I wanted to make sure you understood that policies and rules sometimes have unintended consequences. I don't know if you are considering these restrictions on monocular officers because of some intra-office political storm I don't know about or because of fear of liability or because of a lack of information. Whatever your reasons, you will suffer a great loss if you craft a policy that will leave Lieutenant Lucinda Pierce shackled to a desk.'

'But who could rely on her in the field? Her vision is impaired,' the mayor objected.

'I relied on her in the field – as did sixteen

hostages of a psychopath – including seven children. One hostage died, shot to death before Lieutenant Pierce inserted herself into the situation. The others are alive because she was there. The last life she saved by exercising her expert marksmanship skills. She fired a shot into the elbow of the perpetrator from a long distance. She may only have one eye, ladies and gentlemen, but she's a better shot than a lot of full-sighted officers in the field.

'Some of you might be thinking that Officer Pierce is the exception to the rule – that you can vote in a policy and make an exception for her and any others with her proficiency. But I'll bet if you ask your City Attorney, he'll tell you that exceptions expose you to the most liability.

'So, if you want to punish a heroic officer who willingly puts her life on the line for citizens every day, you go ahead and vote in this policy. But before you do, think about her and think about the loss this city will suffer if you do.'

Jake turned and walked out, hailing another taxi to take him to the hospital. When he walked through the lobby, he saw a young girl arguing with a volunteer at the front desk. When he overheard Lucinda's name, he stopped and entered the fray.

Jake stepped into the room assigned to Lucinda after her surgery. She opened her eyes at his approach and gave him a weak smile. 'Hey,' she said.

'Guess what I found in the lobby?' He stepped to one side and revealed Charley.

Charley tore across the room. 'Lucy, Lucy, are you OK?' She skidded to a stop beside the bed, her exuberance intimidated by the IV tube.

'Yeah, Charley, I'm just fine. C'mon, c'mon, get up on the bed.'

Charley eased up beside her. 'Lucy, you gotta get better.'

'I will, Charley. But how did you get here?'

'I saw the news about the bad man you caught and, instead of getting on the school bus, I got on the city bus and came here.'

'Does your dad know where you are?'

'I called him,' Jake said. 'He wasn't real happy about her independent decision to head over here on her own but he was glad to know where she was.'

'Oh, he'll get over it,' Charley said with a roll of her eyes.

Affection swelled up in Lucinda's chest. If there had ever been time for a child in her life, here was the one she would want. She sighed at the thought.

'Did I hurt you, Lucy?' Charley said in response.

'No, Charley. Not at all.'

'I'm going to go get a cup of coffee and let you two have some time alone.'

They listened to Jake's footsteps go down the hall. 'Lucy?' Charley asked.

'Yeah?'

'I was scared when I saw the news. They showed the stretcher putting you into the helicopter.'

'I'm fine, Charley.'

345

'I know. But I can't lose you, too, Lucy.'

Lucinda grabbed the little girl's hand and squeezed. 'I'm still here.'

'Sometimes I make believe that you are really my mommy and that you live with me.'

'You had a wonderful mommy, Charley.'

'Oh, I know. I'll never forget her. But sometimes I pretend that you marry Daddy and become my second mommy.'

'Well, that's a pretty complicated situation.'

'You don't want to live with me?'

Lucinda ached. As much as it would complicate things, having this child in her life, in her home, every day, would be the answer to a long-forgotten dream. 'Oh, Charley, it's not about you. I would love to live with you.'

'You don't like my daddy?'

'It's not that either, Charley. It's just that your dad needs to have some time to grieve for your mom and put his life back in order before he makes a decision about another wife. He just hasn't had enough time.'

'I think he likes you.'

'Yes, he does and I like him. But that is not enough. You can't rush these kinds of decisions. There needs to be something deeper than just liking each other. If you don't take care, a lot of people can get hurt.'

'Do you think you'll marry my daddy one day?'

'I don't know, sweetie. It's not going to happen any time soon if it ever does. But what happens between your daddy and me doesn't matter. You will always be a part of my life – even if your daddy marries someone else.'

'Promise?'

'Yes. I promise.'

'I think that Special Agent man likes you, too.'

'Jake?'

'Yes. We had a long talk while we waited for you to wake up.'

'You think he likes me?

'Yes. Will you marry him?'

'Charley, I just met him a couple of days ago.'

'Oh. There's that time thing again. It's not easy being a woman is it?'

Lucinda's career and relationship choices ran through her head – and with them, the realization that neither had gone the way she'd planned.

'No, girlfriend. It certainly is not.'